I grew hot, tired, and bored. And, of course, there was that damn front-loading freezer!

Everyone knows that a basement freezer in the South usually contains some part of a deer, some barbecue . . . and *ice cream*.

However, the first thing I noticed when I opened that damn freezer was poor Aunt Jerry. She'd been crammed in there in a fetal position, on her back, so that only a shelf or two had to be removed. Sure enough, above her was a shelf of packages wrapped in white butcher paper and clearly labeled "dear steaks." I can only hope that Ben was a bad speller, and not in the custom of freezing women. But back to Aunt Jerry, I am eternally gratefully that I never saw her face; it was her outfit I recognized, the gorgeous mustard-colored sari. At this point she was minus the paper crown from Burger King, but the orange and purple faux leis still hung from her neck, for when the freezer door opened they spilled forth, adding to the drama.

Was it any wonder that I screamed?

Den of Antiquity Mysteries by
Tamar Myers

TAMAR MYERS

THE
GLASS IS
ALWAYS
GREENER

A DEN OF ANTIQUITY MYSTERY

A V O N

An Imprint of HarperCollinsPublishers

AVON BOOKS
An Imprint of HarperCollins*Publishers*
10 East 53rd Street
New York, New York 10022-5299

Copyright © 2011 by Tamar Myers
ISBN 978-0-06-084661-9
www.avonmystery.com

THE GLASS IS ALWAYS GREENER

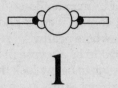

1

I was in the mood for some Ben & Jerry's ice cream; but I most certainly wasn't in the mood to discover Jerry dead in Ben's freezer. Perhaps I'll be forgiven, then, for scraming bloody murder. For those of you unfamiliar with my screams, it may be of interest to learn that—petite though I am—they can knock starlings out of trees, shatter goblets with ease, and even start the kettle to boiling. This is not to brag, mind you; I am merely explaining how it is that everyone in the backyard heard me shrieking, even though I was in the walkout basement of Ben's house.

Trust me, finding a body in a complete stranger's deep freeze could easily happen to *anyone* on a warm summer day—if he, or she, didn't mind his, or her, manners. It wasn't my family gathering—I was only a guest—and I was bored and hungry, as well as hot, and I wandered into the walkout basement to cool off for a few minutes, as well as get away from as big a group of loons as you will ever find on a New England lake. That's when I spotted the freezer, and the thought

1

Tamar Myers

occurred to me that, if I wished hard enough, there might be a pint of Cinnamon Buns–flavored ice cream in there. And, of course, that I'd find a clean sterling silver spoon somewhere nearby.

But no, there had to be a corpse in the front-loading freezer; which seems to be my luck these days. At any rate, due to the extreme stress I've experienced just by describing the above situation, I've gotten slightly ahead of myself. Therefore I shall now backtrack from Charlotte, North Carolina, the scene of the crime, to lovely and gracious Charleston, *South* Carolina.

Both cities are winners, but they are worlds apart and cannot—*should* not—be compared.

What the cities do have in common is that, although they are Southern at the core, in recent years their respective characters have been heavily influenced by Yankee immigration. What Sherman could not accomplish with his army, the Highway Department has accomplished with its interstates. It is almost impossible to hear a native accent in Charlotte these days, and only slightly less so in Charleston.

Thus it was that my petite ear perked up at the dulcet sounds of Dixie as I perused the display of baby eggplant at the Harris Teeter on East Bay Street.

"Well, look what the tide washed in!"

I turned quickly to see the Rob-Bobs, who are two of my closest friends, pushing a shopping buggy of their own. However, it took me a second or two to adjust my thinking, as this was the first time I had ever seen either of them in such a mundane place as a supermarket.

Rob, the tall, handsome one, who looks like an even

2

slimmer George Clooney, and Bob—bless his heart—who is spindly with a balding, oversized head, are both far more sophisticated than I could ever hope to be. I might not be surprised to encounter them at Whole Foods or at the farmers' market; just not here.

"Rob! Bob!"

"Always second," Bob boomed. "What else is new?"

"It was Rob who spoke," I said in my defense. I kissed each man, starting with Bob, so as to allay his jealousy.

"Abby," Bob said, "what are you doing?"

"I'm shopping for dinner; what else? The real question is: what are you two doing here? Bob, don't you usually order your emu meat from a catalogue?"

"No—I mean, yes, but what are you doing to that aubergine? You seem to have a death grip on it."

"Say *what*?"

"He means eggplant," Rob said.

"Oh that." Indeed, I was hugging the shiny black vegetable as if it were a precious child about to be snatched from my arms by a ruthless kidnapper. "Aubergine. I've read that word, but I'm not sure that I've ever heard it pronounced before. I think it would make a lovely girl's name."

"Abby," Rob said, his handsome face lighting up and becoming even more attractive—as if that was possible. "You and your eggplant have just given me a fabulous idea."

"Not moussaka," Bob said. "That is *so* pedestrian. Can't we think of something a little more original, like—"

"Aubergine opossum," Rob said, pronouncing the

O. "Bob, I love you dearly, but please put a sock in it. This is between me and Abby."

"Why, I've never been so insulted in my entire life," Bob said, and taking the buggy he stalked off.

"Rob Goldburg," I said sternly, "that was rude—and unnecessary."

"You really think so?"

"I do."

"He's forever butting in, and it's usually with some damn recipe."

"I know. The thing is that he just wants to be included."

"Well, he is included; he's my partner. That doesn't mean we have to share our friendships equally—does it?"

I sighed. "Of course not. But you will apologize to him, won't you?"

"You know I will. Probably even before we leave this store."

"Good. Now what was your fabulous idea?"

"I want you to come with me to my Aunt Aubergine's party."

I put the eggplant back before it ended on the floor and was suitable only for dip. "Uh—you *have* an Aunt Aubergine? As of when? Five seconds ago?"

My friend smiled, revealing teeth that were even and still exceedingly white. "Actually, I do have an Aunt Aubergine, but she goes by Jerry. Always has, ever since she was a little girl. And she spells it like the boy's name because when she first was learning to write cursive she decided that the letters J and Y were more beautiful than G and I."

4

"Hmm, someone who knows her own mind; I like that."

"I thought you would. And I'm not drawing any parallels here, so don't get me wrong, but Aunt Jerry is also extremely eccentric."

"Okay," I said hesitantly. "Give me an example."

"This party that I'm going to, it's her going-away party."

"That's nice. Where's she going? On a cruise?"

"She's dying—I think. As to where she'll end up is anybody's guess. We Jews don't believe in Hell—not one that lasts for all eternity, at any rate—but Aunt Jerry says that if by chance she gets to Heaven and sees the likes of Pat Robertson, she'll turn right around and go the other way. She can't abide homophobia. And Abby, even though she's almost as old as God and grew up in who knows what century, she's always been in my corner. Right from day one."

"She sounds like a really special— Wait just one cotton-picking minute. What do you mean by 'she's dying, I *think*'?"

"Oh that. Well, you see, Aunt Jerry visited a psychic in Florence, Italy, who predicted that on August tenth she would leave her earthly body behind and begin the next phase of her soul's progression—whatever that means. I'm sure it lost something being translated into English. What matters is that she really believes this. So"—he closed both his eyes and his fist somewhat dramatically—"she has put together this good-bye soiree that is de rigueur for everyone in the family—even the in-laws—but Bob won't attend."

"Why not? You said she isn't prejudiced."

"Yes, she's not, and a lot of them aren't, but there are enough holdouts to make Bob truly uncomfortable—Mama included."

"Oh, her." I'd met Mrs. Goldburg on more than one occasion. Like a category five hurricane, she was a force to be contended with.

"Come on, Abby, my mama's not *that* bad."

"Let's not turn this into a game of Truth or Dare. The bottom line to all this is that I'm to be your backup Bob, am I right? I'm your Bob stand-in."

Rob shifted from one polished Ferragamo to the other. "Must you always be so plainspoken?"

"The truth, Rob. I demand nothing but."

"Okay! All right! I surrender! But will you come? Please? I'll put you up at the Ballantyne Resort Hotel."

"Where's that?"

"Give me a break. You've heard of the Ballantyne Country Club, haven't you? There have been some famous golf tournaments held there. *Everyone* knows where that is."

"Oh yes, of course; it's right next door to the NASCAR Museum of Fame."

"No, it isn't! In fact, it's on the opposite side of Charlotte—touché. Anyway, it's on the south side of town, just off 485, one exit down from Rea Road. That's where you'll be getting off for the big event."

"Wait a minute; I didn't say that I'd come. What do I get out of this? And who is going to mind the Den of Antiquity while I'm gone?"

"How about my credit card for Neiman Marcus? After all, South Park Mall is only twenty minutes from the hotel. Fifteen from Auntie's house. As to minding your shop, you're hardly in there anymore now that you have such a competent staff."

I stared him in disbelief. "That's *it*?"

"Isn't that enough? I'd give you my blood, but I'm squeamish when it comes to needles."

"No, silly, I mean is that all you want to say about your credit card? Don't you want to set a limit?"

"I trust you."

And therein lay the catch. Although Rob was well-off, he knew very well that I would rather spend fifty-nine dollars on a blouse at Stein Mart than twelve hundred dollars on a blouse at Neiman Marcus. Conspicuous consumption has never been my thing. If an item looks good, and feels good, that's all that matters.

"Okay, Rob," I said. "But I'm going whole hog on this. I'm going to Dillard's at Carolina Place Mall, and I might even spend five hundred dollars."

"You go, girl."

"Yippee. So when do we get started?"

"Put down your eggplant and go pack your bag, Abby. My chariot awaits."

"Hey, you can't do that," Bob bellowed. "I have a nice goat testicle stew simmering—"

"Come on, we don't have a moment to waste." Rob grabbed my arm and propelled me past a pile of melons and around a tower of sweet corn. The next thing I knew I was headed up north to Charlotte, my old stomping grounds.

Of course I had to smooth clear the way first with my husband, Greg, and Mama, who lives with us. But since Rob poses no threat at all to Greg, and Mama is a better cook than I am—plus she's been feeling a little bit useless lately—it didn't take all that much convincing. The price I'd pay was that upon my return my dear sweet husband was going to expect a lot more pampering than I was used to giving. Also, I fully expected Mama to have rearranged my kitchen, and maybe even to have gotten rid of my cat, Dmitri—no, she wouldn't dare.

Rob's Mercedes-Benz was so quiet that, when we weren't talking, I could hear the pulse in my ear. I think I heard my pulse for a total of five seconds during the four-hour trip.

"Now spill," I said, as soon as we'd cleared city traffic. "Tell me everything there is to know about your Aunt Jerry. She sounds like quite a character."

"Abby, she is the epitome of eccentric. She married young, to the love of her life, who made his fortune in textiles, but then she was widowed young. And she was very rich at the time. She was also never the same."

"How so?"

"She lives in a parallel world, where there are always parties going on—soirees, she calls them. Her house is always lit up, there is always music playing—from the 1940s—and even though you can have a conversation with her, occasionally she will interrupt it to have another conversation with someone who isn't even there!"

"You mean she's nuts? Oops. I'm sorry! That just slipped out."

"While that wasn't PC, Abby, believe me, it's been said a million times in our family. The thing is, even though she has this alternative universe, she still functions in this one quite well. And in case you're wondering, she can't be committed; she has no children, but her siblings have all tried."

"Hmm. So what's with this good-bye party? Is she planning to commit suicide? Just asking."

"No, not Aunt Jerry. That's not her style. Think Auntie Mame with a Dixie accent. Abby, do you know what a basenji is?"

"Isn't that one of the barkless breeds of dogs?"

"Very good! It's from Africa. They're beautiful little dogs that trot on their tiptoes like Thoroughbreds. Anyway, Aunt Jerry had a basenji named Pagan."

"I love it already!"

"Because Pagan couldn't bark like other dogs, whenever they were out and about the neighborhood and they encountered a barking dog, Aunt Jerry used to do the barking on Pagan's behalf."

"You're joking!"

Rob grinned. "I swear that's the truth. That's the kind of thing she does. Harmless stuff, but really nutty."

"Actually she sounds like fun."

"In small doses. But don't ever cross her; at least not in public. There was this one time, in a home improvement store, where she felt she'd been slighted by a male '*associate*.' She was in the plumbing department at the time, so to demonstrate how she felt about the service she sat on a toilet that was on display."

"She didn't!"

"Don't worry, she kept her skirt down and her knickers up, but she drew quite a crowd. Eventually the store manager had to call the police, because even the store security was unprepared for the tongue lashing they were getting."

"I'll try not to tick her off. So where do you think she's *really* going? On a cruise?"

Rob shook his head, clucking all the while. "No, Abby, you don't seem to get it; Aunt Jerry isn't playing games here. She sincerely expects to die on August tenth. That's what the psychic in Florence said, so that's what's going to happen."

"But that's silly—I mean, well, you know what I mean."

I watched the muscle in Rob's jaw twitch. "Abby, meet my Aunt Jerry first, then you decide."

We stopped at the hotel just long enough for me to check in and drop off my weekend bag in the *suite* that my sweet friend Rob at had reserved for me. No matter how things went over the weekend, at least my accommodations would be very nice indeed.

My smile grew even wider shortly after we turned right on to Rea Road from I–485. The four-lane highway began its life there as a boulevard; the center median lush with crape myrtles and seasonal plantings. Low, wooded hills greeted the eye on either side, and one beheld not the slightest suggestion of urban stress, much less blight of any kind.

"Rob, if every visitor to Charlotte first saw it from this approach, it would always be voted the most beautiful city in the country."

"Amen, hallelujah, and pass the mashed potatoes."

I emitted a small gasp, as behooves a very small

lady. "I totally forgot; should I be bringing food? A dish to share?"

"You're my guest, Abby. You're not going to a community *oneg*."

"A *what*?"

"An *oneg* is kind of like a church coffee hour—but on steroids. At least at Temple Beth El. Do you know that we have our own chef?"

"Now you *are* kidding me."

"Nope. Her name is Lorrie—I think. I've lost track. Anyway, nothing is expected of you, and certainly nothing is required; this affair at my Uncle Ben's house is to be catered."

"Still serious?"

"Oh yeah; we Ovumkophs take our celebrations very seriously."

"Very funny. Ovumkophs indeed. Thought you'd fool me with that one. But *ovum* means egg in Latin and *koph* means head in Yiddish—I'm not exactly a *dumm*kopf, you know."

Rob laughed. "Well, unfortunately, my great-grandfather was. You see, Ovumkoph really is my mother's maiden name."

"No way!"

"Way. Great-granddaddy was a physicist from Germany. He knew Einstein as a matter of fact. He had a sense of humor but very little patience. When he arrived at Ellis Island and the clerk had trouble recording his name, Great-granddaddy suddenly switched it to Ovumkoph. Said later it made more sense anyway since he was a scientist, and scientists are eggheads."

"What was the name originally?"

"That's just it; he wouldn't tell us."

"You've never researched it? If he was a scientist, then there have to be records—especially if he knew Einstein."

"Hey, I'm a Goldburg. But that should show you how self-absorbed the Ovumkophs can be; none of them cared if their dad, or granddad, was a brilliant scientist."

I shook my head in pure wonderment. No one in my family tree ever came close to being a scientist—well, with the one exception of a cousin on Mama's side who raised laboratory rats.

Jerry's youngest brother, Ben had reluctantly offered to host the party at his spacious home in Piper Glen, which is truly one of Charlotte's suburban delights. Large houses sprawl among mature plantings of oak, crape myrtle, holly, camellia, ornamental cherries, and azaleas. Small lakes punctuate the verdant hills like gemstones. I couldn't imagine anything more lovely.

She was standing on a table in the middle of Ben's patio, seemingly as tall and regal as the Statue of Liberty. Aunt Jerry was also dressed in yards and yards of flowing material, but in her case it was a silk sari the color of mustard. Around her neck a tangle of purple and orange faux Hawaiian leis fought to be noticed, and clinging lopsided to the top of her hoary head was a paper crown from Burger King. So much for taking herself seriously, I thought.

"Robbie, is that you?" she called, cupping one hand over her eyes to keep out the glare.

"Yes, Aunt Jerry. And I brought a dear friend. Her name is Abigail."

"Abby," I said.

'Welcome, Abby. Any friend of Robbie's is a friend of mine."

"Aunt Jerry, *please*, it's Rob—not Robbie."

The assemblage—there were thirty-eight, not counting the grande dame and us—laughed. I don't think they were being mean; it was more like an inside joke.

"Well, now that y'all are here, I will begin with my going-away party's most important event. But first, does anyone care to venture a guess as to what it might be?"

Debbie, a girl of five, was pushed forward by her grandfather, Ben. "Is it a treasure hunt?"

Aunt Jerry guffawed and the poor girl was reduced to tears.

"Not exactly Auntie Mame," I whispered.

"Oh honey, please don't cry," Aunt Jerry said, as she teetered dangerously close to the edge of the table. "I didn't mean anything by it; I laugh at everything."

"She does," Rob whispered.

"But no, darling, it's not a treasure *hunt*, because in this case the treasure is coming to you."

Debbie squealed and clapped her hands.

"Oh no, dear, I didn't mean you in the specific sense of the word. Robbie, sugar, give little Debbie here a hundred dollars—I'll repay you shortly—and Ben, sweetheart, tell your daughter to take the precious little one inside and keep her occupied for the next ten minutes or so. I'm afraid this treasure hunt is strictly R-rated."

Ben bristled; there was no question about that. "My daughter's name is Amy. Why don't you try speaking to her directly—Jerry?"

The old woman shaded her eyes again as she scanned her hangdog relations. Even Rob's mom, who can be as snooty as an anteater when she's around Bob, sat shriveled as a dried plum in her chair and pretended to examine her fingernails.

"Which one of you dears is Amy?" Aunt Jerry finally asked. She sounded a bit desperate to me. "You young ladies all look so much alike to me. Too much makeup, too much fast food, too little clothes—it's a wonder y'all don't get arrested. Why in my day—"

"Never mind!" A very round woman in very short shorts struggled to her feet, gathered the small girl in her prodigious but comforting arms, and stomped angrily into the house.

I expected at least one other person to object to Aunt Jerry's rude categorization of the younger generation, but other than Amy's justified outburst, nary a peep was heard.

"Well now," Aunt Jerry said, rubbing her jeweled hands together in exaggerated glee. "Let the good times begin."

2

Aunt Jerry paused for dramatic effect. "You see, my dears, I have given this day a great deal of thought, and I've come to the conclusion that one of the few perks of knowing one's departure date—that's a euphemism for death, by the way—is that one can be present at an early reading of one's will."

"Aunt Jerry! Stop that kind of talk!"

"That's my Uncle Aaron," Rob said, not bothering to whisper this time.

That was hard to believe because he bore absolutely no family resemblance to my friend. Unlike Rob, Aaron Ovumkoph was bald with a large head, a pigeon chest, and spindly arms and legs. In fact, he looked remarkably like Rob's life partner, Bob. But a much older version, of course. Hmm.

"Don't stress yourself, Aaron, sugar; you are in the will. In fact, I believe I'll start with you." Aunt Jerry thrust a ring-bedecked hand deep into the mustard

15

yellow folds of her sari and withdrew a much-creased sheet of college-ruled notebook paper.

"Ahem," she said to get our attention, although it was hardly necessary at that point. "I'm going to skip all that 'being of sound mind' crap—seeing as how y'all won't believe it anyway—but just so you know, I was over to Duke last week and have a stack of notarized test results that affirm my sanity. Now where was I?"

"Aaron's inheritance," said Aaron's wife, Melissa. A first impression of the woman, based only on the amount of flesh she chose to expose, would put her firmly in the trash category. But that would be judgmental, and I have made an effort to give that up ever since Lent.

Aunt Jerry flashed Melissa a smile that may have been a tad insincere. "Oh yes, that's right; thank you, dear. Aaron, you have always been like a little brother to me—"

"That's because I *am* your little brother." He turned his head as if for our benefit. "Senile old woman," he muttered.

"Aaron, darling," Aunt Jerry continued, oblivious to his disparaging aside, "bless your little ol' heart, you have always been a pain in the rear to everyone who's ever known you. Therefore I am bequeathing you one U.S. dollar. It will be up to you to decide whether or not you share it with Melissa."

After maintaining what seemed like a ridiculously long shocked silence, Aunt Jerry's relations erupted into laughter. "That's a good one," Aaron said.

"I'm glad you think so, dear," she said, "because I wasn't joking."

Melissa was on her feet like greased lightning. "No, this can't be! I came over to feed your cat once while you were off in Bali or somewhere. Remember?"

"I'd only gone to Baltimore that weekend, and you claimed to love cats and volunteered to come over every day and spend some time with Xerxes. Instead, you threw a party in my house and one of your guests let my sweet little boy out and he wandered off and got lost. You didn't have the decency to call me."

"He didn't wander off," Melissa said. "He escaped."

"Good one, hon," Aaron said.

I poked Rob. "Your relatives are vicious," I hissed softly. "It's no wonder Bob bowed out."

"Abby, we're just getting started."

"Moving right along," Aunt Jerry said. "This brings me to my dearly departed brother Nathan's son Samuel Abraham Ovumkoph, who now goes by the rather incomprehensible name of Pastor Sam. Not even a last name of any kind, Sammy; how strange indeed."

Sam, who was tall with broad shoulders and blond hair, held up his right hand, with the palm facing Aunt Jerry. "You promised not to get into the religious thing if I showed up."

"Yes, but televangelism, Sammy—your ancestors in the shtetl are turning over in their graves."

"I have to be true to my beliefs, Aunt Jerry."

"So the traditions of your forebears mean nothing?"

Sam smiled. Who am I to say that it was a smarmy smile, but in retrospect I'd have to say it could not have been very friendly.

"Say what you want, Aunt Jerry; I don't need your money."

Tamar Myers

"Perhaps you don't, dear; you've been bilking your congregation for years."

"Then why did you insist that I be here?"

"Because I'd like to give you a million dollars, Sammy—in a manner of speaking."

I'm sure the collective gasps were heard all the way down in Charleston. Mama later said she had to struggle for air at precisely that time in her house just above Broad Street. Of course, in all fairness, the air there *is* a mite rarefied.

"Why him?" Melissa screeched. "He hasn't spoken to any of us in ten years."

Aunt Jerry glowered at Melissa and then plowed right along. "Now you, Tina—bless your heart—have kept me nicely informed of the happenings in your family. Congratulations, by the way, to you and Sammy on the birth of your son Sheldon. That's your eighth child, am I right?"

"Ninth, ma'am."

"My goodness; that's one for every year you've been married. It's no wonder he needs to bilk his congregation."

"Allegedly," Sammy snarled. "You can't prove it."

"Nor do I want to. Think of the shame it would bring to this family. No, what I'm going to do, Sammy, as head of this family, is give your wife, Tina, a million dollars. She, in turn, will do her best to parse it out to the congregants whom she thinks that you—uh—well, *screwed* is as good a word as any. You may not like it, but it will keep me from turning you in to the authorities, and you from going to jail. Let's face it, Sammy; with those blond good looks of yours, you'd be mighty

18

popular." She laughed raucously. "I've no doubt that some tattooed gangster type would love to make you his be-yotch."

There followed only laughter, albeit of the nervous sort. Apparently the assembled folks were used to Aunt Jerry's streetwise vocabulary. So far the old woman appeared to be addressing only her siblings and the one nephew. Cousins were apparently not included in her will, a fact that seemed to make some of the more optimistic ones anxious to be noticed. Others—perhaps people who had at one time or another pissed the grande dame off—tried hard to blend in with the scenery.

Aunt Jerry, however, remained focused. "I'm glad we got that settled, Sammy." She licked her thin but cherry red lips. "And now I wish to address my only sister, Chanti Ovumkoph Goldburg."

"*Chanti?*" I whispered. "Did I hear right?"

"Short for Chanteuse," Rob said.

"Quiet in the peanut gallery," Aunt Jerry said. Although she didn't sound angry, she was clearly not amused.

"Sorry," Rob said.

Aunt Jerry had a steady gaze, one that would have very much pleased a portrait painter. Altogether she was a good subject for a painting. I made a mental note of it; I'd suggest it to Rob as a postparty gift idea. Executed by the right artist, I could imagine a portrait of eccentric Aunt Jerry hanging in the Mint Museum of Art in Charlotte, maybe even in the National Gallery at the Smithsonian.

"*Well?*"

I awoke from my daydream to discover that there were three dozen pairs of eyes plus one (Cousin Remus poked an eye out on his house key one night) staring at me. I checked my chin for drool and then glanced down to see if the sisters were still safely cosseted.

"She's waiting for you to apologize," Rob whispered.

"Apologize for what?" I said aloud.

"For interrupting me with your incessant chitter-chatter," Aunt Jerry said.

"Then I apologize; I really do." When someone my size gets cut down to size, we don't need a very wide crack into which we can disappear.

"Then moving right along, Chanti, you have never been unkind to me; really, I couldn't ask for a better older sister."

"Jerry, how could you!" Rob's mother shrieked and ran inside the house, slamming the door behind her.

In the stunned silence that followed, one could have heard a frog fart. Then everyone spoke at once, just not to me.

"What's going on?" I demanded. "What's everyone so worked up about?"

"Children!" Aunt Jerry clapped her hands, her heavy gold bangles clinking together melodiously, as anything gold is wont to do. "Listen up. Okay, so I let the cat out of the bag, and apparently I wasn't supposed to. But honestly, I thought y'all knew that Chanti was my older sister. Why, she'll be eighty—oops, there, I did it again.

"Oh fiddlesticks and a bucket full of toe jam, seems like I'm always misspeaking when it comes to my big

20

sis, so really, I can't believe I haven't let that slip before. Anyway, you have to admire her doctor's handiwork. And yes, he practices right here in Charlotte, which proves we *are* a city to be reckoned with; we don't have to go to Atlanta for the important stuff after all." She paused to make eye contact with my handsome companion.

"Rob darling, you knew I was the younger of the sisters, didn't you?"

"Uh—no, ma'am."

"There, you see? This surgeon does really good work—although personally, I eschew the practice of chopping up one's face for the viewing pleasure of others. I mean, who gets to see it more, you or the girlfriends you lunch with? Anyway, if any of you gals—you guys are included as well—want his name, see me afterward. Now where was I?"

"You were skewering my mother," Rob said. Talk about sounding pissed.

"I was just stating a fact, darling. I look up to Chanti. Never mind that she is a bit judgmental and is against gay marriage—did you know that, Robbie?"

"Yes, but—"

"But I know for a fact that your dear mother has poured herself into a number of United Way charities, and in particular has a soft spot for Charlotte's homeless. In the meantime, her beautiful house in Myers Park is getting a bit run-down. So, I am leaving her a million dollars. She can either pay someone to do upkeep on that house, or buy herself a nice new condo where everything will be done for her."

"What are the strings?" Rob asked.

"*Strings?* There are no strings, young man. Oh—well, I am leaving her an extra ten thousand dollars."

"Yes?"

"That's for poisoning your father like I asked her to do some thirty years ago."

3

Rob blanched and I pushed him toward the nearest chair. It was occupied by two pubescent girls in belly-baring T-shirts and miniskirts. I shooed them away with four words guaranteed to clear a room, much less a lawn chair.

"He might throw up," I said. He really did look that bad.

"A-Abby," Rob finally croaked. "Ask her what the hell she means."

"She hears just fine, thank you," Aunt Jerry said. "I was referring to the fact that I couldn't stand your father—may he rest in peace. Your mother—well, all of my loser siblings and I had inherited a healthy little grubstake from our own parents—may they rest in peace—who'd arrived in this country with absolutely *nothing* in their pockets. Anyway, your father was a schemer.

"Now a dreamer, I can stomach. The Wright brothers were dreamers, and just look at their legacy. But your father was more like Bernie Madoff—but without the smarts. Yes, I know, you lived in a nice house in Myers Park while growing up, and you weren't bright enough to get a scholarship to N.C. State, but they managed to pay for that—except that they didn't."

Aunt Jerry paused to let the horrible truth settle on Rob like a cold fog. He tried several times to speak, but it appeared as if it was too much effort for him. Meanwhile his normally rather haughty mother, bless her heart, who had emerged timidly from the kitchen, was mewling like a newly born kitten.

"I told your mother to poison him with her terrible cooking," Aunt Jerry said. "I didn't mean it literally, but that's exactly what she did. Everything had to have at least a pound of butter in it, didn't it, Chanti?" She was shouting through cupped hands by then. "That somehow made it French, didn't it? And of course garlic. Garlic and butter—"

"Aunt Jerry," Rob said, finally starting to get his mojo back, "I think that's quite enough." His relatives twittered in the background—and I mean that in the old-fashioned sense of the word.

"Enough?" she said, recoiling as if from a snake strike. "Oh dear, and here I thought that I was being ever so gentle."

"If I may," I said, "and I'm a total stranger here, you're not just reading a will, you seem to have an axe to grind, and are taking great pleasure in doing so."

The old lady smiled broadly. "I think I like you, Annie. I think you have a lot of spunk for being just a no-account, two-pint Gidget."

"*I beg your pardon?*"

"Oh, didn't Robbie tell you? When you moved to Charleston—"

"Aunt Jerry, stop! I forbid you!"

Everyone froze. It was like we were all playing that game called Statues that we used to play on long summer evenings when we were kids.

"No one forbids *me*," Aunt Jerry said. "Annie," she commanded, "come up here."

"With all due respect, ma'am," I said, "my name is Abby, not Annie."

"Well, whatever. I said to come up here."

"No, Aunt Jersey, I will not. Not unless you ask me nicely."

"Jersey? Is that what you said?"

There was a smattering of applause and not a few giggles.

"I may have, ma'am. If you come down here, I'll repeat myself."

"Why shoot a monkey!" Aunt Jerry said. "If that don't beat all. This gal is no two-pint, no-account Gidget; she's more like a gallon of—of—well, name your favorite flavor. Personally, that new Cinnamon Buns flavor can't be beat."

"So now she's talking about ice cream," Rob said. "That's why you shouldn't listen to a word she says."

I scrambled atop the table with just a little help from Aunt Jerry. "So," I said to her, "tell me what happened when I moved to Charleston five years ago."

"Well, you wanted Robbie to move down there too."

"Of course; I wanted all my friends to move down there. What's wrong with that? I didn't force them to come."

"Yes, but I had other plans for them. Robbie was supposed to be my companion during these golden years—seeing as how he had chosen not to take on the burdens of a wife."

"But he had a partner!"

"Oh Lord, now look what Jerry's done," Rob's mother said, frantically scanning the yard for someplace other than this table under which to hide. "Rob, she's outed you!"

"Is Cousin Rob gay?" a teenage boy asked.

"Yes, dear, now shush," his mother said.

"Cool! 'Cause so am I."

"You see what you've done!" the boy's distraught mother shouted.

"It's your fault," the boy's father said to his wife. "I read that in a book."

"Rob didn't do anything to turn your son gay," I said. "It just happens. Now go on with your story, Aunt Jenny."

"That's Jerry—oh, the heck with it. I deserve whatever name you choose to call me. There's not much to the story. I offered Robbie an enormous amount of money if he'd stay in Charlotte and squire me to the occasional event—you know, charity balls and such, and make himself available for a dinner party now and then. But oh no, he turned me down for you. Of course I took it very hard, so that's when he tried to make me feel better by putting you down—you know, with the two-pint comment."

Words can describe how I felt, but I would never share such vulgar thoughts with anyone. Rob's betrayal had hit me in the pit of my stomach, and that's the doorway to bile. The best thing for everyone was for me to just keep my mouth shut—for now.

"Listen to me, Abby," Rob pleaded, "I didn't mean it. I just said it to get her off my back. I mean the proof is in the pudding, right? I moved down to Charleston, didn't I? I sold my shop up here, and bought a new one down there. Hell, that's more than most men would do for their spouses *and* I got Bob to move down there as well."

"That's right. What was he, a three-quart Moon-doggie?"

"Don't be ridiculous, Abby. Moondoggie was Gidget's boyfriend."

I turned to Aunt Jerry. "You can have him back. Of course, with the real estate slump it might take him a while to unload his shop down there."

"Oh honey, where I'm going he can't follow."

"You going to Columbia?" someone called out. "I hear that's built over the gates of Hell."

Aunt Jerry smiled, revealing lovely laugh lines. "That's what they say, all right: Columbia, South Carolina is *the* most miserable place to spend a summer. But I've already been there, done that. But you know what, Allie? Not only can't Robbie come with me, but none of my stuff can come with me either—not just my money. So here, I want you to have this." Having said that, she slipped off an enormous emerald ring and tried to slip it on one of my fingers.

"No, no, I can't."

"Don't be silly, of course you can."

"Something like that should be kept in the family."

"This family should be kept to themselves, that's what. Here, take it. I *insist*."

"But that's got to be a ten-carat stone—at least."

"Twenty-two-point-five-carat, grass green, and almost eye-clean. Even Queen Elizabeth doesn't have one this nice—okay, so maybe she does, but I very much doubt if anyone else in Charlotte has one that comes even close to this."

"All the more reason for you to keep it. It must be worth a queen's ransom."

"Seven figures."

I felt my knees go weak, which is not such a good state of affairs when one is viewing the world from atop a picnic table. "Well then you *can't* give it to me. I'm not related."

"I can give it to whomever I want, and I want to give it to you. But since you'd rather not wear it now, then fine; I'll wear it in the meantime. But it is still yours."

"Fine," I said, and jumped off the table. That was the last time I saw Aunt Jerry alive.

I am not one for gruesome details; therefore I feel no compelling reason to describe the scene of the crime in all its grisly accuracy. I shall, however, describe it truthfully, for the two terms are not mutually exclusive.

Because of our rift I was pretty much stuck at the event until I prevailed upon Rob to return me to the hotel, or until I could arrange for a cab. But it occurred to me early on in the game that this two-pint player stood a better chance of winning by not only outlasting my opponent, but appearing to have a better time.

To that end that I flitted and flirted about, making talk so small that even a microbe couldn't hear it. The more I laughed and giggled, the more Rob glared. And even though Jerry was nowhere to be seen following the tabletop performance, not a soul left the premises. It seemed that the Ovumkoph clan desperately needed an excuse—any excuse—to party. Besides, there was always the chance Aunt Jerry might change her mind, return, and make someone's day.

Eventually, however, I grew hot, tired, and bored. I can see how being the guest at someone else's family gathering might possibly be fun for a gossip columnist, or maybe even a novelist, but for a little ol' no-account antiques dealer, it's about as much fun as a Brazilian wax, and without the benefits. Yes, I'd been given that fabulous emerald ring—but bear in mind, the giver was a lunatic; that gift was never going to be accepted as valid by the rest of the clan.

So at any rate, when no one was looking, I ducked into the walkout basement. It was hard to believe that I was the only one there. For heaven's sake, there was a Ping-Pong table, an air hockey table, an enormous flat-screen TV! And, of course, there was that damn front-loading freezer!

Of course there was a refrigerator, and it was well stocked with beverages of many varieties, both alcoholic and non, and there were dips, and cheeses, and summer sausages, and who knows all what—it's not like I took inventory. But everyone knows that a basement freezer in the South usually contains some part of a deer, some barbecue, and *ice cream*.

However, the first thing I noticed when I opened

that damn freezer was poor Aunt Jerry. She'd been crammed in there in a fetal position, on her back, her face turned away from the door, so that only a shelf or two had to be removed. Sure enough, above her was a shelf of packages wrapped in white butcher paper and clearly labeled "dear steaks." I can only hope that Ben was a bad speller, and not in the custom of freezing women. But back to Aunt Jerry, I am eternally grateful that I never saw her face; it was her outfit I recognized, the gorgeous mustard-colored sari. At this point she was minus the paper crown from Burger King, but the orange and purple faux leis still hung from her neck, for when the freezer door opened they spilled forth, adding to the drama. Again, was it any wonder that I screamed?

But try getting any sympathy from homicide detectives Krupp and Wimbler. They were polite enough, but I needed more than politeness; what I needed was a hug from my husband, Greg. At the very least I needed to have him talk to them—but these two detectives didn't care two ripe figs that I was married to a former member of their department. They couldn't even be bothered to call him to verify my claim.

Using the one-way glass wall of the interrogation room as a mirror, Detective Krupp scratched a bit of crusted makeup from the corner of her mouth with her pinkie fingernail before speaking. "So what were you doing in the basement, Mrs. Timberlake?"

"My answer is the same as the last time you asked," I said, trying to both express my exasperation yet not be too antagonistic. "It was hot. I was bored. The basement door was unlocked."

Detective Wimbler was a small man who seemed delighted by the fact that I was even much smaller than he. This went unsaid, but I had a strong hunch that if we'd met under other circumstances, and if I wasn't married (he wasn't wearing a ring), he would have asked me out.

"Mrs. Timberlake, were you aware that there was a large watermelon on a tub of ice in the kitchen?"

"Yes—sir. But I was a bit upset, and when I get upset, my metabolism speeds up—never mind. I guess I was operating on automatic when I cut myself a slice of watermelon." How stupid was that, telling him I was upset? I may as well have painted a bull's-eye on my forehead in neon orange!

"I hear you. Being smaller means we have to eat more often; it's not something the rest can understand."

"Give me a break," Detective Krupp muttered, as she gouged the crud from the other side of her mouth. "Ma'am, how did you manage to sneak the knife downstairs? Did you hide it under your clothing?"

"I beg your pardon?"

"The one you used to stab the victim—before she was dumped in the freezer."

"Your prints are all over the handle," Detective Wimbler said.

"You mean the watermelon knife?" I asked. "*That* was the murder weapon?"

"No, it was the candlestick in the drawing room," Detective Krupp said. "Give us a break, Mrs. Timberlake. For someone who is supposedly married to a former detective, you ought to know that playing coy will get you nowhere."

"Not just *supposedly*," I said hotly. "Greg *was* on this force. And he was one of the best, unlike some—"

"Small people like us have a hard time catching a break sometimes, don't we, Mrs. Timberlake?" Detective Wimbler had placed a miniature man's hand on my shoulder in an effort to calm me. Whatever the department height requirements were, he had to have been fully extended—*on a good day*—in order to meet them.

"Oh shut up with that tiny crap," Detective Krupp said. "Five dollars and a stepladder will still buy you a cup of coffee at Starbucks—*if* they notice you." She laughed, snorting like a horse. "Just so you know, Mrs. *Timberlake*, there has never been a Detective Greg Timberlake on this force."

"That may be," I said, "but Greg's last name is Washburn."

Judging by Detective Krupp's face, she didn't like being bested. "Why didn't you tell me that?"

"You didn't ask—ma'am."

"That's right," Detective Wimbler said. "We just assumed. When we assume, my mama always said, one makes an *ass* out of *u* and *me*. Put the three of them together and you get—"

"An ass," Detective Krupp said. "Really, Wimbler, how *did* you make it on the force? Are you the chief's nephew or something?"

"It's my ex-husband's name," I said.

They both returned their focus to me.

"What?" Detective Krupp said.

"My ex-husband is the notorious divorce lawyer Buford Timberlake. I'm sure you see his smarmy ads every time you turn on the TV."

"Yeah, that's right," said Detective Wimbler. "*Is your husband a bum? Get rid of that scum—with Timberlake. Is your wife a nag? Get rid of that hag—with Timberlake.* Those are the kind of jingles that stick with you."

"That stick in your craw," I said. "When I was forty, Buford traded me for a younger model that was twenty percent silicone—if you get my drift. At least that. But Tweetie—may she rest in peace—met her Maker in a suit of armor—"

Detective Krupp sprang to life. "Not Tweetie Byrd Simpson from Blowing Rock High!"

"You knew her?"

"Knew her?" Detective Krupp cried. "Why we grew up together. Our houses backed up to one another. We had a ton of sleepovers and we used to take baths together as little girls. Right up until high school as a matter of fact. But I lost track of her after we graduated and she moved to Charlotte. She wanted to make something of herself—and I guess she kind of did. I read about it in the paper when she died. That's when I decided to move down here and become a detective so I could solve murders like hers."

"Well, you know, it was me who solved Tweetie's murder."

"Get out of town and back! That was *you*?"

"Yes, ma'am."

"You hear that, Wimbler? We have ourselves a genuine celebrity on our hands!"

"Speaking of which," Detective Wimbler said, "there is absolutely no scientific proof equating hand size with—well, you know what."

"Detective Wimbler has *issues*," Detective Krupp

said in a loud stage whisper, "in case you haven't noticed."

"I do not."

"The best thing is to just ignore him. A lot of the really tall suspects try to sleep with him—go figure—but you're the first one in a long time who is significantly shorter than he is. I think you've thrown him for a loop."

"Just shut up," Detective Wimbler said. His face was pomegranate pink.

Detective Krupp walked over to the one-way glass window and pulled down a shade. "Mrs. Timberlake, because you knew Tweetie that makes you like family to me."

"Uh—listen. I didn't like Tweetie in the beginning. How could I? She stole my husband. Sure, my feelings softened somewhat later on when Buford cheated on her, but I don't think you should count me as family."

"But I do, and I'm going to take care of you."

"Me too," said Detective Wimbler. "Research does show that tall people—especially tall men—get all the breaks. Did you know that they're much more likely to get promoted?"

"Maybe that's because they have larger brains," Detective Krupp said. She sounded quite serious. Then again, she was at least five inches taller than her partner.

"You're probably wondering why I didn't bother to legally change my name from Timberlake to Washburn when I remarried."

"Actually, I hadn't," said Detective Krupp.

"My late mother kept her maiden name," said Detective Wimbler. "It was Wiggins."

I didn't dare tell the poor man that this was also *my* maiden name. Perhaps my late daddy, who was also diminutive, had been kin to Mrs. Wimbler. The revelation of such a possibility was sure to start a never-ending conversation—on second thought, that little tidbit would be my ace in the hole.

Detective Krupp was clearly annoyed whenever the conversation veered from her control. "What I'm trying to say, Mrs. Timberlake, is that Wallace here and I have your back."

Wallace? How cruel can some parents get? (June and Ward Cleaver exempted.) No wonder the poor man had a complex; it wasn't his height after all. Daddy was only five feet, and that included the one-inch chip on his shoulder—but it came from the fact that the service wouldn't take him, not because of his stature per se.

"Mrs. Timberlake," Detective Krupp said, her annoyance clearly growing, "are you even listening to me?"

"Yes, ma'am, I am."

"Good. Because I'm trying to tell you that my partner and I are going to take it easy on you, on account of you and I have this special connection. And you're a native Southerner—like us. It's not like you just moved down here six months ago from someplace like Boston or New York, and started calling yourself a North Carolinian."

"Or worse yet," Detective Wimbler said, "is when you don't."

"Yeah, you've got that right."

"And this means exactly what?" I said. I knew I was being played, and not like a Stradivarius either.

"It means we're going to release you on your own recognizance," Detective Krupp said, "but we want you to stay in the area."

"That means no taking any side trips to visit LEGO-LAND," Detective Wimbler said.

I couldn't help but raise my eyebrows. "Isn't that the miniature village built out of LEGO blocks that's in Denmark?"

"Sometimes it's best just to ignore him," Detective Krupp said. "Like now." She moved to the door, indicating my interrogation was over. "Oh, just one more thing," she said. "Her bazoomas were real."

"I beg to differ, Detective Krupp. That's how I caught my husband having the affair. The bill from the plastic surgeon came to our house; it was for nine thousand dollars."

"Did you take the time to read it carefully, Mrs. Timberlake? I bet dollars to doughnuts that was for Tweetie's reduction surgery. In the fourth grade that girl began to blossom like nobody's business, and by the time we started middle school she could have posed for *Playboy*. Then they just got out of control—her breasts I mean. They were right painful, I suppose. I know she got excused from gym on that account."

"Why, slap me up the side of the head with a mess of greens and call me late for dinner."

"Are you mocking me, Mrs. Timberlake, because I'm trying to like you?"

"I'm sorry. I'm just ashamed of myself for having

been so judgmental of her, and didn't know what else to say."

"Just lay low, Mrs. Timberlake," Detective Wimbler said. "Don't say anything more here; we'll be in touch with you."

When I returned to the grand lobby of my hotel, I expected to get on the elevator, walk down a long plushy carpet to my door, enter my suite of rooms, take a scalding hot shower, and then flop onto my bed with the remote in one hand and a contraband bag of Peanut M&M's in the other. Instead I was accosted. Right there in the lobby, I was practically jumped by three people—one of whom had been stalking me virtually my entire life!

4

"S urprise!" Mama said.

"I don't like surprises, Mama. You know that."

"Abby, don't be such a grouch," Wynnell said. After Rob, she was my closest friend in the whole wide world, and knew a lot better than to drive up from Charleston unannounced like that.

"We're your backup team," C.J. said. C.J. is my ex-sister-in-law, but a dear friend as well. She is also from Shelby, North Carolina, and has the stories to prove it.

The three of them had surrounded me, but I managed to slip under C.J.'s long, gangly arms. "What the heck is going on? Who called you?"

"Why nobody, dear," Mama said. "You know how I have this ability to smell trouble? Well, I began to get a whiff of it last night when I was watching TV, so I called C.J. and Wynnell and told them to be on standby, and then this morning when I was frying bacon I couldn't even smell it on account of the scent of trouble was so strong."

"Perhaps you were smelling something rotten in Denmark," I said with just a hint of sarcasm.

"Shame on you, Abby," Wynnell said. "If my mama was alive, I'd never talk to her like that. Oh Lordy, how I miss that woman."

"Wynnell, your mama used to whip you with a braid made from rawhide strips just because you left water spots in the sink."

"Well, I still miss her, Abby—just not in a good way."

"At least y'all had mamas," C.J. said. "I was raised by Granny Ledbetter who learned her mothering from her mama who learned hers from a she-wolf."

"Oy vey," I said. "I feel a Shelby story coming on."

"But Abby," C.J. insisted, "this one is true. You see, there was this band of Gypsies traveling through Shelby—this was back around 1900. Anyways, they accidentally left a little baby behind at their campgrounds and it was adopted by this alpha she-wolf and her pack. A couple of years later this Italian family built a house out in the forest, near the wolf's den, and discovered Great-granny running wild through the trees. They caught her, raised her up like one of their own, and then took her along with them to Italy on a trip to visit relatives when Great-granny was about nineteen years old."

"Let me guess how this ends," Wynnell said. "Your great-granny fell in love with an Italian sculptor who made a statue of her, and another human child, as they were both nursing from a wolf."

C.J. nearly fainted from surprise. "How did you

39

know? Honest to Pete, Wynnell, I've never told *anyone* that story before. Granny Ledbetter made me promise never to tell it on account of it was just too personal to share—what with the nursing and all."

"I think your granny was right," I said. "So don't tell anyone else." I put my hands on my hips in the most unladylike of stances and gave them each a frank stare, but not one of them even had the courtesy to blink. "Okay, given that y'all are such good liars, maybe y'all will be of some help—*down the line*. But I need to collect my thoughts first. In the meantime, you might wish to drive back to I–77 and go north an exit or two. I seem to remember some chain motels up there."

"That's all right, dear," Mama said. "We're already checked in here. I'm bunking with you, of course—my bags are already in the room—and Wynnell and C.J. will be sharing a room."

"Of course," I said. There went any hope of unwinding.

"In case you're wondering how we're going to pay for these fancy-schmancy digs," Wynnell said, without a trace of sarcasm, "I've been squirreling away money for a long time in hopes of a 'girls' weekend' getaway. And this, Abby, certainly fits the bill."

I urged my lips to form a smile, even just a small one. "But who's minding the shop, Wynnell? Both of my employees are standing right here."

"Ooh, Abby, guess," C.J. said, suddenly animated again. "You'll never guess who."

"Mayor Riley?"

"Good one, Abby! I did ask him," she said guilelessly, "but he said his schedule had been filled for some time. Guess again!"

"Oh what the heck, I guess Greg."

"Abby! How did you do it? Are you psychic like your mama?"

"Wait just one cotton-pickin' minute! My *husband*, Greg, is minding *my* shop, the Den of Antiquity?"

C.J. nodded happily, while Wynnell nodded sheepishly.

"Don't worry," Wynnell said. "He'll be fine. My Ed will be checking in on him from time to time—and Booger is there as well."

"What's this world coming to," I said. "My beloved shop is in the hands of a man who hates antiques. But I shouldn't worry because his best buddy—who goes by the name of Booger—is there to help him."

"Well, when you put it that way," Wynnell said.

"If you'll excuse me, ladies," I said, "I'm going to the bar."

"Ooh, goody," C.J. said.

"*Alone,*" I said.

The clock was stopped for Mama the day Daddy was killed by a kamikaze gull with a brain tumor the size of a walnut. June Cleaver and Margaret Anderson were Mama's role models, and to this day my dear little mama, who stands just five feet tall in her nylons, vacuums the house wearing high-heeled pumps and a single strand of pearls. Of course she wears a good deal more than that as well, including a cone-shaped bra built using hurricane-proof construction methods and a full circle skirt shirtdress with a matching belt

41

cinched so tight it appears to bisect her waist. Beneath that skirt (holding it out to at least a forty-five-degree angle) is a crinoline so heavily starched that the carbohydrates in it could feed Paris Hilton for a year.

When I returned to the room I found five of these crinolines lined up, standing upright on my bed. Mama, on the other hand, was curled up under a blanket on the sofa in the sitting room of my suite. Believe me, her sweet dreams soured rather quickly upon my arrival.

"Mama!" I had to shake her as hard as a paint mixer just to get her to open her eyes. "You didn't take a pill, did you?"

She sat up groggily, pulling the blanket over her bust. The modesty move was so unnecessary given the fact that she wears the twin cones to bed under her nightgown. After all, Deborah Kerr wouldn't be caught braless. What if her lover—Deborah's, not Mama's—were to come pounding on the hotel door, demanding to take her into his strong, business suit–clad arms . . .

"Mama, I'm talking to you. Did you take a sleeping pill?"

"No, dear. It's just that I didn't get much sleep last night, what with all the worrying I had to do about you."

"*Had* to do? No one's forcing you to worry, Mama!"

"It's a mother's job, dear; it comes with the territory. Don't you worry about Charlie and Susan?"

"Well, of course I do, but that's different; they're only in their twenties."

"It never ends, Abby. The problem is that there isn't anything you can say to anybody before they—well, you know, do it—that will truly make them under-stand this. That parenthood is forever."

"I thought that only applied to Jewish mothers."

"Who knows? Maybe so—but remind me to discuss that further with you tomorrow."

"What?"

"Abby, I'm really awfully tired. Can't we just go to sleep?"

"Where, Mama? The bed has been taken over by a company of crinolines. I know that if I were to set them on the floor there would be all heck to pay."

"Well, dear," said Mama becoming suddenly, and suspiciously, wide-awake, "this couch opens into a full-queen size bed. We could stand the crinolines on this and I could sleep with you on the king."

I sighed. "Okay, Mama. But no spooning. Last time those cones dug a hole in my back that took two weeks to plump out again."

"Deal," Mama said happily.

When I'm with her, Mama makes me drive. C.J. and Wynnell drove separately. That said, we had breakfast at the Flying Biscuit in the Stonecrest Shopping Center. The biscuits there are the size of small pillows, and I'd forgotten just how much food my compatriots could put away in a single meal. Even more surprised at their combined intake was the somewhat distraught manager of that fine establishment. Understandably, she was trying to urge us along.

I shared her frame of mind. "So," I said, "we best be getting this show on the road. We have a lot of sleuth-ing ahead of us."

Tamar Myers

"More biscuits, please," Mama said nonchalantly. Given that my minimadre has a waist that would make Scarlett O'Hara look positively chubby, it is a wonderment where she stores all this.

Wynnell fixed her unibrow on the manager, which sent the poor gal scurrying back to the kitchen. "The problem is," she said, when the coast was clear, "that we're here as Abby's backup team. But according to that fellow who grilled me like a well-seasoned tenderloin this morning, my petite friend here, my best buddy, my galloping gal pal—"

"Okay, we get it," Mama said. "Could you just get to the point, dear?"

"Well, the point is that your daughter is the number one suspect."

"*What?*" I cried. In my distress I stood so abruptly that I tipped our table, causing empty, but nonetheless sticky and gooey plates to slide into C.J.'s and Wynnell's laps.

Wynnell ignored the egg yolk on her white cotton blouse and the syrup on the lap of her blue bias-cut skirt. "He knocked on the door at six-thirty, Abby, and made it sound like I had to speak to him. You know, down at the station. I didn't know what else to do."

"What did he ask, and what did you tell him?"

"He asked mostly stupid stuff, like how long had I known you, did I ever hear you talk about the victim, did I think you were capable of killing anyone—that kind of thing."

"And what did you say? About me killing someone?"

"I said that it was theoretically possible, but ex-

44

tremely doubtful. I told him about the time we found a mouse in the storeroom and you insisted that we catch the little fellow in one of those humane traps and release it in the black neighborhood."

"*What?*"

"Well, you did; that's where the vacant lot was."

"Wynnell, dearest, I merely directed you to release the critter in the *nearest* vacant lot. Now the detective is going to think that I'm a racist. C.J., were you grilled as well before breakfast?"

The galoot had crammed half a biscuit into her mouth and was having trouble swallowing it. I waited patiently while she chased the pastry down with half a tumbler of milk and a glass of ice water.

"I have my own room now, Abby, on account of Wynnell snores like an asthmatic orangutan. Anyway, he knocked on my door at six thirty-five, only he was a she in my case. I know because I was on the phone with my ex—your brother—and I had my eye on the clock. It isn't cheap calling the Congo."

"Toy is in the *Congo*?"

"My only *son* is in the Congo?" Mama wailed.

"The Democratic Republic of the Congo—which is anything but. There are two countries that call themselves Congo, Abby. This is the by far the bigger one; this is the one most people think of when they hear that name."

"Fascinating geography lesson, C.J., but what's my brother—your ex—and mama's son—doing there?"

"He's delivering mosquito nets to remote villages. Malaria kills thousands of people over there every year."

"My son the saint," Mama said.

"How did he get to the Congo?" I asked. "Did he walk across the Atlantic?"

"Good one," C.J. said. "I'm sure he took a plane, Abby. But my cousin Malcolm Ledbetter up in Shelby can walk on water."

"That's very interesting," I said. "What questions did the detective ask you?"

"You don't believe me, do you, Abby?"

"Well—"

"You've never believed any of my Shelby stories, have you?"

"Never say never, right? Right, Mama? Right, Wynnell?"

"If y'all will excuse me, I need to use the little girls' room," Mama said.

"I'm coming with you," Wynnell said. "Somewhere it's written that we ladies of a certain generation must always do this in pairs."

"You're not that old, dear," Mama said, "but come along. And do hurry. This is one conversation that I'd prefer to miss out on."

Apparently C.J. was not in a waiting mood. "Well *what*?" she said before Mama was even safely to her feet.

"Well," I said, "some of your stories are a little far-fetched."

"Just name me one!"

"For instance, you don't have goat DNA, C.J. That's physically impossible—not to mention that's a lot of initials."

"I have horns and a tail, Abby. What further proof do you want?"

I glanced around the room. I saw normal people eating pillow-size biscuits having normal conversations. It was probably a safe bet that none of them was claiming to have barnyard kin.

"C.J., I've said this before—and you know that I say this out of love, as your friend, and not as your ex-sister-in-law—that I know someone in Charleston who is excellent. I can recommend her personally, because I am one of her patients. It's strictly talk therapy, mind you, nothing—"

That's when she lunged. She threw herself across the table and grabbed my right hand, which she then forcibly placed on her head.

"Feel that," she bellowed.

"Ouch!" I tried in vain to yank my hand away. "What is it?"

"Get a good feel," she ordered.

"Okay, okay. You can let up."

"No, you have to feel the other side. And push the hair away too, and tell me what you see."

"Gross! C.J., they make special shampoos for this condition—oh my fathers, what the hell? C.J., is this *really* a horn? No, that's ridiculous! You've obviously glued something to your head."

"Uh-uh, Abby. Here, I have a tail too. You gotta feel that."

"Get out of town and back! A tail?"

"That's not so uncommon, Abby. Like one in a hundred thousand people is born with a little extra something that needs to be removed, but this—Abby, you really need to feel it."

This was getting surreal. The only pills I'd taken that morning were a multivitamin and extra vitamin C, but they were Mama's pills, ones that she'd brought with her and foisted on me. Left to my own devices, I picked up my nutrients via a glass of orange juice and healthy eating choices (which did not include pillow-size biscuits, no matter how tasty). My point is that I had not, to my knowledge, ingested a hallucinogen, nor was I still asleep and having a nightmare. I knew the latter because I could smell bacon, and I don't smell anything when I dream.

"C.J., I'm not going to go feeling around in your pants—not here, at any rate."

5

The pseudo-giantess from Shelby pivoted around the table and would have forced my hand down the back of her Gloria Vanderbilt denim jeans had not Mama and Wynnell returned from the ladies' room. As it was, we presented quite a spectacle and had the attention of everyone in the restaurant.

"What's going on?" Mama said in a tone that only a mama can muster.

"Nothing, ma'am," I said.

"Then why is your face the color of a raw pork chop, and why is everyone staring at you?"

"C.J. and I were arm wrestling," I said. "I lost badly—of course."

"Why Abigail Wiggins Timberlake and Oughta-Be-Washburn, you're lying to me, as sure as Sherman razed Atlanta. C.J., you wouldn't lie to an old woman, now would you?"

"Yes, ma'am, I would."

Mama turned and faced the other customers. "Y'all see what I have to put up with? Have y'all ever seen

49

such an incorrigible pair of twins? Oh yes, they are twins—normally they're as close as Frick and Frack. I guess they're just overly excited about this being their thirtieth birthday; I know, it doesn't seem possible— but Abby here played in the sun a lot as a baby. Plus she used to smoke. There's a lesson there, folks."

"I am not C.J.'s twin!" I cried. "I'm practically old enough to be her mother!"

"You said it, dear, I didn't."

At that Mama gathered her crinolines in both hands and glided from the room like a swan on ice skates. Wynnell hurried after Mama, and C.J., bleating a pathetic apology, trotted three steps behind.

I was stuck with the check.

Toy and I never got along—except late on Christmas Eve day, when we could be found canoodling over a puzzle, or playing Go Fish (a tradition we kept up all the way through high school). The rest of the year we were sworn enemies, if not out for blood, then at least out for revenge.

It was during my so-called Toy years that I learned how to be sneaky and tap into all my baser instincts. I had to, because it was a matter of survival. Essentially then, this darker side of me is all his fault. At least that's my story, and I'm sticking to it.

After I paid the bill, rather than exit through the front door where I knew the rest of my group were waiting, I fabricated a story about a competition and a race, and was ushered through to a back door, which also happened to be a shortcut to where I'd parked the car. By the time the others came back in to inquire about me, I was long gone in Mama's car. As a matter of fact, I was probably halfway to the shabby-chic home of Chanteuse Ovumkoph Goldburg.

Rob's mom lives in a 1940s traditional two-story brick that is now sandwiched between a pair of McMansions. The effect is immediately unsettling, as the brain has trouble sorting out which of the residences is out of place. As I understand it, Chanti has been offered a substantial amount of money for her house by someone who wishes to bulldoze it and erect a third McMansion in its place. So far memories have triumphed over money.

A boxwood hedge flanked Chanti's restrained brick path, in contrast to the imported river-stone walks and dwarf gardenia borders of both overstated productions on either side. Yet I would rather be walking up to the door of either stucco palace, with the intent of selling skin products, than facing the woman who produced my best friend. To put it succinctly, Chanti had never liked me.

Actually, I can't recall anyone she's liked other than her Robbie. If the word *possessive* had a picture next to it in *Webster's Collegiate Dictionary*, it would be Chanti's stern visage. I realize this description makes their relationship sound like it leaps off the pages of some 1950s psychological review of homosexuality, but I'm just calling a queen a queen.

But I wanted to know where Rob was, and since he hadn't answered either his room phone or his cell phone, I was willing to bet dollars to doughnuts that the good ol' boy was at his mama's. And while I was betting greenbacks against my favorite fat-laden sugary treats, I'd go so far as to say that he'd already confronted his mama about the food-poisoning charge and was now curled up on his bed, in a fetal position under the covers, reading ancient copies of *Mad* magazine by flashlight. It is self-medicating habits like this that keep the man trim and fit-looking, while the rest of the walking wounded sport spare tires and double chins.

Chanteuse Goldburg answered the door looking as if she were about to head out to South Park Mall. In fact, her purse was waiting in the howdah of a wicker elephant just inside the door. South Park, for anyone who is unfamiliar with area shopping, is *the* place to shop in Charlotte. Another way to put it is thusly; that's where Neiman Marcus is located.

"It's you," she said, and nothing more. She didn't even stand slightly aside.

"And it's you."

"Look, Addie, I'm not receiving *unexpected* visitors today."

"Mrs. Goldburg, you know very well that my name is Abby. We've known each other for years. May I come in?"

"No." *No?* For heaven's sake, the woman was as Southern as sweet tea, and here she was refusing to invite me in? What on earth was going on? Was she being held hostage? Was there a gunman hiding behind the thick, genuine silk, floor-to-ceiling drapes?

"I just wish to speak to Rob," I said quickly, fearing the door might be slammed in my face. "We can do it out here on the porch—if you prefer."

"You can't."

"I beg your pardon?"

"Mrs. Washtub, do you have any idea how much that emerald ring means to me?"

"The name is Wash*burn*, dear, and I'm sure I don't understand how the ring's sentimental value has anything to do with you allowing me to talk with your son."

"Why you arrogant little—*tiny*—woman, you. I never really liked you, from the moment I met you. I don't think my Robbie was truly gay until you got your hooks into him. You're what they call a fag hag, aren't you?"

Me? A fag hag? Was that a pejorative term? And if so, for whom? For little, tiny me, or for my gay friends? Well, it certainly wasn't cool for Rob's mother to be calling me that, because it was clear that her intent was unkind.

"Mrs. Goldburg, your son is certain that he was born gay; he experienced same-sex feelings from a very early age. And he was certainly acting out on those feelings long before he met me. Like decades before."

She bit her lip and shuddered. "Enough with that crude talk. Come in—but just for a second."

Stepping into the house was like entering a mausoleum to good taste. Chanti had been a high-end interior decorator who'd retired from the business in the mid-1970s. During her working life she'd acquired some very nice pieces, some unusual ones as well. However, Chanti was still using 1970s wallpaper and fabrics, so that the overall affect was somewhat discombobulating. *Depressing* was another word that immediately sprung to mind.

The second she closed the door, Chanti grabbed both my hands. "Where is it?"

"Where is *what*?"

"Don't be obtuse, Mrs. Washbum. Where's the ring?"

I yanked my hands away and put them behind my back. "*What* ring, damn it?"

"The emerald ring, you blockhead! The one my sister gave you. The one she should have given to me. It belonged to our grandmother, you know."

"No, I didn't know. And please read my lips—*I don't have your ring.*"

"I heard her leave it to you in the will. We all did."

"Yes, but I refused to accept it. You all heard that as well."

"Look, missy," Chanti snarled, as she leaned over my airspace, "you can play games all you want; but I know the truth. I am family after all. I officially identified my sister's remains."

I shrank back toward the door. "The truth? What's that supposed to mean?"

"The ring was missing, you imbecile!"

"Finally! A three-syllable insult. Of course it was missing, Chanti. The police always remove the valuables from the victim for safekeeping. Did you ask about it?"

"You exasperating, harebrained twerp!" she screamed. "I don't know what my son sees in you."

And there, as if by magic, the fruit of her womb appeared on the staircase behind her. He was dressed in chinos and a pale blue chambray shirt that set off his deep salon bed tan. Since sandals—without socks, of course—have, as of late, been given a thumbs-up by the mavens of the fashion world, Rob sported an extravagant pair of designer straps. Even from this short distance he appeared cool, elegant, and unflappable.

"Good morning, Mama. Good morning, Abby."

Since Rob hung the sun it was only natural for Chanti to turn and greet him. I could have used those precious seconds to scoot out the door, but I had come to see my friend, damn it.

"*Boker tov*," I said.

"*Boker or*," Rob said, and laughed.

"What was that?" Chanti barked.

"That was Hebrew," I said.

"I learned it in NFTY," Rob said. "You know, Mama, my Reform Jewish youth group."

"Abby's not Jewish," Chanti said. "You shouldn't be teaching her things."

It was an absurd statement, but one not to be argued with. I'd just hit a home run in the game of "irritate Chanteuse Goldburg," and I sure the heck wasn't going to rub my victory in.

"Abby," Rob said. "Come with me to the back porch."

I needed no further urging.

Once we'd settled into some comfortable recliners, and were sipping mimosas, Rob cleared his throat.

"Uh-oh," I said.

"Uh-oh, what?"

"You're not going to yell at me for getting into it with your mother?"

"If *that* was getting *into it*, then I'm going to insist

you come back home with me every time I visit. Her imperial highness thrives on discord, as you might have noticed. When she went to finishing school she got an A+ in How to Make People Miserable. By the way, I'm all for you having that ring; that's what Aunt Jerry wanted. But I am curious as to how you managed to get to Aunt Jerry and get the ring before she was—I mean, you didn't take it off *after*, did you?"

I may be a petite woman, but my mouth opened wide enough to swallow the state of Delaware. "Rob Goldburg! You're not suggesting that I killed your aunt, are you? Because if you are, I'll—I'll—let's just say that Dick Cheney will wish he'd had me working for him."

"Ouch! So much meanness in such a small package of pleasantly arranged molecules. Abigail, darling, it didn't even flash across my mind—not for a microsecond—that you had anything to do with Aunt Jerry's horrible send-off. I only meant that, given both your love of jewelry and knowledge of gems, you might have felt tempted to slip that boulder off her finger before screaming bloody murder. It was, after all, your ring."

I carefully set my champagne flute on an onyx coaster before getting up. When I leaned to give Rob a hug, he virtually pulled me into his chair.

"You don't need to be forgiven," he said. "But you need to join me. It's times like this that I feel very much alone."

"Oh Rob—"

"She left me a million dollars, Abby. Free and clear. No strings attached."

"She did? Where was I?"

"You'd jumped off the table and run into the house for some reason. What did you do, go to the bathroom?"

"No. I was embarrassed by that ring episode. So, who else was named a beneficiary?"

"Uncle Ben, of course. The catastrophe was held at his house, so you can guess that they were kind of close—well, he got along with her better than anyone else in the family did. Anyway, she left him two million dollars—also free and clear."

"Anyone else?"

"The Mecklenburg County SPCA."

"Really? For how much?"

"Approximately three million in real estate."

I sipped my drink. "No offense, Rob, but your aunt was loaded."

"None taken."

"Do you think your family will object to the dogs and cats of Mecklenburg County sharing in her largesse?"

Rob's laugh was as hollow as a store-bought cheese straw. "Three lawsuits have already been filed—and no, none of them are mine."

"So that means your bobble-headed Uncle Aaron—well hush my mouth, how shallow can one get? Sorry, Rob, that just slipped out."

Rob laughed. "Not to worry, Abby. We call him Bobby on that account. Not to his face, of course."

"Who is we?"

"Why Bob, of course." The irony—and perhaps Rob didn't see it—is that if Aaron shaved his mustache, he and Bob Steuben could pass for identical twin brothers.

"So far that's one. Who are the other two?"

"My righteous cousin, the pastor; and The-One-to-Whom-All-Is-Owed—that would be my mother."

"You're kidding! Your mother, who just inherited a million dollars—plus ten thousand for supposedly—well, you know—anyway, *she's* contesting the will? Doesn't that seem just a little bit—uh—"

"Not as long as the animals of Mecklenburg County get more. We've never been an animal-oriented family, Abby. No pets of any kind. That was such a hard and fast rule that when I was in the third grade and every kid got head lice, I was the only kid who didn't; they didn't dare violate Chanti's 'no pet' rule. Once I found a carp swimming in the bathtub. I got so excited, thinking I was finally getting a pet. I named the behemoth Moby. It ended up the next day on my plate as gefilte fish."

"That's a sad story, Rob."

"Too bad it's not true," a female voice said.

6

I was so startled that I literally tossed the rest of my mimosa in the air, glass and all; a stranger might even have guessed that I had a small role in an ABBA movie and that he or she had caught me rehearsing. But believe me, the worst part about being vertically challenged is that I will forever have to look up to individuals like Chanteuse Goldburg.

"Sorry," I said. "I really didn't mean to get that all over your clothes. If you'd leaned just a little bit lower, I might have been able to get most of my drink down your cleavage."

Rob's mother can recoil faster than a striking cobra. "I beg your pardon! What did you say? Robbie, did you hear what this white trash just said to me?"

"Not now, Mama; I'm still laughing!"

"Why I never! Not in all my born days! Abby, do you treat your mama like this?"

"Oh no, ma'am. When she asks me a direct question, I always answer; no matter how hard I've been laughing."

"No, I meant—well, never mind what I meant. I'm just glad to know that you respect your mama. Robbie, did you hear that? Abigail wouldn't dream of being so rude. Honestly, I don't know where I went wrong. You had the very best of everything. And I mean *everything*—yet, ironically, it's like you didn't want much of anything. He was a very hard child to please, Abby, because he had no desires. Can you imagine that?"

"And who says mankind is incapable of change?" I said. The Rob I knew was a collector of everything beautiful, both for his home and for his shop, The Finer Things. In fact, at this stage of his life, his desires had moved beyond a lust for the exquisite, and into the realm of the limitless. I knew for a fact that he'd recently spent ten grand on a silver flask said to have touched the lips of Marilyn Monroe on the night of her tragic demise. When I asked him why he wished to own such an object in the first place—never mind pay such an exorbitant price—his answer was simply "Well, somebody has to own it, so why not me?"

"Mama, that's a dig," Rob said. "Abby's picking on me."

Poor Chanteuse, I almost felt sorry for her. Her fierce love for her son would have been admirable had not some of that ferocity traditionally been reserved for me. But now we were allies, were we not? Surely that presented her with a dilemma.

"Get out of my house, you gold-digging little strumpet," she barked. "How dare you cuddle up to my son in the same chair, pressed against his manly chest, like a young nubile Jewish woman—which you are anything but! It's temptresses like you, Ms. Timberquake, who have convinced my dear Robert that he is a homosexual. So if you don't leave before I count to ten, I will—"

She'd stopped to give her son a meaningful look. Meanwhile she was huffing and puffing like the Little Engine That Could.

"You'll what?" Rob said casually.

Just to be safe, I got out of the chair and backed well away onto the lawn.

"I'll call the police, dear. You know I will."

"I dare you to call them, Mama."

Chanteuse disappeared into the house but returned just a few seconds later bearing a cordless phone. Already she was speaking to someone on the other end.

"Of *course* this woman is an intruder," she said. "Would I have called you otherwise? She was in my living room just a few minutes ago—I'll swear to that in court. Yes, I think she's armed. I mean she definitely looks the type. You know, beady eyes, scar across the left cheek, that kind of thing."

Rob hoisted himself out of the recliner. "Mama, I'm leaving," he said.

"But darling, I only want what's best for you—and a grandchild! Is that too much to ask?"

"Yes, it is."

"Come on, Abby, we can leave through the back gate."

"But what about your stuff? Didn't you bring in your suitcase?"

"Screw my stuff," Rob said.

Rob said he needed to work off some steam so I left

him to hike the greenway that begins across from Trader Joe's and ends approximately six miles later on Johnston Road, not far from Pike's Nursery. Meanwhile I dropped in on Tuesday Morning. I remembered Lauren Bacall doing the TV ads for these stores a couple of years back, but had never taken the time to visit one.

My verdict, based on this one store, is that they are fabulous *if*, like Rob, your need for things is endless. Since the merchandise in Tuesday Morning is always changing, it is hard to shop for specifics, although one will always find something that is *indispensable*. It's when our desires become our needs that we're in trouble, if you ask me.

Chanteuse Goldburg wanted a grandchild, although she couldn't have one; as a consequence she was becoming mean. Rob wanted just about anything, and as for me, well, there was a piece of resin sculpture in Tuesday Morning that spoke to my soul. It was a particularly well-crafted Southern magnolia blossom displayed against a background of the dark shiny leaves that characterize this species.

The sculpture had probably been mass-produced in China. The truth is that some beautiful things are being cast in resin today; if this technology had been available three hundred years ago, and just a few pieces had been made, only kings would have owned them. But unfortunately beautiful items are available to the masses, and in my Charleston home I had room to showcase only the *rare* and valuable, no matter how homely those collectibles might be.

I fondled the delicate sculpture, turning it this way

and that. This magnolia blossom could pass for a real one and never wilt, and it was only $26.99. I could buy it and use it as a paperweight—but to weigh down my papers from what? The breath of a giant? A hurricane? I never kept my windows open; it was always too hot, or too cold, or too buggy. Call me wasteful, but I loved my air—

"Do ya honestly think," said a woman turning into my aisle, "that *I* would do something like that?" She was of sufficient girth to appreciate the benefit of leaning on her shopping buggy.

"Honey," said her male companion, "I honestly believe that *anyone* is capable of *anything.*"

"Uh-uh, ya did not just say that, because that's a flat-out accusation."

"I call them as I see them, dear."

"Then screw ya, Malcolm, and the horse ya rode in on!"

The fellow—who was actually quite handsome—took off at a lope, and without another word.

"Damn him," the woman said as she approached me. "Damn his sensitive hide."

I sucked in all my vibes, willing a shield of invisibility to surround me. It was soon clear that I was out of practice.

"Can ya believe that?" she said to me.

I said nothing.

"Ya don't have to be rude," she said.

"Oh, sorry," I said. "I've been a mite distracted lately. Yesterday I found a dead woman in a freezer, and I think I might be a suspect in her murder, and now my best friend left home because his mother thinks I

63

turned him gay, even though he's almost fifty and I've only known him a dozen years, and my own mother tracked me to town along with my second best friend and ex-sister-in-law who really is part goat—although I refuse to believe that. You wouldn't believe *that*, would you?"

"Say, you gonna buy that magnolia or not?"

"Well, I—"

"Because that piece of junk looks just like the one my mother-in-law used to have until I broke it. Of course it was an accident—sort of." She laughed. "That's what me and my husband was fighting about. He thinks he seen me do it, and maybe he did. But I'm just messing with his head. If I buy this one and put it where the old used to be, that will really get him good."

"Ah, too bad," I said, "that I already have my little heart set on buying this for myself."

"Ya sure? I'll pay ya ten bucks more than it's worth."

"No thanks. I've got a spot already picked out for it."

"Bitch."

"You've got that right."

I had some time to kill before I had to pick up Rob, and what better way to kill it than at a coffee shop? There is something about purchasing a cup of overpriced java and sipping it on the premises that makes it feel like a mini-event, rather than a first-rate rip-off—which it is. I, for one, like to imagine that the folks hunched over their laptops are serious novelists and that if I affect a distinctive set of mannerisms while sipping my brew,

I might just show up in a book as part of a character.

"Why are you twitching, Abby?"

Holy crap, I thought, what did I do to deserve this? "Mama," I exclaimed. "Where did you come from?"

"The ladies' room. You know what caffeine does to me, dear."

"Where are the others?"

"Wynnell is getting her upper lip waxed just up the road from here and C.J. is still in the ladies' room. Apparently there was some graffiti in one of the stalls that read something like: 'I'm being held prisoner; call me at blah, blah, blah.' She's taking it seriously. You know how she is."

"Oy vey," I said. "What are we going to do with the big galoot?"

"Love her; that's all we can do. She's not dangerous, and she can clearly function on her own. What is her IQ anyway?"

"One sixty-five. I think that's part of her problem. It's kind of lonely up there at the top, so she invents these stories to amuse herself."

"Speaking of stories, dear, you'll never guess what the latest one is that's making the rounds."

"That I took an emerald ring off a dead woman?"

Mama wears a string of pearls given to her by Daddy decades ago. She has never removed them—not once. Not even to shower. The fact that the gems look as splendid as they did the day that Daddy lifted them from the blue velvet box and hung them around Mama's alabaster neck, is, in my humble opinion, every bit as miraculous as the images of Mary, Joseph, and baby Jesus that appeared on Grace Wilder's cornbread when she took it from the oven on the stroke of midnight, December 24, 1966.

At any rate, when Mama gets agitated she pats her pearls. When she's very excited she twirls them. Until then, I had never seen her stroke them like one would stroke a kitten.

"Mama, what's wrong?"

"That's exactly it, Abby; that's the story."

"So how did you hear?"

"That awful Mrs. Goldburg. She called the hotel just before we left. She said to tell you that unless you give it back, she's going to call the police."

"So let her. Of course she won't; she already made that threat to me. Besides I didn't take it." I shuddered. "Mama, that would be macabre; removing something from the finger of a dead woman."

"Shhh, dear."

Oops. She'd been right to shush me. In my agitation—lacking pearls to pat—I'd spoken far too loudly. Apparently nothing pulls in an audience quite as well in a coffee shop as talk of robbing the dead. One of the keyboard pounders actually changed seats, moving to the one just behind me. Either he really was a novelist in need of a plot, or I was being followed.

"And then I put the bomb inside a frozen turkey," I said, "which I shipped by Bactrian camel to his summer house in Uzbekistan."

Mama's fingers tapped a rapid rhythm on her mollusk secretions. "Abby, honey, you're not making a lick of sense."

I rolled my eyes. "Behind me," I mouthed. "What's up with the guy sitting behind me?"

Mama sighed. "Maybe Toy was right; I do need to get my hearing checked. First you practically break my eardrums, and now I can't even hear you. I used to think I'd be a good lip-reader, but I can cross that off my list of accomplishments; I mean surely you wouldn't prattle on about the gentleman sitting behind you."

"Mama!"

"Now I hear that; nice and loud too."

"I give up."

"Please don't," the man behind me said. "If you do, my story will be too short."

I stood, which frankly doesn't make me a whole lot taller than when I'm sitting; it certainly doesn't make me more imposing. "*What* story? Are you from the *Charlotte Observer*?"

7

Oh no, ma'am. I'm taking a creative writing class and my assignment was to listen to some dialogue in a public place and to use it in a story of my own. You and your sister were da bomb."

"She's not my sister; she's my mother! And the bomb is in the turkey, for crying out loud."

"It's an honest mistake, young man," Mama said, as she went from patting her pearls to patting her hair. Trust me; I was never going to hear the end of this.

I took a twenty-dollar bill from my wallet and held it out to the young man. He was about the age of my son, Charlie, which made him perhaps twenty.

"Here," I said, "take this. It might help move dialogue along—like back to the table where you started."

The kid remained seated. His eyes were uncomprehending; I may as well have been speaking Cantonese.

"Abby," Mama whispered, "I don't think that money talks as loud as it used to."

I pulled out another twenty, followed by a ten. "Either you take a hike now, junior, or we do."

He was a good Southern boy. "Thank you, ma'am," he said, before skedaddling.

"Who was that young stud muffin?"

I looked up from my café latte to see a strange woman with familiar eyes standing inside my comfort zone. Even worse, after brazenly bumping my shoulder with her hips, she slid into the booth next to me.

"*Excusez-moi*," I said, "but have we met?"

"Abby, it's me!"

"Wynnell? B-but you have two eyebrows!"

"I know," Mama purred, "doesn't she look fabulous? I was lying about the lip wax."

"Is that what you said, Mozella? And you believed that, Abby? I don't have a mustache, do I?"

"Of course not, dear." The fact that, upon occasion, I've had to reach over and whisk the crumbs off my dear friend's face was not relevant at the moment. What mattered was that her feelings not be hurt.

"It hurt like the dickens," Wynnell said. "I don't think I'll have it done again."

"But you look like a movie star," I said. "Really."

"Oh Abby, you really should stop lying. With your height, someone with a nose that long will not look in proportion." She glanced around. "Ahem—speaking of truth stretching, where is the maestro?"

"She's in the ladies' room answering a call of distress."

"Serves her right; I told her that eating the entire 'blooming onion' by herself was not such a good idea."

Mama sighed wearily. "No, it's— Oh, there she is.

C.J., darling, I was about to send a plumber in there after you."

"That was sweet of you, Mozella," C.J. said, and slid in next to Mama, "but I'm too big to be flushed down a toilet." Enormous tears suddenly filled her eyes and shook her gargantuan head slowly from side to side. "If only the same could be said for poor Cousin Theopolous Ledbetter. He was as thin as a rail, so thin, in fact, that if you looked at him from above you might mistake him for a crack in the sidewalk. One day he rode his mule into town, to one of those stores where the toilets have the automatic flushing."

"Let me guess," I said. "Poor Cousin Theopolous got flushed down the toilet and was never heard from again."

My former sister-in-law and current very dear friend turned her wounded eyes on me. "You don't need to be so rude, Abby. Besides, you're wrong; he did turn up again. He turned up in a sewer in Flushing, New York. That's how the town got its name."

"Ah," the three of us said.

"You guys don't believe me, do you?"

We nodded this way and that, neither confirming nor denying anything. Since our response was all too familiar, C.J. wisely let it go.

"I called that number in the stall," she said. "It was for Domino's Pizza. Can you believe someone would pull a prank like that?"

"Yes," we all said in concert again.

This time the big gal bristled. "Don't think I'm naive, ladies, because I'm not. Granny Ledbetter didn't raise any fools. I saw right through Uncle Rufus Ledbetter's scheme to get investors for the Trans-Atlantic Tunnel Project. New York to Paris in three days by car, he said. Underwater hotels. Every room would offer a fantastic opportunity for viewing deep-sea life."

"It sounds great," Wynnell said, "if you're not claustrophobic."

"It might have been a good idea at one time," Mama said sadly. "But nowadays—with the threat of terrorism—I wouldn't want to be stuck at the bottom of the ocean."

"I wouldn't either," I said. "And I'm sure you saw the drawbacks, C.J., which is why I want you on my team."

"Teams," Mama said. "Are we going to play games?"

"That's exactly right, and it's going to be you and Wynnell and against C.J. and me."

"Ooh," C.J. cooed. "I love it when Abby gets like this."

"I'm trying to frown," Wynnell said, "but I can't feel my brow scrunch up. Having two brows is for the birds."

"It's very becoming," I said. "Isn't it, ladies?"

"I liked the unibrow better," C.J. said. "It was more—uh—distinctive. Now you're actually kind of pretty."

"Beautiful, in fact," I said.

"Mozella, you see what you did?" Wynnell cried accusingly. "You made me beautiful! Now, if I'm not careful, I might get prideful; all on account of you."

Wynnell's outburst got the attention of everyone in the coffee shop. Their stares made my dear friend all the more uncomfortable. As usual, it was time for me to step in.

I jumped on the banquette. "Please, folks," I said, waving my arms, "can't you see this woman is distressed. The poor woman has just found out she's the inadvertent mother of Sarah Palin. Let's give her some privacy, shall we?"

"Oh come on," a beefy man in khaki shorts and wife-beater T-shirt said. "That's a bunch of bull."

"It is *not*," I said. "Wynnell, what is the capital of Africa?"

Wynnell is a staunch Republican and we have agreed never to discuss politics. However, if there is one thing she can't stand, it's a fat man in a wife-beater T-shirt butting into her business.

"The capital of Africa is Nairobi," she said, utterly deadpan.

"You see?" I said. "Now leave her alone, y'all."

I slid back into the booth. "Okay, gals, where were we?"

"The game," Mama said. "Do we need a deck of cards?" She reached into her handbag and pulled out two pill cases, a battery-powered fan, three pairs of drugstore reading glasses, a six-inch bust of Nefertiti, an oversized Christmas card, and a Portuguese language thesaurus. But no deck of playing cards.

"Mama, why so many pairs of glasses?"

"Frankly, dear, I'm too lazy to check, and since I'd rather be safe than sorry, I throw an extra pair in."

"Gotcha. And no, we don't need cards. The game is solving a murder."

Everyone groaned.

"Okay, so y'all have been there, done that; but this time it's different. We're working in two teams, and we're going to solve it in eight hours. It is now ten o'clock—give or take a couple of minutes, at least by that the clock on the wall—and by six o'clock tonight, we'll have this case cracked."

"Can we go to dinner then and celebrate?" Mama said. She's always concerned that I'm not eating enough—well, that's when she isn't concerned that I'm eating too much.

"What makes you think we can crack this case if the police haven't so far?" Wynnell said.

"The murder only happened *yesterday*," I said. "By the way, you scowl much better with the unibrow; I vote that you grow it back."

"Hear, hear," the others said in unison.

"So anyway, here are the players, guys." I proceeded to tell them everything I knew about the Ovumkoph family, naming Ben, Aaron, Melissa, Sam, Tina, and Chanti as possible suspects. I didn't mention Rob, because I knew he was on all of our minds anyway, and because we all loved him, and most of all, it would have been a betrayal to even breathe his name in that context.

"Okay, so we have the suspects," Mama said. She'd been taking careful but microscopic notes on the back of the Christmas card. "Now we need a motive."

"What about humiliation?" Wynnell said.

"Rob's Aunt Jerry was just telling it like she saw it," I said. It was amazing, but here I was feeling protective of a dead woman's reputation, and I'd only known her for a few minutes. Strictly speaking, make that a few seconds.

"Then the motive has to be greed," C.J. said. "Every-

73

body wanted more than their share, and they felt—Mozella, Abby, close your ears—stiffed."

"And I feel annoyed. C.J., first of all, I heard that. Second, how does one close their ears? And third, why didn't Wynnell have to close her ears?"

"Wynnell is hip, Abby. I didn't want to offend you and your mother with the S word, that's all."

"The S word?" Mama said.

"She means *stiffed*," I said.

Wynnell and C.J. sound absolutely wicked when they laugh in unison, especially when the laughter is directed at *me*. "You sound like a couple of fourth-graders," I said.

"And I, for one, am not at all offended," Mama said. "I think *stiff* is a lovely word. You know, I've been searching for years, and just last month now I finally found a man who does it right."

I clamped my hands over my ears. If only I *could* close them; if only we humans came equipped with "earlids."

"Mama," I moaned. "Why must you mortify me like this?"

"Oh Abby, you're such a prude. A well-starched crinoline is something of which to be proud. I used to do it myself, but frankly it's a messy job that I'd just rather not be doing at my age. So when I discovered that new full-service laundry up there on East Bay—"

Of course covered ears are only symbolic; they don't stop one from being able to hear. "Is that *all*, Mama? Stiff crinolines?"

"Why Abby, dear, whatever else could I possibly mean?"

I presented her with a blank face, one honed by my years as her teenage daughter. "Beats me, Mama."

"Oh, by the way, dear, I decided not to report my car stolen if you'll do my crinolines for the next three months. I figure that with the money I'll save I can have a nice little visit with your cousin down in Savannah. Do we have a deal, or should I beat Chanti to the punch?"

"Mama, you wouldn't! *Would* you?"

"Beats me, Abby."

"She's got you, Abby," Wynnell said. "She does your blank face even better than you do."

C.J. sighed. "I wish that I had me a mama—especially a young-looking one like you, Mozella. Granny Ledbetter has so many wrinkles that you never know which one's going to open when she talks—bless her heart."

"Bless her heart," we echoed in unison.

I clapped my hands. "Okay ladies, time's a-wasting, so here's the deal. Jerry Ovumkoph was murdered so that someone could take possession of a ring she was wearing."

"Diamond?" Mama asked.

"An emerald—practically the size of an egg. She wanted to give it to me, but I refused to take it."

Mama clucked like the hen that might have laid such an egg. "Talk about looking a gift horse in the mouth—not to speak ill of the dead." She opened one of the two pill cases and flung its contents over her shoulder.

"Hey! What was that?" The beefy man in the wifebeater T-shirt was out of his banquette and looming over our table.

"It was salt," Mama said calmly.

"It was to ward off bad luck," Wynnell said.

"Back in Shelby we once had a horse with no mouth," C.J. said, apropos of nothing. "We had to feed it through—"

"*What'd* you say?" Big and Beefy demanded.

"Don't mind her," I said. "She claims to be part Nubian—goat, that is—and may even have the horns to prove it."

"Cousin Calamity Jane Ledbetter Cox, is that *you*?"

"Cousin Rufus Horatio Ledbetter III Junior, is that *you*?"

"Lord have mercy," Mama said, "I think I'm going to be sick."

By then the big galoot and the big bully were wrapped around each other like clumps of kelp washed up on the beach after a storm. What were the odds that we'd run into another one of *the* Ledbetters, one of Granny's direct descendants, in a great big city like Charlotte, North Carolina? And in a sophisticated place like an overpriced gourmet coffee shop of all places?

"I don't get it," I said. "How can someone be designated the III and still be a Junior?"

"Sh-Sh-Shelby," Wynnell hissed.

The cousins disengaged. "Hey, don't be insulting our hometown. It's as fine a place as any to grow up. And you," he said to Mama in particular, "don't be tossing sodium chloride into folks' faces—sorry about the alliteration." Then he grabbed his coffee container and was off.

8

C.J. was still beaming half an hour later when we got to the Tabernacle of Joy Through Giving. It wasn't just that we had run into someone from her past—a cousin no less—but his brutish nature aside, this man was rather normal. Sure, it was a reference to owning a horse with no mouth that made it possible for him to recognize her, but if we're really honest about it, we've all had experiences every bit as bizarre. Haven't we?

Thus it was that when we entered the sanctuary she was at her most socially acceptable level of behavior, if I might use that term. I'd even go so far as to say that we were virtually indistinguishable from any other of the worshippers. We both were decked out in polyester flowered dresses with high necklines and distressingly low hemlines (for a shrimpette like me, at any rate). We both tied the frocks in back, but loosely, so as not to accentuate our provocative feminine attributes. Our sleeves were supposed to come down to our elbows, but in my case, they reached almost to my wrists. We even pinned our hair atop our heads, and fastened tightly rolled falls above our crowns to simulate "holy roller" buns.

I was wearing one extra element of disguise, one that I am ashamed to admit to possessing. Just about a month prior, my optometrist, a pleasant presbyopic Presbyterian, had given me a prescription for bifocals. It was hard to adjust to the darn things, and I usually kept them in my purse, but now was as good a time as any to give them the old college try.

But sad to say, I hadn't been to church in a long while—certainly not one as conservative as Pastor Sam's—so I'd plumb forgotten that we would have done well to bring our own Bibles as part of our illusion. This omission of detail earned us both looks of mild suspicion, and in C.J.'s case, an all too firm handshake. When the big gal winces, the game is on.

"Good morning, sisters," the deacon who greeted us said. "Where are y'all from?"

"We're from the Holy City," C.J. said without missing a beat. And indeed, the Holy City is a popular name for South Carolina's largest metropolis, on account of the plethora of churches to be found there.

"Well, I doubt that," the man said with a chuckle. "Youse look like lovely ladies, but real angels is men." His accent, by the way, marked him as a former Bostonian to my ears; that would explain his lack of Carolina knowledge.

"Why bless your heart," I said, as I snatched up a Sunday morning bulletin from a stack by the door and sailed right on past.

As soon as C.J. could disengage from the iron grip

of doubt, she joined me in the very front pew. Experience has taught me that these seats are the last to fill up in an ecclesiastical venue. After all, nobody wants the preacher to glance down during his sermon and spot that you have fallen asleep or, worse yet, are the one whispering dating advice to her BFF in a stage whisper. Today, however, I suppose it would be texting and tweeting that would get you into hot water.

At any rate, the service started right on the dot. From somewhere far to our rear a great organ pealed. After a few stirring notes, a youthful worship minister, dressed in an expensive suit and Ferragamo loafers, ran out to the center of the stage.

"Put your hands together for Jesus!" he cried.

The response was both invigorating and deafening. For the next half hour we clapped, swayed, and sang ourselves into a spiritual frenzy. Only then did Pastor Sam make an appearance and, in keeping with the mood that had been created, it was no ordinary entrance.

First, two very young boys (perhaps no older than six) ran across the stage carrying red pendants. Abruptly the music stopped. Three very buff young men (possibly in their twenties) materialized suddenly from either side. They wore only white loincloths and carried long-stemmed trumpets, upon which they played a single triumphant note.

All eyes gazed upward, for descending from the rafters on a platform jazzed up to look like a cloud was none other than Rob's first cousin, Pastor Sam. Undoubtedly the majority of the folks there had seen this mockery in the sky a thousand times, but from the hoopla it created, one would have thought it was indeed the Second Coming. C.J., on the other hand, was livid.

"Abby," she shouted into my ear, "there ought to be a law against this."

"This is America; we have the freedom to get as carried away as we want. Doesn't your granny's church use snakes in their worship service?"

But she was too mesmerized to answer. I'll say this, Pastor Sam had a first-rate makeup artist at his disposal; the man appeared positively radiant. Even his robes were dazzling white. If I'd tried to imagine a celestial being, this might have been the image I would have come up with.

Just as the cloud was about to touch the stage floor, Pastor Sam stepped lightly off and faced his congregation with a smile as dazzling as his robes. I even found myself smiling back. Pastor Sam's smile grew even wider and he locked his eyes on mine. No, it couldn't have been me he was gazing at so tenderly.

But then, sure enough, he was walking my way, his eyes still on mine, his right hand extended.

"Uh-oh, Spaghetti Os," I said. "What do I do now?"

"Run, Abby, run," C.J. said. "I'll try and hold him off."

Her advice only added to my panic. "I haven't done anything—except to impersonate someone of deeper devotion. That isn't a crime, is it?"

"Actually, I think it might be a crime in Idaho—or is that Montana? You know, where that senator's from; the one with such a wide stance. Personally, Abby, I never did see anything wrong with having a wide stance.

Cousin Leopold Singleton Ledbetter back in Shelby had a wide stance; of course he had three legs—"

But I wasn't really listening, because my thoughts were on Sam. And that's exactly where he wanted them to be, because the next thing I knew, that young, blond-haired devil had taken my right hand in his and was leading me up to the stage. I'll be the first to admit that I'm no longer a young chickadee, one that can be easily overwhelmed by a stud muffin's charisma, but I felt like a virgin bride being led to her bed. That man could generate enough electricity to light up Idaho, or Montana, or wherever it was that folks tend to have wide stances—bless their hearts.

We climbed a short flight of stairs and kept walking until we reached our mark in the center of the stage. Then Sam slid his arm around my shoulders. I was reminded of the story of Eve in the Garden of Eden and the treacherous serpent. But unlike the first woman ever created, I was no dithering innocent; I knew that the slithering arm spelled trouble, yet I could not bring myself to run. It is no accident, I think, that the first syllable of the word *hormones* is what it is.

"Brothers and sisters," Sam said into his handheld microphone, "y'all know what today's service is all about!"

"Healing!" the crowd managed to roar, even though it is fairly difficult to do so without any R's in the word.

"That's right. There will be no sermon today, no plea for funds—although the Good Lord knows we are always in need, and the ushers *will* be passing buckets around during the offertory. Today it is about healing; healing of the spirit, and healing of the body."

Pastor Sam turned to me. "Ma'am, are you saved?"

The truth is that I'm a lapsed Episcopalian, and one who prefers different terminology; but I knew what he meant. I also knew better than to argue theology with him.

"Yes!" I shouted.

"Glory hallelujah!"

"Glory hallelujah!" The crowd was on their feet, stamping and shouting, and the organist was playing victory music lifted straight from the ball park.

Sam waved his hypnotic arms. "Then what we got here, folks, is a healing of the body; a genuine miracle that y'all will be privileged to witness."

"Amen!"

"Quick," Pastor Sam said to me, "what's your illness?"

"My *what*?"

"Your sickness. Hurry up, ma'am, spit it out."

"I'm sorry, sir, but I don't have the foggiest notion what you mean."

"The front row is reserved for folks who are sick. Didn't the ushers screen y'all?"

"Well—"

"Think of a disease right quick," Sam growled under his breath.

"Floccinaucinihilipilification," I said. "It's gotten into my bloodstream and my doctors think that I might not last through the night." I doubled over as I grabbed my gut and let out a heart-wrenching moan.

"You hear that folks? This little gal has flocci—uh—help me out here, little lady."

"Naucinihilipilification," I said. "The pain is excruciating! Oh Pastor, do something. Please! I beseech you!" By the way, it is a real English word and references the act of making something worthless.

"Easy does it," Pastor Sam said under his breath. "Overacting will get the reporters' attention; and believe me there are always a few embedded in a group this size." He held the mike closer to his heavily rouged lips. "All in good time, my dear, all in good time," he said.

"Praise the Lord and pass the apple Danish," I said.

"You see, folks," Pastor Sam said, "the poor woman's delirious from all that pain."

"And how much wood *would* a woodchuck chuck?" I said. "How come nobody ever answers that?"

"Dial it back, sister," he grunted. "You're about to blow my cover. Pastor Sam does not like exposés."

"Meet me in your office after services, Pastor, or you'll get an Oscar-worthy show."

"So," he hissed, "you *are* a reporter."

"Absolutely not. I am, however, the woman who inherited your Aunt Jerry's fabulous emerald ring!" I whipped off my irritating bifocals. "Do you remember me now?"

"Get out of my church!"

I threw my arms in the air. "I feel a healing coming on! Say it, Pastor! *Heal*-ing!" I grabbed the mike from the flummoxed flimflam conman. "Come on, people. Put your hands together. *Heal*-ing! *Heal*-ing!"

The congregation clapped and stomped their feet. They chanted to the boisterous beat of the organ, which sounded more human than instrumental. Meanwhile C.J. had joined me onstage, where she was waving her gigantic arms like they were flesh-covered batons. I immediately discovered that the big gal didn't need a microphone to be heard all the way back to the farthest reaches of the stadium-size sanctuary, but I tossed it to her anyway.

"Come here, child," she said to me.

I stood dangerously close, which is anywhere within reach. She laid a ham-size mitt on my head, and to be honest, I felt another electrical charge run through my body.

"Naucinihilipilification, be gone," she said.

I felt like I'd been kicked by a horse. "Whoa!"

"Are you healed?" she demanded.

I pushed the mike away. "C.J., darling, naucinihilipilification isn't a disease."

"Don't be silly, Abby; of course it is. Granny runs an awful fever each time she gets it." She felt my forehead, and in the process nearly knocked me over. "Nope; you're not running a temperature. In fact," she said, "you're as cool as a maggot on a week-old corpse. Hallelujah," she yelled through the microphone, blowing out at least one of the speakers. "This little no-account woman has been completely healed."

"No-account? I took you into the business and taught you everything you know. Ergo the goat girl from Shelby is now one of the most respected antiques dealers in all of the Southeast. I also introduced you to my brother, Toy, and to hear him tell it, you toyed with his heart, yet I stuck up for you, even though you changed your race in the middle of your short-lived marriage and declared that European-American men smelled like wet dogs."

"Oy vey," Sam said into his hands, which covered his face. "This has got to be hell."

"Excuse me," someone with a thick Gastonia accent said, "but is this the healing line? Sister Eliza's goiter is growing by leaps and bounds. She refuses to eat any salt—even the kind containing iodine—on account of she heard on television that eating salt is bad for us."

"Bring her on up here," C.J. said, "and let the goiter be gone!"

"C.J.," I growled, "you can't promise that."

"Abby, I have the *gift*, so let me be." The big galoot's steel gray eyes seemed to bore right through mine, giving me an instant headache.

This was a different woman than the one that I knew as Calamity Jane. Intense, focused, charismatic, magnetic, supercharged—a genuine healer! Pastor Sam and I stepped back and observed from a respectful distance, but what we witnessed for the next hour was unbelievable! Indescribable, even, although I shall try.

I saw a woman with a shriveled arm return to her seat, tears streaming down her face, marveling at the perfectly normal limb that she now possessed. I saw a teenager who had never walked a step rise out of a wheelchair and dance for joy, while his parents wept in each other's arms, because they too were so overcome with emotion.

And I saw what C.J.'s intercession did for the woman with the goiter. She approached the stage wearing a blue silk scarf that covered but did not camouflage a huge lump on her neck. After C.J. did her thing, the woman tugged at the scarf, and as it came undone, you could see the goiter disappear in front of your eyes. I was stunned! I mean, there's simply no faking that. And when the scarf came all the way off you could see that the woman's neck was as bare and smooth as the top of Aaron Ovumkoph's head.

"Wow!" I said.

"Your friend really *does* have the gift," Pastor Sam said. "I'd say only forty percent of those folks in the line were plants."

"*Excuse* me?"

"You know, shills. Nothing opens their wallets like a good old-fashioned sob story. Of course you, and your partner, know all about that."

"She's not my partner—not that there's anything wrong with that! Unless you meant *partner in crime*. But again she wouldn't be my partner—oh, the heck with explaining myself. We're not scam artists like you. Whatever you saw actually happened."

"Give me a break," Pastor Sam said, and rolled his eyes.

"Hey, you're the man of the cloth; you're supposed to believe in this stuff. Tell me something. Was the woman with the goiter a shill?"

"Roberta?" He sighed. "Yeah, she ties a bubble in the scarf. It's one of my oldest scams."

C.J. had been giving a final blessing of some kind, but now that she was through, she loped over to us. Gone was the fire in her eyes; also gone was my headache.

"I've changed my mind," I said. "Instead of talking to you in your office, might we treat you and your wife to lunch?"

THE GLASS IS ALWAYS GREENER

Pastor Sam might not have believed in miracles, but it was clear from his demeanor that he was in awe of the woman from Shelby. He glanced from her, to his departing flock, and then back to her.

"Just let me call my wife," he said.

9

In the olden days, when I was growing up, we womenfolk rose at the crack of dawn to prepare the beef roast (we'd killed and butchered the cow the day before) for the oven, peel the potatoes, carrots, and onions that went in with it, *plus* make a hot breakfast for everyone, find their missing shoes, walk the dog because some eight-year-old had reneged on her agreement, and do whatever else needed to be done. In other words, we (oops, or our mothers) did enough tasks to run a cruise ship *before* heading off to church.

Today it is perfectly acceptable to run through McDonald's on the way to church, and Burger King on the way back home (although moms still have to look for the missing shoes and walk the dog). No longer does a good Christian housewife need to slave before church, and again during cleanup, while her master snores in bed, or later sprawled across the couch on the pretext of watching the Sunday afternoon ball game. What legislation wasn't able to accomplish, innovation did. Fast food freed a generation of women who might otherwise have been chained to their stoves.

Because she had not cooked a Sunday dinner, Tina Ovumkoph, bless her heart, was perfectly amenable to my offer. She quickly farmed all her children out to friends and relatives and off we went, riding in two cars. Our destination was the Viet Thai Noodle House at the rear of McMullen Creek Shopping Center.

"Used to be there were no really good authentically Asian restaurants in town," Sam said. "Now there is a plethora, but this one is special; this one is primarily frequented by other Asians. It's not like Bubba's China Gourmet. You ever been to Bubba's?"

"Gag me with a spoon," C.J. said.

"What a gross expression," Tina said.

"No," I said, "she means that she literally choked on a spoon at that establishment. It was one of those porcelain deals and C.J. had never seen one before, and thought it might be edible. Anyway, we had to call the paramedics, but by then it was too late—for the spoon; obviously not for C.J. Bubba, being the parsimonious dear that he is, has hung on to the spoon—even though it came out in five pieces—and glued it back together. If you're lucky enough to grab it with your place setting when you're in the buffet line, Bubba will give you an extra fortune cookie."

"Ugh," Tina said.

I made up my mind to hush my mouth before I ruined everything. Usually I can be such a delightful dinner companion, skilled as I am at small talk.

At the door to the Viet Thai Noodle House we were greeted warmly and shown to a booth with a view of a large fish tank. The Ovumkophs, who'd dined there numerous times, ordered "bubble drinks," fruit-flavored concoctions embedded with "pearls" of tapioca. C.J. was denied her request for a "tall glass of refreshing goat's milk" and settled for a Diet Coke. I asked for a glass of water with lemon and a Vietnamese ice coffee.

"You like?" the waitress asked.

"I'd never had it," I said.

"You will like," she said. Her enthusiasm for my beverage choice was encouraging.

"Are you originally from Vietnam?" I asked.

"No, we are Laotian. You know where Laos is?"

"Yes," I said, "above Thailand, and to the west of Vietnam."

Her face glowed. "Very good," she said. "Most Americans, they don't know. If we make restaurant Laotian, they not come."

"We would," Tina said. "The food here is divine—oops, sorry honey, that word just slipped out."

Sam squeezed out what just barely passed for a smile. "Let's order, shall we? We'll have number thirty-four all around."

"But honey—"

"Yes, sir." The waitress bobbed her head and scurried off to the kitchen. No doubt she was glad to be shed of what could have blossomed into a full-blown domestic scene. In fact, it *would* have done so for sure, had I been writing the script. I mean, what chutzpah for him to not even *consult* us about our meal choices when I was the one paying for lunch.

"I hope I like whatever it is," I said with a laugh.

One must appear to keep it light, especially when one is the gift horse. This etiquette rule is found in *The Moron's Guide to Southern Manners*, the handbook given to every baby born south of the Mason-Dixon Line.

But I didn't like what Sam had ordered for me; I *loved* it. Never mind what it was called. It was strips of tender grilled steak served over a bed of steamed rice, accompanied by a mixed green salad. There was a small bowl of sweet yet tangy dipping sauce for the beef. The flavor of this meat was so fabulous that my tongue couldn't stand it, and wanted to come out and box my ears silly.

As for the coffee, it arrived in a cute metal drip pot set atop a glass that contained sweetened condensed milk. When all the water had been put through the press, I stirred the milk and coffee mixture and poured it into a much larger glass that was filled with ice cubes. I stirred that. The result of this minimum amount of effort was a party for the mouth, making my tongue quite glad she'd played by the rules and stuck around.

Of course we engaged in a lot of conversation. Pastor Sam tried to steer the talk to the moneymaking possibilities of C.J.'s miraculous power. C.J. wanted to talk about new technological development in the direct reduction of iron ore using microwaves. Then there was Tina Ovumkoph, who was dying to get a word in edgewise about her nine children.

Tina, bless her heart, was as homely as stump full of spiders; honestly, there is just no kinder way to describe her. No doubt when she was born, her mama had to borrow a baby to take to church. Such mean

observations on my part may seem uncalled for, so I'll
come right out and say that I'm no prize myself. But I
did bring up Tina, and I did so because she was married to a very handsome man. Think of Sam Cham-
pion with six-inch lifts in his shoes; this man really
was a head turner. Right away this begged the question, how did someone like Tina, bless her heart again,
snag a looker like that? And one to the manor born, to
boot?

To put it another way, what did Sam see in Tina? In
my opinion the Ovumkoph family kept more secrets
than a stadium full of mummies. Anything they had
to say could, and would, be used against them, until
they were proven not guilty by a court of law.

"I hate to bring this up," I said, after I'd eaten enough
of my steak to be fully nourished, "but have you heard
the news?"

Tina pressed her hands to her cheeks. "You mean
about them tornadoes over ta Oklahoma? Warn't that
just terrible? 'Twas like the Devil was wrasslin' with
the breath of God."

"How very poetic," I said, "but that's not the news I
meant. Sam, didn't anyone tell you that your aunt's
green ring has gone missing?"

"Say *what*?"

"She means the emerald ring," C.J. said, just before I
kicked her.

"Ouch, Abby, what was that for?"

"I'm sorry, C.J., I guess there's just enough room on
this banquette for one murder suspect who's trying
hard to clear herself. Everyone else is going to have to
stand."

"But Abby, I wasn't even at the good-bye party. How could I be a suspect?"

"C.J.," I said, "remind me what your IQ is again."

"Hold everything," Sam said. "I think the rules of this game have just changed. If you're a murder suspect, then you're no better than the rest of us."

"Except that this isn't a game," I said. "Not for me. I hadn't even met your aunt until that afternoon, and I sure the heck didn't know she was in possession of a ring that valuable."

"One sixty-five," C.J. said. "My low score was such a disappointment for Granny. I'm telling you, Abby, she wept bitterly the day those test scores came back."

"So how'd you do it?" Sam said to me. "Aunt Jerry wasn't alive when you put her in the freezer chest, was she?"

I drew upon what little experience I'd had in acting in Sunday school pageants: one year I got to play a bleating sheep, another year a silent Mary; and in elementary school plays: one year as a snowflake, two years as pilgrim, and one year as a leprechaun. Unfortunately my roles didn't improve much in high school or college.

"She struggled," I said, "and please keep in mind that she was much bigger than I—of course everyone is—but what else could I do? I'd forced her to rewrite her will, right there in front of the watermelon, at knifepoint, so I couldn't very well let her blab to everyone, now could I?"

"Ooh, Abby," C.J. moaned, "your mama's going to be so disappointed. But I promise you that I will come to see you every visiting day, and if you marry someone from the outside—like one of the Menendez brothers did—I'll still come to see you, unless it's your turn to do the bird with two backs."

"That's *beast*, not bird," I said. "No wait; you probably know of some exotic bird that procreates in mid-air."

"Your nose is as long as a telephone wire," Tina said, before C.J. could respond. It was the most grammatically correct sentence I'd heard come out of her mouth.

"*Excuse* me?" I said.

"It's from a children's saying," C.J. explained, "only instead of 'nose' we used to say 'ears' on account of—"

"Hush," I said gently. "Mrs. Ovumkoph, are you calling me a liar?"

"I are."

"On what grounds?"

Tina stared at her husband. "I just know that you ain't tellin' the truth; you ain't the killer."

"Maybe you should hush as well, baby doll," he said. He had his arm around her with his hand on her shoulder. As he told his wife to stifle it, Pastor Sam's fingers dug into her shoulder, causing her to wince. I could see the tendons in his talons; every one of them was clearly delineated.

Nothing gets under my skin quite like a bully. As a miniature person of so-called normal proportions I was still tormented beyond endurance. I had a very robust brother, but he was younger, his name was Toy, and his sexual preferences were yet undecided. He had his own battles to fight.

So the teasing persisted, and sometimes it progressed to worse things, like when Sarah Newhart and her cronies tied me up and put me on the top shelf of the paper supply closet. This was on a *Friday* afternoon. Thank heavens Mr. Sodt wanted to mimeograph some handouts at the beginning of eighth period. Right or wrong, I skipped school for the next two weeks.

To this day the issue of school bullies raises a visceral response in me, but now that I am a woman of means and am married to a very buff man who is six feet four, I no longer have to put up with it. I also learned that bullying doesn't stop just because one becomes an adult. Nor does it happen just to those people with obvious differences. There are those folks who will bully anyone who will allow them to get away with it. Apparently Pastor Sam was just that sort.

"Get your manipulative mitt off her," I said.

"Beg pardon?" he said.

"You heard me," I said. "Now process it. And you, Mrs. Ovumkoph, don't let him stifle you like that."

There were tears in her eyes. "But ma'am, you just told your friend to hush."

"Touché," I said.

"But that was different," C.J. said. "Abby and I have this agreement; anytime I go off on a tangent with one of my Shelby stories, then she has the right to tell me to put a lid on it."

Tina's right homely face got within six shades of pretty. "Are you from Shelby, North Carolina?"

"Yes, ma'am."

"By jingle, so am I!"

"You wouldn't, by any chance, happen ta know

Lyudmila Parsons Ledbetter, would ya, 'cause she's my granny."

"Get out of town on a dirt road! She's my granny too!"

"Why shoot a monkey, but don't hurt it none! If this don't beat all! Cousin!"

"Cousin!"

The women flew at each other across the table, and dishes and food flew to both sides. Due to the ruckus that they caused I insisted that we move the show outside, and since Pastor Sam pretended to have left his wallet at home that morning, I also paid for the broken crockery—in addition to the meals, of course.

"Is there a Shelby dialect?" I asked Pastor Sam as we walked behind the two very animated ladies to the car.

He laughed, sounding almost pleasant. "Maybe it's a Ledbetter thing. Have you ever met any others in her family?"

"Yes, an aunt. But she wasn't much for talking."

"Mr. Ovumkoph, how is it that you manage to live with yourself?"

"Dagnabit, Mrs. Timberlake, I thought I'd made it clear that I did *not* murder my aunt. She was always a favorite, by the way."

"No, what I mean is: how can you fleece your own flock, shear your own sheep, hide your own herd as it were, and not feel guilty?"

"Give me a break, Mrs. Timberlake, will you? Tina's going to be giving the money back on my behalf, remember?"

"Yes, but how can *you* possibly remember everyone you've ever bilked? After all, you do it on a weekly basis."

We were almost to the car, where the ladies had stopped and were carrying on an animated conversation, so Pastor Sam put a hand gently on my arm and we slowed our pace considerably. Fortunately the weather was fabulous and there were no biting insects about.

"It's like this, Mrs. Timberlake," Pastor Sam said, turning to face me. He had the whitest, straightest set of chompers I'd ever seen this side of a TV camera. "I was never good at school. And I really sucked at sports. But I did have a gift for remembering people's names and faces. When you're part of a four-thousand-member congregation, Mrs. Timberlake, and the pastor remembers your name, and possibly a little something personal about yourself, that's when you feel important. You feel singled out and special. You're in denial that he can do the same in regards to everyone else there."

By then we'd caught up with the others. "And you can do that?" I said. "You can remember all four thousand of your congregants by name?"

"That's how I make my living." He chuckled. "And I keep track of who's been healed of what, and when. Call it my gift. And just so you know, I never 'heal' anyone who I know to be really ill. That would be just plain wrong." He tried to lock his blue eyes on mine, but I refused to let him. "I only bring my brand of healing to those folks who are already whole in body

97

and spirit, and together we dance in the light. If in the process I help them be shed of some collateral ailment, then I say praise the Lord!"

"Hallelujah!" Tina said.

"Ooh Abby, wasn't that just the most inspiring thing you ever heard?" C.J. moaned.

"Au contraire, my dear," I said. "That was a bucket of *merde."*

10

"Ooh, Abby, you better explain yourself," C.J. said. "Those are fighting words and this man's kinfolk now."

"C.J.," I said calmly, "get ahold of yourself. He's a con man. Surely you didn't buy that 'dancing in the light' baloney."

"Abby, aren't you the big liberal that's always preaching that 'hey, whatever works, that's what counts'? If Cousin Sam's congregants feel better after dancing in the light with him, then it really isn't your business, is it?"

"C.J., don't desert me. We're supposed to solve Aunt Jerry's murder before six. Time's a-wasting."

"Abby, let me be," my buddy said, her voice quavering. "You know how important family is to me."

Indeed I did. My ex-sister-in-law wants nothing more than to *belong*. Maybe it's the herd instinct she got from that supposed goat DNA, or maybe it's because she grew up believing that it really was a stork that dropped her off on Granny Ledbetter's doorstep.

Whatever the reason, she has a thirst for roots and a hunger for the type of validation that can never be awarded her in the city she chooses to call home.

In Charleston, South Carolina, a newcomer is anyone whose people arrived after the War of Northern Aggression. For a handful of the elite, it is the War for Independence from Britain that is the marker. Charleston is "it," the epicenter of creation, the mile marker from which everywhere else must be measured, for to be from anywhere else is to be from "off." This is not merely hubris on the part of Charlestonians, mind you; to be fair, one must keep in mind that Charleston is where the Ashley and Cooper rivers join together to form the Atlantic Ocean.

So, yes, I understood where my dear friend was coming from. However, that didn't mean I had to like it.

"Mr. and Mrs. Ovumkoph," I said. "Somehow I don't think this is the last you'll be seeing of me. And just so you know, if you harm even one hair on C.J.'s chinny-chin-chin, you'll have me to answer to."

"Ooh, Abby," C.J. squealed, "you're the best friend ever!"

"Yeah," I said, as I gave her a great big old hug. But if that was really true, then why did I feel like I had a flock of Canada geese wearing miniature army boots marching over my grave?

Melissa Ovumkoph answered the door with freshly painted toenails. I know this because she told me so, although I might have guessed that by the special thongs she was wearing: there was a division between each toe. Her hair was in curlers and there was something on her face resembling egg white. Perhaps the most disturbing thing about her appearance was her lips. Whereas they had once been enormous, they were now leaking collagen, and resembled half-inflated inner tubes. She shared that with me too.

In short, I would not have answered my doorbell looking like that, so I gave her extra points to start with. Melissa was either a very self-confident woman, and to be admired, or extremely depressed, and to be treated lightly.

"Life really sucks when you don't even have the money for a pedicure," she said, waving a foot through the crack in the door.

"I know what you mean. I had to do my own highlights one year when my kids were in high school; it was the pits."

"Hey, you're serious, aren't ya?"

"You're darn tooting, I am. I snagged too much hair through the cap with that thingie and ended up looking like a skunk."

She opened the door wide. "Fiddle-dee-dee. Wherever are my manners? Please come in. You must be Robbie's friend. Aggie, isn't it?"

"Abby."

"Ya sure?" Her speech was somewhat muffled, given the challenge of speaking with flapping, out-of-control lips. "I mean, ya look more like an Aggie ta me. You know, old-fashioned like. Now myself, I always thought I looked more like a Caitlyn instead of a Melissa. Ugh, Melissa, I can't stand my name."

"Then why don't you change it?" I said.

"I just might," she said. "Now that the old lady didn't leave me nothing."

I cringed at hearing her callousness, even though I'd come prepared for just that. But somehow I wasn't prepared to see how utterly middle class Aaron and Melissa Ovumkoph lived. Family money had either not trickled down to this branch, or had run right through them like a sieve. It was no wonder they'd been so disappointed not to be mentioned in the will.

Melissa threw several armloads of clothes off a sagging purple and brown plaid sofa. "I was doing laundry and hadn't gotten around to folding yet. Heck, I'm always doing laundry. Betcha ain't never seen a man sweat as much as Aaron."

"I won't contest that," I said. I glanced around the room. Their decorating style consisted of dark, faux wood paneling and cheaply framed prints of dogs playing cards.

"Ain'tcha gonna sit?" she said.

"Thanks," I said.

"Ain't them pictures cute?" she said. "We seen them at a garage sale. Aaron says we oughta hang on ta them 'cause someday some snooty professor type will say that they're folk art, and then even copies like these will be valuable. I tell ya, Aggie, he ain't worth much as a husband, but that Aaron is pretty smart. Hey, ya want something ta drink? Got some red wine, and some white wine, and some Cheerwine." Cheerwine is a popular Southern soft drink that goes well with Moon Pies in the event that RC Cola is unavailable.

One of the tricks to good sleuthing is to always accept an offer of refreshments. That allows one at least a modicum of time to do some snooping. A body should take care, however, not to ingest the comestibles—unless said goodies are also consumed by the host or hostess—lest one should awaken in a crate in the port of Shanghai, staring up at the face of a Cantonese madam named Huang Lu. Been there, done that, is all I want to say about that experience.

"Yes, ma'am," I said. "Do any of those wines come with a cork—no offense."

"Oh, none taken. I just hate them uppity folks and their corky ways, don't you? Screw them, I say!" She roared with laughter, as she tossed back her long bleached mane and slapped her thighs.

"Yeah, what a bunch of winers," I said, and pretended to carry on as well.

Laughter is indeed contagious, and it is best caught from our own selves. Just by pretending to laugh, I began to laugh, and soon I forgot that I was pretending. Then suddenly Melissa and I were laughing at cues taken from each other, and then we just couldn't stop. Together we laughed until there were tears in our eyes, and I felt my bladder dangerously constrict.

"If you don't quit making me laugh, I'm going to—"

"What? Pee in your pants?"

And then we were off again, me and the woman who had egg white on her face and curlers in her hair, and with whom I had nothing in common. But I had a job to do, so after several minutes of shamelessly rolling about on the brown and purple plaid sofa like a college student stoned on pot, I got it back together enough to ask for wine in a box—color unimportant—and some Moon Pies if she had some.

Then, as soon as she'd padded out of sight, I was all business. A more careful look around the room confirmed my initial impression: this was a family that either had no assets, or chose not to invest them in feathering their nest. If suddenly handed a thumbnail-size bar of soap and a towel no larger than a dinner napkin, I might be persuaded that I was back in the one-star West Virginia motel in which Buford Timberlake and I spent our honeymoon—oh, but there had to be a footprint on the ceiling to complete the mood.

Of course poverty doesn't necessarily equate with pedestrian taste. We've all heard of folks down on their luck who've still managed, through creativity, to build very attractive and sometimes astonishingly beautiful spaces for themselves. But not so Aaron and Melissa Ovumkoph. I even did a two-second reconnaissance of their downstairs powder room. The only bit of decorating in there was a hand-lettered sign hanging over the toilet that read: JUST DO IT!

"Here we go," Melissa said, barely giving me time to throw myself back on the sofa. This second time around I learned that there was a broken spring.

"This is mighty gracious of you," I said.

"'Tain't nothing." She handed me a glass tumbler half filled with a murky, deep maroon substance. It looked like the fake wine we used in high school plays, and which was supplied by Miss Odell Jordan, one of the English teachers. We were instructed not to drink the foul fluid, so of course we did, and we all got sick, but we never did find out what it was.

"To *chai*-yum," she said, murdering the pronunciation of a great Jewish toast.

"Skoal," I said.

"Well, drink up. It's fresh. I just now broke the seal on the box."

"Yes, ma'am." I took a sip. Whatever harmful parasites I might have been harboring at the moment were, without a doubt, instantly killed. Ditto the good ones. It was going to be a yogurt kind of evening for me once I returned to the hotel—assuming I survived. The wine I'd swallowed wasn't rotgut bad, it was eat-a-hole through my guts bad.

"Good, ain't it?" she said. "One night Aaron didn't come home, and I just knew he was cheating on me with that no good sister-in-law of mine, so I drank me two boxes of this stuff. Got me a good buzz going that night, I tell ya."

"I bet you did," I said. "Say, Caitlyn—I'm sorry, but you really do look like one—I mean, Melissa, what did you think of Aunt Jerry's taste in jewelry? Pretty gaudy, if you ask me."

"Oh no, hon, ain't no such thing as too gaudy when it comes to hot rocks—that's what I call them big stones. The bigger, the better. They's some that just goes in for diamonds, but Aaron says you gotta keep an eye out for them colored rocks too, because some of them is just as valuable."

"Like the emerald ring she tried to give me?"

"Yeah. But you didn't want it. You said that loud and clear in front of God and everybody. Tell me, Aggie, are you nuts, or what?"

"Probably the what. But I didn't refuse it; I just refused to wear it then."

"Oh no, ma'am. We all heard you tell her that you

didn't like them big stones and that she could shove it up her you-know-what."

"I did not!" I said.

"Cheese and crackers, you don't need to get so worked up about it none. I'm just saying that's what it sounded like to some. Personally, I didn't hear exactly what you said—uh, anyway, that was the impression I got."

"Well, hear me now, please. The ring is still legally mine."

She stared at me. "Yeah, like whatever."

I tried out various smiles, but after getting no reaction after far too long a period of time, dove back into the fray. "Did you know that the ring was stolen off her cold dead finger sometime before the police arrived yesterday? Of course there is an excellent chance that the thief and the killer are one and the same person."

Melissa's eyes grew as wide as dessert plates, and her mouth gaped open to the point that I could see what she'd had for breakfast. Seriously, I am entirely certain that she was genuinely shocked by the news.

"H-how do ya know?" she finally gasped. "Who told ya the ring was missing?"

"The police told me."

"Wh-when did they tell ya?"

"Last night. I'm a suspect too, you know."

She deftly snatched my glass of maroon poison away from me. "Just one minute there, hon. Maybe *you're* a suspect, but we ain't."

"You mean the police haven't interviewed you?"

She was on her feet in a clichéd flash, motioning

vigorously toward the door. "You need to be leaving now, Aggie; our visit is over."

I took my time standing. "Mind if I have a Moon Pie for the road?" I said.

She held out the plate of pies, still in their cellophane wrappers. "Take two—three if you wish," she said. "I ain't trying to be dis-sociable-like, you understand?"

"Indeed I do," I said.

"Maybe under different circumstances, Aggie, you and I might have been good friends—best girlfriends even, on account of we're so much alike. But this suspect stuff—Aaron and I can't handle none of that. The old lady got bumped off because somebody had it in for her. So be it. We say leave it at that. We ain't even going ta her funeral."

I slipped three pies in my purse; no telling when and where supper would be. "If you hear anything else about my ring," I said, "please let me know."

"Bye now, Aggie," she said, and practically pushed me out the door.

Aaron Ovumkoph owns and operates his own business in a strip mall on Sardis Road. If I have a hard time describing his business, it is because Aaron had a hard time deciding what exactly his business should be. The end result was one quarter watch repair business, one quarter shoe repair business, and half gift card and sundries shop. This mishmash might have succeeded in less throwaway times, but it was my guess that the repair jobs barely paid for his overhead. As for the cards and sundries; the former turned yellow and curled in the sunlight and the latter turned thick or watery in their tubes or jars. To be succinct, nothing sold.

This would explain why Aaron alighted on me like a mosquito after a rain the second I walked in the door. "Yes, ma'am, how can I help you? Everything you see here is fifty percent off—today only."

"Very nice," I said, lying through my small, but fairly even, teeth. "However, I'm really here just to—"

"Uh-oh, look at those shoes. Houston, I think we have a problem."

I looked down at a perfectly good pair of dress sandals. "What's wrong with them?"

"Well, look how your heel wants to turn in. You know what that means, don't you?"

I did indeed. It meant he was going to try and sell me some unneeded shoe repair.

"Of course I know what it means," I said. "It means that I have a very advanced case of naucinihilipilification."

"Uh—"

"Believe me, you don't want to even touch these sandals. But don't worry; you can't catch it just from being in the same room. So where were we? Oh yes, Mr. Ovumkoph, my name is Abigail Timberlake. I'm a friend of your cousin Rob Goldburg. I'm also—"

But before I could utter another word, Aaron began to sputter like a campfire when it rains. All that lip motion set his oversized head to bobbling in all directions on his spindly neck, and I had to look away lest I get vertigo and give seven Moon Pies another shot at daylight (yes, I may have fibbed earlier a wee bit).

There were a number of things that Aaron tried to say, and some that he eventually managed to say, none of which a Southern lady of good repute would dare repeat. In fact, I suppose that a woman of my generation should plead ignorance to even being familiar with a few of his choice words.

The gist of it could be boiled down to two sentences, composed of four words. They are: "Get out! Stay away!"

My response, stripped of its invectives, was even briefer: "Gladly."

Honest-to-goodness Pete. Aunt Jerry was stabbed to death, then allowed to bleed out before being moved to the freezer. There was no telltale trail of blood, or someone would have noticed. Clearly both Aaron and Melissa Ovumkoph were too stupid to have accomplished something that tricky.

But there were two more suspects who, at least superficially, appeared to be somewhat normal. It was time to revisit the scene of the crime.

11

Uncle Ben had just returned from a golf outing with the Brotherhood of Temple Beth El when I showed up. However, he acted like he was expecting me, and ushered me right in.

"Strictly speaking, I shouldn't have gone," he said, pointing at the torn black square of cloth pinned to his shirt. "I'm in mourning for my sister, and I should be sitting shivah. The truth is, though, that I had to clear my head. Like everyone, I had a lot of conflicted feelings about Jerry before her murder; now I feel a lot of guilt and—heck"—he choked back a sob—"already I miss her like crazy."

I nodded. "Mr. Ovumkoph—"

"Please, call me Ben."

"Ben. We haven't been properly introduced. My name is Abigail Timberlake, and I'm a friend of your nephew Rob Goldburg."

"Yes, you're the sprite to whom my sister tried to give away that very clever fake of hers. Brava, I say, for not letting her make a fool of you."

I'll admit to being a bit taken aback by these comments. The man was an older, heavier version of my best friend, Rob, but if Rob had referred to me as an elfish person, I might have punched him on the arm with one of my wee little fists. As for the emerald being a fake, how in tarnation did he know? What was he, a jeweler?

"I mean no disrespect, Ben," I said, and tried to disguise my antagonistic tone with an insincere smile, "but I think we should leave the identification of that particular stone up to a certified gemologist—one who is certified in colored gemstones."

Ben even produced Rob's self-righteous little victory grin. "I've been a board-certified gemologist—colored stones and diamonds—for the past forty-five years. Would you like to see my diplomas? We can run down to the shop; it's only a five-minute drive. Less if we hit the lights right."

My knees felt weak. When I made it back to Charleston—not *if*—I was going to barricade myself in my home with my husband and cat and never, ever set foot outside again. I could be happy doing that. I was sure of it. We could order in, watch our big-screen TV, and make whoopee all we wanted (which thankfully was less as the years went by). We didn't need the outside world. If I never set foot outside again, I could never risk being arrested, or have all the other frightening and life-threatening things happen to me, that have happened because of my insatiable curiosity and reputation as an outstanding sleuth. From here on, I could live joyously as a nobody, just as long as danger left me alone.

"Mrs. Timberlake," Ben said, "are you all right? You have a distant look in your eyes."

"I'm good; sometimes I just spaz out. As regards your certification—I believe you."

"Thank you," he said.

Since I had not had a chance to view the front rooms the day before, I took my time gazing at my very spacious surroundings. At one point a woman had had her say in choosing the decorating scheme. But that woman had been absent for a good ten years and it appeared as if nothing had changed. Although the decor was still very much this century, at the same time it was tired and outdated.

"My Judy had fabulous taste, didn't she?" he said.

"That she did," I said. "Amy, then, was your daughter? Yours together, I mean?"

Ben's eyes twinkled. "Yes, ma'am. And that was unforgivable what my sister did; forgetting Amy's name like that. At the same time it's vintage Jerry; she had a two-hundred-watt personality and she was always on. But boy howdy, you let yourself get too close to her and you get burned. Say, I've been kinda rude here; would you like something to drink? Maybe some sweet tea or a beer?"

I may have emitted a soft gasp of pleasure. "A beer would be nice. Anything you happen to have."

"Chips and salsa? Chips and ranch dressing? I'm going to have some of each."

"You've twisted my arm."

Ben disappeared for five minutes or so, during which time I did my best to case the great room without leaving my very green velvet armchair by the fireplace. Of course, these being the dog days of summer, the latter was not in operation.

At any rate, despite the fact that nothing appeared to have been changed since his wife's absence, there wasn't a speck of dust to be seen. Therefore I was able to deduce that either Ben was unusually fastidious for a widower, or he was solvent enough to hire a maid service. In either case, I was dealing with someone whose lifestyle approximated mine, more than it did either of his two nephews'.

"I'm divorced," he said, causing me to jump half my body height.

"Jeepers," I said, "you just took ten years off my life."

"Sorry." He handed me a Budweiser in a Panthers foam cozy. "She ran off to Australia with a twenty-one-year-old surfing instructor for whom she was booking a flight. Judy was a travel agent, you see. Now she's a washed-up cougar outside of Brisbane trying to get permanent resident status in Australia. Sixty-two years old she was when she chased after that hunk of melanoma-in-the-making."

"Wow, and can you spell *bitter*?"

He laughed. "I like you. I wouldn't expect that of someone who found my aunt dead in my downstairs freezer. Although I must confess, Mrs. Timberlake—"

"Please, call me Abby. Just don't call me Aggie, like your sister-in-law Melissa does."

Ben laughed again. "She's a mess, isn't she? Aaron never was what you'd call an overachiever, but still, marrying Melissa—now that took the cake. She's not Jewish, you know."

"Are you prejudiced?"

"I'd like to think not. But we Reform Jews have an almost fifty percent intermarriage rate. Anyway, it broke his mother's heart."

"How about your Brisbane cougar?"

"Oh yes, she was of the faith; it just goes to show you that nuttiness knows no religious boundaries. But hey, I was about to ask you—and this is not to put you in that category—but why are you involving yourself in this family's *meshugas*? That means—"

"I know what that means, and the answer is simple: I've been made a suspect in your aunt's murder. Until I can clear my name, I'm stuck in Charlotte. Now mind you, this is not a bad place to be, but I miss home. I miss my husband. I miss my cat, Dmitri!"

"Well then I guess we're in this together—you and me. Unfortunately, Abby, if I was at a roulette table and had to put money down on any one of those five: Aaron, Melissa, Sam, Tina, or Chanti, I'd have to do it with my eyes closed. I really couldn't choose. They all had it in for Jerry."

"And not Rob?"

He closed his eyes for a couple of seconds and then blinked as they opened. "Rob is as fine a young man as they come," Ben said. Never mind that Rob was fifty. "If I had a son—well, I couldn't ask for a better one than Rob. And even our rabbi, who is a terrific young gal—she's also named Judy—is very inclusive toward gays and lesbians—and that's the way the Reform movement has decided to go, but sometimes you just can't teach an old dog new tricks."

I found myself unconsciously pushing back into the

green lushness of my well-padded chair. "Does this mean that you have something against gays?"

"Well, not against them—not personally—just their lifestyle. It makes my skin crawl to think about *it*."

"Believe me, dear, it made my skin crawl to think of your cougar wife and her babycakes surfer dude and I didn't say anything. But let's bring it back to Rob, you don't think he could possibly be guilty—do you?"

"Not in a million years."

"So that leaves only you."

After a stunned silence, which was only appropriate, Ben roared. "Good one, Abby! But let's not forget you! *Sospechoso número uno.*"

I took a long, much-needed swig of my good buddy Bud. "How well acquainted were you with your late sister's ring? May she rest in peace."

"Yes, may she rest in peace. Ah, the ring—after Jerry's husband died, she waited a suitable length of time—several years, at least—and then had a series of lovers. One of them was a Colombian gentleman whom I always suspected of being a drug lord—then again, I have an active imagination. Someone told me once that I should be a novelist."

"Oh, you don't need an imagination for that anymore. I've thought about doing that myself. I read about a book called *101 Plot Ideas for the Uninspired*. The whole premise is that with the help of this book, and Internet publishing opportunities, anyone can be a published author."

"That's really cool. I'll have to remember that. Anyway, this guy, Carlos, gave her this ring like on their second date. Now mind you, Colombian emeralds at their finest are the best in the world. Their color simply cannot be matched."

"Because their color comes from chromium," I said, "and not vanadium like Zambian emeralds."

"Whoa," Ben said. "You do know something about colored stones."

"A tiny bit. I get them in my shop now and then."

"And what shop would that be?"

"The Den of Antiquity. It's an antiques store—obviously—on King Street, in Charleston. It's right down the street from Rob's."

"Yeah, I know it! And darn if I don't know you. I'm a Citadel grad and have good friends down in Charleston, and I come and stay with them. I wouldn't want to impose myself on Rob—not since he has a—well, you know."

"Partner?"

"I guess that's what they call them."

"They do. And Bob is a terrific guy—he'd be straight as an arrow if he wasn't—you know."

Ben winced. "Anyway, these friends have a house in Mount Pleasant and go into town every whipstitch to eat. I've wandered into your shop on numerous occasions. I thought you looked familiar."

Unfortunately I couldn't say the same for him; I get hundreds, if not thousands, of tourists through my shop every year. However, very few of the men are dead ringers for someone as handsome as Rob. This just proves how busy—or how unfocused—I am.

"I can only hope that your multiple visits were because you enjoyed my shop, and not out of some morbid desire to look at a train wreck in progress. We at the Den try our best."

"And you succeed! I've bought a number of small pieces there as gifts for my hosts. I've especially enjoyed dealing with a rather tall—how shall I describe this gently—"

"Goofy gal who says preposterous things?"

"That's the one! B.J., or something like that, am I right?"

"C.J. It stands for Calamity Jane. She's a real hoot, isn't she? She's here, you know. By that I mean she's consorting with your nephew Sam and his wife, Tina, at this very moment. She only met them this morning, but then instantly discovered that she and Tina were cousins through their Granny Ledbetter over in Shelby."

Ben cleared his throat and grinned broadly. A somewhat vain man, he'd taken good care of his teeth and they gleamed, white, straight, and indigenous to his mouth.

"Shelby, eh? Did she talk like a poor country hick with a third-grade education? Kind of like Granny on *Beverly Hillbillies*?"

"Exactly!"

"Abby, there's no way to break it to you gently; my nephew's wife, Tina Ovumkoph, is a scam artist."

12

Get out of town and back! And take the scenic way, will you?" I took a deep breath, grateful that I was already sitting down. "Details, please," I said.

"Those good folks in Shelby ought to tar and feather her the next time she passes through town on her way up to the mountains," Ben said. "That woman is a Southern Baptist, but she's from Atlanta, and she has a master's degree in clinical psychology from the University of Pittsburgh. I've met her parents; her mother is from Atlanta—old school—and her father from somewhere in southwestern Pennsylvania."

"Uh-oh. Poor C.J."

"When Tina first clamped on to Sammy—and I mean clamped, just like a vise—I thought she was English. You should have heard that accent—and all the references to crumpets and marmite, bubble and squeak, and toad in the hole."

"Okay, now you've lost me."

"English comestibles, all of them."

"Oh, so that's how you pronounce comestibles."

He winked. "I daresay."

"So when did she switch continents—so to speak?"

"About a week later—or never. That all depends. If Tina thinks someone from the family's listening, then her accent is English again; if it will raise money for the 'cause'—that would be her cause, not God's—then she's from some holler so far back in the mountains that you have to cross the Pacific Ocean first to get there."

"That's pretty far back." I chuckled. "I must say, though, Ben, you are given to some hyperbole."

"Ma'am?" He looked absolutely wounded.

"With your Pacific Ocean comment," I said.

"Oh no, Abby, those are her words, not mine. But hyperbole is it in a nutshell. In fact, that's what the others call her: Perbole. 'Hi Perbole,' they say. 'Bye Perbole.' Of course she doesn't get it; she thinks they're just being friendly—but weird. You can see why nobody can stand her."

"Uh, I hate to disagree," I said, "and may she rest in peace and whatever else I'm supposed to say at a time like this, but it seems that your Aunt Jerry could. She put Tina in charge of a lot of money—wait a minute! You mean to say that Aunt Jerry couldn't see through Tina's ruse?"

Ben slapped his thigh he laughed so hard, and then abruptly caught himself. "Sorry, that was totally inappropriate. And here I am supposed to be planning her funeral, which is the moment the police release her body. In Judaism we try to bury our dead as soon as possible. We don't embalm, you know."

"I didn't know that," I said. Sadly, what I knew about other religions, or even my own for that matter, was next to nothing. But I can see two church steeples from my front porch!

"You're right," Ben said. "Jerry didn't see through Tina, even though she thought of herself as very savvy in the ways of the world."

"Or maybe," I offered, "she didn't see through her act until the end, and that million-dollar bequest was a test of some sort."

"A posthumous test?" he asked. "What good would that do?"

"I didn't mean it that literally; I meant that the test came at the good-bye party. Maybe it involved seeing how Tina would react to the bequest. Oh grrr, I've got to go rescue C.J. from that woman's conniving claws."

"Don't forget Sammy's slimy paws. He's so slippery he could hold his own in a pond full of eels."

I jumped to my feet. "Oh shoot a monkey," I cried, "I plumb forgot!"

Ben's face mirrored my alarm. "What's that?"

"I was supposed to pick Rob up hours ago; I've left him stuck without a ride at the end of the greenbelt trail. My phone's been off the entire time—dang it—yes, there are two new messages."

Ben shook his head as he grinned. "No need to worry about Rob, sweetheart. This is his hometown; this is where he grew up. He's got more connections here than a dump truck full of Tinktertoys. Plus a wallet full of gold and platinum credit cards. He's not stuck anywhere that he doesn't want to be."

"Hmm, good point. Still, I need to be going."

Ben walked me to the door, and by the time we'd finished saying good-bye we were "cheek-pecking acquaintances" which is only one step away from being friends—at least "outer-circle friends." Even just that was saying a lot, given that I'd been the one to find his aunt stuffed in his upright freezer.

Don't get me wrong; I didn't for a second believe that Ben suspected me of murder. However, the phenomenon of wanting to kill the messenger is probably as old as mankind, so it would only be natural for Ben to bear a natural antipathy toward me, unless—wait just one hog-sloppin' minute—unless he was trying to play *me* like a country fiddle.

Sure enough, the calls were from Rob. The first one was from the trail and he was calling to apologize because he wasn't going to be able to meet me at the end. He'd met a friend along the way and the two of them would be brunching together. The second call involved another apology; brunch was over, but now they were headed up to Metrolina, which is a humongous antiques market just north of where I–85 crosses I–77. Thanks for helping to solve his aunt's murder, he said; there was no better sleuth in all of Charlotte at the moment—even though I was untrained.

There was some other bit about my sleuthing skills stemming from the fact that I excelled at being nosy, but I chose to take those words in the spirit in which they were intended. Alas, choosing does not always mean achieving. Nonetheless, when my nose was sufficiently back into joint to hold up a pair of sunglasses, I set my GPS to the address that Ben had so thoughtfully supplied for his nephew Sam. Thank heavens he'd also supplied me with the entry code I needed to get past security.

In case anyone has ever thought otherwise, now would be a good time to dissuade them of the notion that I am above reproach. I am particularly vulnerable to house envy. Even though I currently own a beautiful house in the most desirable part of Charleston, South Carolina (without a doubt *the* most desirable city on the planet), I find myself lusting in my heart after some of the megamansions that I see from time to time. I am particularly charmed by the current Charlotte fad of Spanish–Tucson–medieval castle fusion, characterized by stucco walls, clay tile roofs, balustrade balconies, and towers galore. Clearly some poor architect has turrets syndrome, and to that I say, "Bless his heart."

Sam and Tina lived in a gated community that was so ritzy, even the wind needed the entry code in order to blow through. As I drove slowly along the winding road, mouth open and drooling, I kept hoping that number 8369 would be the smallest house on the so-called block. I was overjoyed, therefore, to discover that was indeed the case. I was dumbfounded, thunderstruck, and downright gobsmacked when just a few seconds later I realized that the mini-megamansion that I thought was Sam's was actually his own private guard shack. Complete with its own garage!

"Excuse me, ma'am," said a woman about my age. "This is private property." She'd stepped out from what at first glance had looked to be the front door of the house. It was only then that I noticed there was a wooden bar across the driveway, and it was much like the barriers one sees across a railroad track, but without the stripes painted on it.

"Is this Sam Ovumkoph's house?"

"I'm afraid you'll have to be moving along."

"I'm a friend of Sam's Uncle Ben—like the rice, but, of course, this Ben is a real man—and I'm best friends with his cousin Rob. Actually, you might say that I'm friends with Sam and Tina too, since I just had lunch with them at the Viet Thai Noodle House, which isn't fancy by any means, but they thought the food was really good. Oh, by the way, as it turns out, I was there with my third best friend in the whole world, C.J. from Shelby, and she and Tina figured out that they were first cousins. Can you imagine that?"

The guard's response was to walk slowly around the car and, I presumed, record my license plate number. When she was done making her circuit, she rapped on my window.

"You look kind of familiar. Have you ever been here before?"

"No, ma'am. I have not."

"Maybe selling cosmetics to the missus, or something like that? Lord knows I don't mean to be ugly about it, but she sure can use a little help—you know what I mean?" She gestured with her thumb up the road.

"Indeed I do, missy!" I pushed my door open with my left hand as my right hand undid my seat belt. The badmouthing guard was caught by surprise and fell back on her butt. Quick as double-geared lightning I was out of the car and standing over her with my hands on my hips. When viewed from that angle, and if I exert enough attitude, I can give the appearance of a much larger woman. I know it may sound hard to believe, but it really is all in the " 'tude," as my son, Charlie, likes to say. Why, in that particular instance, I wouldn't be surprised to learn that I came across as being five-four!

"What the H," she said. She actually said a whole lot worse, but since I don't possess a potty mouth, it is hard to repeat it exactly.

"Put up that crossbar or I'm telling Tina what you just said. That poor girl can't help what nature dealt her; just because her parents had to tie a pork chop around her neck to get the dog to play with her—well, that was no fault of hers, now was it?"

"No, ma'am."

"So what will it be? Up goes the crossbar and we're all happy, or—"

"Yes, ma'am."

I stepped back and let her struggle to her feet, but sure enough, as soon as she was up, up went the bar.

"Tootles, darling," I said as I hopped back in the car. Then off I sped up the yellow brick road.

Upscale neighborhoods have covenants, written rules that one must abide by that are specific to that area. South of Broad, in Charleston, we even abide by unwritten covenants that govern certain social customs. For instance, one simply does not hang a Christmas wreath on the door more than a fortnight before Christmas. To do so is to invite a gentle rebuke via a handwritten note on scented stationery, or perhaps a soft knock on the door and a few kind words of disap-proval. Those are the short-term ramifications, of course. Long term—well, the occupants of said house are clearly from "off" and need not expect an invita-tion to any holiday party or oyster roast anytime soon (so what are a few generations in the grand scheme of things?).

But covenants, like many aspiring congressmen (and women), can be shaped by a sufficient influx of cash. "The bucks stop here" is really a much older phrase than the one made popular by Harry Truman, and the more money that is to be had, the further the rules can be bent. This might explain how it was that the yellow brick road that led up the hill to the Ovum-koph monstrosity was literally that: yellow and brick.

Although I was a child of the seventies, and had in my college years dabbled a *wee* bit in mind-altering substances, and had always prided myself on an active imagination, nothing I'd experienced could have pre-pared me for the Ovumkoph creation they called home. Once, on a trip to Portugal, I'd been privileged to travel to the mountainous city of Sintra, and from there up to the Pena Palace, which is a fantasy that combines Moorish, Gothic, and Manueline motifs. That multicolored, domed, gabled, and crenulated structure perhaps comes closest to resembling Sam and Tina's act of stewardship gone awry.

Instead of ringing of a doorbell I had the pleasure of yanking on a rope. This set into motion a graduated series of bells, each with a different tone. I think that the tune they produced was the first measure of "America the Beautiful"; then again, it might have

Tamar Myers

been the title song from *Beauty and the Beast*. After several long minutes, when the door went unanswered I pulled the rope again. Apparently the bells had not stopped vibrating from their first go-around, because the resultant sound was even more garbled. It struck me that this was a very clever way to discourage unwanted visitors—possibly including myself.

I was fixing to give the rope a third tug when the massive door inched open. Out poked an immense proboscis followed by curtains of hair. My first impression was that the Ovumkophs had a sheepdog trained as a butler.

"I'm here to speak to either the pastor or his wife," I said.

"Come in," the sheepdog said.

13

It stood aside as the door opened wider. My eyes opened wider as well. The Ovumkophs, bless their hearts, did not abide by the "less is more" principle. Instead they believed in gilding the lily, the furniture, the walls, even the floor tiles. If they did make it to Heaven and were privileged to walk the celestial golden streets, how would they ever know when they'd arrived?

"Wow," I finally said.

"You don't think it's too much, do you?" There was an unmistakable challenge in the sheepdog's voice, and a familiar Piedmont accent.

I gave the odd butler a closer look. It wasn't really a dog, *of course*. It was a woman with an unfortunately large nose and volumes of hair—goodness gracious, and a bucket full of kittens! It was none other than Tina Ovumkoph herself! And in skintight jeans and—oops, when her hair parted for a second, I could see a shamefully low-cut blouse that displayed acres of boobelege. Okay, so maybe that's not a real word, but it ought to be. This was serious hoochie-mama stuff that shimmied and shook, and which *briefly* made me consider batting for the other team. But only briefly, mind you.

"*Tina?* Is that really you?"

She sighed. "I'm afraid so, Mrs. Timberlake. Sunday is Oscar's day off, on account of the Bible says we need to give our servants and beasts time to rest too. Oscar's our butler, by the way."

"But just out of curiosity, do you have a beast as well? Pastor Sam excluded for now."

She didn't even crack a smile. "Oh Mrs. Timberlake, I'm afraid you got the wrong impression somehow. Sam really is the kindest, most gentle man I know."

"Then you must know some real brutes."

She stiffened, an act that set the curtains of hair into motion. "I beg your pardon?"

"I saw how he tried, and succeeded, in controlling you at the restaurant. Or was that an act as well?"

Tina brushed a curtain of hair away from her face and practically jammed it behind her left ear. Meanwhile her gaze flitted side to side as if scanning the gold walls for the telltale reflection of a third party.

"I'm fixing to leave him just as soon as I can," she whispered. "Believe me, I've been prayin' about it right hard, and then today the Lord sends my dear cousin Calamity Jane, like an angel sent from Heaven, to show me the way. I just know it's a sign. And now you sayin' this." She grabbed my hands and held them tightly. "Mrs. Timberlake, you too are like an angel— well, maybe a cherub. You know, one of them baby angels, on account of you being so petite and all."

At that moment C.J. quietly entered the hall from somewhere behind her, and I desperately wanted to get her attention. I jerked my hands loose from Tina's and reached up and patted—none too gently—her somewhat drooping cheeks.

"And you, my dear, are the biggest fraud since Bernard Madoff. And stop looking so surprised, will you? I know for a fact that you are not from Shelby, North Carolina. Neither are you related to the legendary, and practically sainted, Granny Ledbetter."

I'll say this for Tina. She was smart enough to know that she'd been bested. Rather than deny involvement and dig her hole deeper, she immediately sang like a velvet-throated canary.

"Okay, you've caught me; but if your people can cut me a deal, I'll tell them everything there is to know about that thieving son of a—"

"Bless his mama's heart," I said. "I'm sure he broke it a million times when she was alive."

At that point the big galoot was upon us, but I could tell by her expression that she was not yet a believer. "Abby, why don't you want me to be happy?" she demanded.

"C.J., I *do* want you to be happy. I want you to be over-the-moon giddy with happiness, but Tina here is not your cousin. Go ahead and tell her, Tina."

Tina nodded her confirmation. No doubt she was too embarrassed to turn around and speak.

"Look, C.J.," I said, as I opened my pocketbook and withdrew a thick brown root that I'd purchased in the produce department at the Colony Square Harris Teeter on my way over to the Ovumkophs' exclusive neighborhood. "I'm going to give Tina the Granny Ledbetter proof of kinship test."

"What's that?" Tina said. She held her hands up in front of her face.

"It's a horseradish root. There isn't a descendant of C.J.'s Granny Ledbetter—by birth or adoption—who isn't capable of chewing his or her way through a root this size in two minutes flat. And then you have to sing the Ledbetter family anthem—backward and in Mandarin Chinese. Of course you already know all that."

"But Abby," C.J. said, "we—"

"Shhh, hush, sweetie. This is between Tina and me. Go ahead, Tina. Chomp away. I'll start timing you."

Tina waved her arms wildly above her head. "I can't eat horseradish! Get that thing away from me." She had, by the way, totally lost her strong Carolina accent. If anything, she sounded a bit South Bronx.

"You see," I said.

"And anyway, I already told you that I wasn't an ignorant hick like that one."

"*That* one?" I couldn't believe how rude Tina was; it was further proof that she came from up the road apiece. All right, not everyone from up the road apiece is rude, or vice versa, but overall I think we Southerners are better at camouflaging our ugly feelings beneath a veneer of perceived manners. As Dr. Phil once said, "Perception is nine tenths of the law"—or something like that.

"Let me show you what a *real* Ledbetter can do," C.J. said, and threw herself into the thick of things. Before I could react she'd snatched the horseradish root from me and had crunched her way through half of it.

"C.J., stop! I was just making that up! There is no such thing as a Granny Ledbetter kinship test; you ought to know that."

She shoved the rest of the pungent root into her mouth, chewed a couple of times, and then swallowed. "Of course I know that, Abby. Granny makes them drink an entire pot of road apple tea. So far there's not been one person willing to try the tea, not even when Granny found an emerald mine on her north forty."

"North forty what?" I said.

C.J. gave me a pitying look. "Honestly, Abby, sometimes I worry about you."

"She means her north forty acres of land," Tina said. "Even a city slicker like me knows that. Honestly, Mrs. Timberlake, I see what she means about you."

"Oh give it a rest," I said. But I said it with a warm smile and stretched it out to nine syllables, so it wasn't like I was being mean.

"Abby," C.J. said, as soon as her car door slammed shut, "what took you so long?"

"So *long*? What on earth do you mean?"

"I expected you to pick me up at least an hour ago," C.J. said.

"You did?" I said. "Did you call?"

"Abby, I'm only human; I forgot to plug my phone in last night. But I've been sending you signals."

"Well," I said, "I must have picked up on them eventually, because here I am. So, tell me, what was it like deep inside the Golden Palace of Excess?"

"You won't believe what I saw, Abby."

"Try me," I said. "I've seen some pretty magnificent

edifices: I've been to Versailles, the Vatican, Buckingham Palace, and of course our very own Biltmore Estate. At one time it was the largest private home in the country. So I can believe just about anything right now."

C.J. chortled. "Ooh, Abby, I win! Think opposites."

"*What?*"

"Drywall and cinder blocks; that's it in all the other rooms. And linoleum floors—if they have any at all. Abby, that monstrosity back there is just an empty shell! It's like the facade of a movie set."

"It is?" I said. "No way! The guard shack is as big and comfy as my old house in Charlotte."

"Yes," C.J. said, "but it's just for show. First of all, they didn't want me tagging home with them, they just wanted a loan—a million-dollar loan. They said that they could tell by your handbag that we were loaded."

"Huh?"

"Abby," C.J. said accusingly, "isn't that a twenty-thousand-dollar Bons Laeppa bag you're carrying?"

"Yes, but I didn't buy it, for crying out loud! Mr. Laeppa came into my shop one day and we started talking, and sort of hit it off, and then—well, how can I help it if the bonny Bons with the tight pair of buns found me a mite attractive?"

"Ooh, Abby, you're awful. You better hope that Greg never hears you talking that way."

"But C.J.," I protested, "these guys are big-time con artists; they can't be broke."

"Yes, they can, Abby. They're stealing from church folks, remember? And Granny said I should never be vain about my gift but, to put it plainly, their victims aren't the brightest coals in the weenie-roasting pit."

"You can say amen to that, sister."

"Amen. Besides, Abby, just paying for the upkeep of the huge church, and then the outside of this place, and the gatehouse—"

"And property taxes," I reminded her. "They're immensely high in Charlotte, as you know, and yada, yada. But you certainly have a good point. Theoretically, at least, the not-so-good reverend and his two-toned wife could very well have needed that emerald ring in order to finish decorating."

"Abby, you talk in riddles, you know that? Besides, Tina was supposed to inherit a million dollars—or have you forgotten?"

"Don't sound so gleeful at the prospect of my memory failing. The thing is, she is not going to get that money for a long time—if ever now. And even if she does, she'll have to be accountable for every penny. It's not hers to keep, remember?"

"Duh," C.J. said, and slapped herself up the side of the head with enough force to knock the average man off his feet. She often does this to acknowledge the times when she's been the one to say something foolish. I hate it when she does so. A woman of lesser brainpower would have the knocked the smarts right out of herself years ago.

"Stop that," I said. "Did they say anything that might implicate them in the murder of Sam's poor Aunt Jerry—may she rest in peace?"

"Thanks for fitting that lowercase P in there; it makes it easier to read."

"Say what?" I said.

"Never mind," C.J. said. "But to answer your question: on the way over to their house, before I knew they were really poorer than church mice—well, than *most* church mice, on account of there are a couple of mice up in Shelby—"

"C.J.," I said, "if you don't put a lid on that Shelby story I'll pull into the driveway of that really big house over there, open all the windows, and scream."

"Abby, that's not a house; it's an assisted living home."

"All the better," I said.

"Okay, okay, you don't need to get your Spanx in such a snit. What I was about to say is that I asked Tina to recommend a really fine jeweler, and she didn't even have to think about it. Of course when she did think about it she got mad and accused me of setting a trap; but I just continued to play the part of the dumb hick and said it was on account of I needed to sell some scrap gold. I think she was so relieved that she didn't ask why I needed a fine jeweler for that."

"Why I declare," I said. "You really are as smart as a tree full of owls."

"Thank you, Abby. Although adult owls—when not rearing chicks—are usually solitary. You must be thinking of starlings, which are not native to this country, and are—"

"What's the name of the jewelers?"

"Temptation Rocks. It's at South Park Mall and it's open until six. But be a pal and drop me off at the library first; it's right on the way. There are four books in there I have yet to read."

I smiled. "Will do."

14

There are those who love to shop at South Park Mall. Then there are those who are afraid to enter without an exit plan, such as a line tied around her waist, a GPS, and a flock of homing pigeons. I say this with great respect, as I am a woman who loves to shop. And while there are probably worse fates than a life lived out wandering in perpetual search of a mall exit (assuming the food court is half decent and the restroom stocked with paper and seat liners), I do have a hunk of a husband waiting for me back in Charleston. There is also a very handsome, very hairy, younger male whom I would miss terribly: my cat, Dmitri. (And yes, I do think that the pronoun *whom* should be used with cats; they are just as human as many men I've known.)

But in order to get to Temptation Rocks I had to traverse a labyrinth of hallways laid out in what was, to me, a very confusing floor plan. The layout was rendered even more torturous because the stores are upscale establishments like Neiman Marcus and _calls# Tamar Myers

Tiffany's; places where I would normally not shop, but can't help popping into nonetheless. This is where the GPS comes in helpful, especially if you get the kind that scolds you harshly for deviating from the proscribed path.

At any rate, Temptation Rocks had an understated display window, and I walked past the space twice without noticing it. It was essentially just a gray satin background punctuated by one recessed, brightly lit niche about the size of a PC monitor screen and perhaps six inches deep. The interior of the niche was lined in pale blue velvet and showcased just one gem: a knock-your-socks-off ruby and diamond necklace that was priced at a mere $899,999.99.

As when entering a few other fine shops of its ilk, I had to be buzzed into Temptation Rocks. The woman who let me in wore a badge that proclaimed her to be Hildegard. Her long, golden brown hair was braided tightly and coiled on the crown of her head like the beginnings of a folk art basket. Her perfectly round cheeks were heavily rouged and brought to mind the pair of Gala apples I'd packed in Greg's lunch bucket before leaving to drive up here.

Hildegard immediately held out a silver tray bearing Baccarat crystal champagne glasses that were certainly no more than half full. "Would you care for some champagne, madam?"

"No thank you; I'm more of beer gal."

Hildegard recoiled as if she'd been approached by an untouchable. "There is a food court at the end of this hall, and to the left. Perhaps they serve that beverage there."

"I didn't come here to drink."

She appeared to sniff the air as she surveyed the rather impressive rock on my left ring finger. "Oh. Then how may I be of service?"

I made a show of trying to look around her. "Is there a jeweler on the premises?"

"Why do you wish to speak to a jeweler?"

There is an art to delivering that "just so" dismissive look, the one that says that the speaker had no business asking such an impertinent question, and would do well to mind her own business from here on out. I learned that art by watching Rob, who learned it from a former lover who was purportedly minor royalty: he would have been a Portuguese prince had that country kept its king.

"Very well, madam," Hildegard said. She set the silvery tray on a mahogany stand by the door to the shop. Then she carefully locked that door, before trotting around the counters and through a velvet curtain. Did I mention that she trotted on three-thousand-dollar high-heeled sandals by Victor Illuminati, the blind, but oh-so-gifted Italian designer who is all the rage this year among those who are truly in the know?

I didn't have to wait long. In fact, I was having a good time admiring the pretties in the nearest case when out from behind the curtain hurried a middle-aged man who carried with him the look of a hunted animal. Right behind him trotted the expensively dressed hostess. She cast me an evil look before resuming her post right inside the door.

"Yes? How can I help you?" The jeweler spoke with

the slightest of foreign accents; not Yankee, mind you, but possibly Eastern European.

I held out my hand in the limp fish position. Much to my pleasure, he actually took and kissed it.

"My name is Abigail Louise Wiggins Timberlake Washburn," I said. After all, European society is ancient, and Europeans respect people with family connections and complicated genealogies.

"Ghurtpen Chergonia." I had him print it for me. Even then I wasn't quite sure of his first name.

"Mr. Chergonia, I have heard wonderful things about your work."

"My work?"

"Your skill! You're supposed to be the best, you know. Everyone says that."

"Who is *everyone*, madam?"

"Connoisseurs of fine workmanship, that's who. Like the Ovumkophs, for instance."

"Forgive me, madam, but I do not know these people." He turned away and began a slow sideways retreat.

"Oh well, Ovumkoph is just one of many names, of course." I put my hands to my mouth as if I wished to whisper in his ear. "I can hardly use their *real* names now, can I?" The low-pitched, cultivated chuckle I emitted was also learned from Rob, who no doubt also picked it up from his Portuguese paramour, he of the purified plasma.

The jeweler turned and beckoned me to follow him. As I did so, the hostess became quite agitated.

"You can't go back there, ma'am." Her accent, by the way, had shifted suddenly from BBC British to Piedmont American. "Mr. Hunter, the owner, will be very upset."

"Oh? Where is he? I'll ask his permission first."

"He don't work on Sundays. It's just me and this foreign guy. Look, I don't want no trouble. I don't want to get in any trouble with Mr. Hunter neither."

"Either."

"What?"

"I think you meant *either*. Anyway, I have no desire to get you into trouble. I just want to see a sample of Mr. Chergonia's craftsmanship. He's an artist, you know."

"Uh-uh, get out of town!" she said to the jeweler. "What do you paint? Can you paint a picture of my mama's dog, Cotton? It's Mama's birthday the day after Labor Day but we're fixin' to have a cookout down at my cousin Trudy's place over in Tega Cay. It's right on Lake Wylie. I mean the deck actually extends right over the water; you can spit right down on the fish if you're so inclined. And they actually go for it, like it was fish food. I guess they ain't very smart."

"What an interesting idea—spitting on the fish; I'll have to keep that in mind should my husband and I ever decide to build on the water. Or swim in it."

Hildegard glanced at the door, and seeing it still securely locked, risked a bawdy laugh. "Oh honey, that water has seen a lot worse than that, and folks still swim in it. It's the lake; not the shower."

"Gotcha," I said with a knowing wink. I gave her what I hope was interpreted as a friendly wave and trotted off after the mysterious European on my $39.99 Naturalizers.

* * *

I am not so stupid as to reveal the exact location of the safe in the backroom at Temptation Rocks, but I will say this about its contents; many of the rocks I beheld were so beautiful that I was sorely tempted to—well, to drop a wad of cash. What else? The trouble was that even though I am well-off, I am not *that* well-off.

It used to be that glittering gems advertised personal wealth, but that was back in the cavemen days before the technology existed to make cheap fakes—and I mean really cheap. It's possible to pick up some rings for five bucks or less in tourist traps that will make heads turn, if only for a minute. Because this is the case, because the bling factor can be achieved for so little, there really isn't a whole of impetus to spend huge amounts on the real thing. Not when there are lots of other status symbols to spend it on. I, for one, would only pay a fortune for the real McCoy when it came to rocks, if I'd checked everything else off my want list, and that included a new Mercedes-Benz.

Nonetheless, I gasped in reverent appreciation, in part because of the elegant gold settings that surrounded so many of the stones. I was particularly fascinated by a ring that looked identical to the one that Aunt Jerry had wished to bequeath me, except that this treasure sported a golden centerpiece.

"It's a twenty-two-carat golden beryl from Namibia. German cut. Here, hold it up to this light so that you can see the facets. Beautiful, no?"

"Beautiful, yes. Did you make the setting?"

"Yes, madam. Lost wax process. It is an original

design, although I have used it since on five other rings."

I shivered with delight. Surely this feeling was akin to what matadors felt when they were finally coming in for the kill.

"Were they all golden beryl?" I asked.

He made a clicking sound with his tongue. "No. One was aquamarine—that is a kind of beryl too, you know."

"Yes."

I may have sounded impatient, because his rejoinder was slightly combative. "You don't see good aquamarine in American stores; not like in Europe. Now in Japan—only the best there. The Japanese know their stones. Here, mostly the stores sell junk. A good aquamarine is—"

"—deep blue, the color of the ocean when you've sailed out beyond the continental shelf."

He stared at me. "Ah, so you are not a dilettante!"

"Nor an expert either. I'm just a lover of gems."

He motioned for me to sit on a padded stool that had arms and a back. After I'd hoisted my petite patootie into place, he perched on an identical stool.

"Which is your favorite gemstone?" he asked.

"That depends. Can we, for the sake of this discussion, eliminate the human suffering aspect?" I was dead serious. Most gemstones come to us from Third World countries where they are "mined" under appalling conditions. The workers—often children—are little more than slaves, working twelve-hour days either under the blazing tropical sun or deep under the earth in danger of suffocation at any time. For their labor they are a paid a pittance, sometimes not even enough to sustain them physically. After all, what does it really matter if they die on the job? There is always someone to take their place.

"I guess that we would almost have to eliminate the human suffering element, or we wouldn't have any gems, would we?"

"Actually, there is a lot of gem mining in parts of North Carolina. Some of it is essentially backyard pits. But honestly, what I'd really like, if the human suffering factor was not an issue, would be a Mogok ruby from Burma."

He nodded. "That famous 'pigeon blood' red. The stones with the fluorescence that can't be matched by their Thai counterparts."

"Yes, and all we see are Thai rubies, am I right? Little, itty-bitty ones."

He laughed. "So you like big stones—like this."

"Unfortunately, I do. And what's that famous saying? You can have anything you want in life; just not everything. An eye-clean Mogok ruby the size of this golden beryl would cost five times as much as my house in Charleston—*South* of Broad Street. What about you? What's your favorite stone?"

"Madam, I do not know anything about the house prices in Charleston, but I too would not be able to afford my first choice of an emerald from the famous Muzo mine in Colombia. If it were eye-clean—impossible! But with a garden of slight inclusions, then maybe. Emerald is a beryl too, you know."

"Yes, I know."

"Madam, you know everything." He sounded astonished rather than miffed.

"No, but I know a lot." Play your cards close to your chest, I reminded myself; there was no point in divulging to Mr. Chergonia that my well of knowledge was about to run dry.

He sighed, and locking his fingers, put his hands behind his head. "Then you must know that some gemstones are easier to replicate than others, and that a lab-created emerald has the same physical properties—that is the word, yes?"

"Yes. And yes, it is exactly the same as a natural emerald, except that it took months to grow, rather than tens of thousands of years."

"There are many times I cannot tell a good synthetic emerald from a natural one, except for under the microscope. As for the glass imitations, they are always greener. Ha, now I make a little joke."

"Excuse me?"

"You have a saying, yes? The glass is always greener on the other side of the wall."

I thought of correcting him, but thankfully thought better of it. "That is what we said in my country," he said. "We had many prisons. But now I want to tell you something truly amazing. This emerald that I desire, the one from Muzo with just a little bit of garden and which is the perfect color of ferns—you know what are ferns?"

I leaned forward on my stool. "Yes. I know what ferns are."

He leaned forward as well. "I have seen this emerald—right here in my shop. I have held it my hands; I have touched it to my lips. I am telling you, madam, it exists. This fabulous stone is right here in Charlotte, North Carolina."

"Yes, I know."

He recoiled ever so slightly. "You have seen it?"

"Yes. I believe that I own it."

The jeweler shook his head wearily. "Madam, please, it has been a long day. Either you know that this stone is yours, or you do not. It is not a matter of faith."

"Well, it's kind of a long story—but I'll give you the short version. It was given to me by an eccentric woman named Jerry Ovumkoph—an older woman in her seventies—"

"Yes, yes, she is the one! She brings in this ring; at first I think that she has been misinformed; many clients come in with synthetic stones and they do not know it. When I tell them that their stones are worthless, they are, of course, very angry with me." He shrugged. "But some do know that the stones they have are counterfeits, and their intention is to cheat. Anyway, I studied Ms. Ovumkoph's stone carefully, and I even asked the opinion of some of my colleagues, and yes, madam—it is real."

"Did she want to sell it?"

"Madam, you are very charming; a native of the South, yes? But, you still have not stated your business. Are you a buyer, or a seller?"

I thought back to my college days, and what different connotations those words had then. But it was stupid of me to waste even a nanosecond on such memories. I decided to come clean with the jeweler with the vaguely

Eastern European accent—well, partway clean, at least. Any Dixie chick with a speck of starch in her crinolines knows better than to spill all her beans at once, even if she has to murder her metaphors.

"I'm neither a buyer nor a seller. You see, the woman who was here—Jerry Ovumkoph—left me that ring in her will. But she's dead now, and the ring is missing. I'm trying to trace down the origin of that ring for insurance purposes so I can get a replacement value."

He stared at me. I knew he was trying to read me, to see if I was lying. Of course I was, but I wasn't trying to scam him out of any money. He didn't have a thing to lose by telling me the truth. Surely he could sense that.

"She wanted a glass copy made," he said. "Glass!"

"Scandalous," I said.

"Are you mocking me, madam?"

"No, sir. I'm quite serious; to put a glass center stone in that gorgeous design of yours would be like hanging a Jackson Pollock painting in the Hermitage. How many diamonds are in the border?"

"Forty-two. Each one is VVSI or better. It is twenty-two-karat Italian gold—not fourteen-karat like the cheap rings one sees everywhere."

I glanced down at the cheap ring my sweetie gave me. Well, it would take more knocks than a more expensive ring without getting bent out of shape. That's what I was trying to do in this new marriage: not get all bent out of shape. But as for the knocks—just one literal tap and Greg was out of there. I'd survived one abusive marriage, and I was not going to be a punching bag, for *anyone*, ever again.

145

"Of course you Americans are very smart," Mr. Chergonia said. "You spend thousands of dollars on the dress, which the bride will never wear again. But it is big, and every one can see it even from the back of the church. The ring not so much—even though when the revolution comes, the bride can run and hide with her ring, and then sell it across the border and buy bread for her children if it is high-quality gold."

"Your point is well-taken, sir. I concede—that means that you win."

"So—Mrs. Abigail Louise Wiggins Timberlake Washburn—what else do you want to know?"

It took me a minute to scoop up my lower jaw and slap it back into place. "Wow! You've got quite a memory for names."

"And you have an impressive knowledge of stones—for an amateur, yes?"

"Yes, although I do own an antiques store and from time to time I come into possession of estate jewelry. Anyway, what I really came here to find out is if anyone has been trying to unload this ring in the last day or two."

"Madam?" He appeared to be genuinely startled.

"You see, Jerry Ovumkoph passed—that is to say, she's dead—and she left me her ring in her will, but it was stolen."

His dark eyes flashed angrily. "I do not deal in stolen goods! *Never!*"

"I know that, sir. I'm just wondering if someone— maybe another Ovumkoph—tried to sell you this ring."

His response was to hold one of his long, slender, if

slightly crooked fingers to his lips. The dark eyes directed me to look at the curtained doorway. There was a gap toward the bottom where the heaven curtains fell apart, and in that space was the hideously expensive toe of a Victor Illuminati sandal.

I smiled and nodded. "Then I dragged the body to the car," I practically shouted. "Of course I couldn't lift it into the trunk by myself, so I had to call someone from the *family* to help me. You wouldn't believe how fast they showed up. Being the Godfather's real daughter has its perks, you know. I just wish I'd kept my maiden name, and not those of all my former husbands. Oh well, at least they're no longer around to bother me."

By then Mr. Chergonia had risen to his feet. The poor man's face was as white as parboiled grits and he'd begun to sway like a palmetto in a category four storm. I have never taken a bona fide CPR class; all I really know is that the techniques have changed a bit over the years and—thank heavens—giving mouth-to-mouth is no longer de rigueur. Then again, like I said, I really know squat. I just knew enough to dig my cell phone out of my purse and mentally review the procedure for dialing 911.

"I think you need to sit back down," I whispered.

"Yah, mebbe, dats a goot idea," he said.

By then the ridiculously expensive footwear was no longer to be seen. Having caused such consternation, I took it upon myself to at least see what, if any, the lasting damages were, so I crept to the doorway and gradually peeled back enough of one panel to allow me to peep into the showroom. You can imagine my relief then when I saw the hostess cleaning the top of a display case at the far end of the room. She looked entirely absorbed in her task; calm and peaceful even. The tray of champagne glasses waited nearby on another countertop. All was well with the world.

I scurried soundlessly back to my source of information. "So? Have you been contacted?"

"Ahuuug—" he said, and slid to the floor.

15

It was already past six when the police let me go. Ergo I didn't stand a chance of winning the bet.

"Abby, darling," Mama said, over her fillet at the Texas Roadhouse, "you should lock yourself up in your hotel room until Greg gets up here. Bodies are dropping like flies wherever you go."

"*Please*, Mama," I said, "the waiter might hear you."

"Did you say you wanted fries, ma'am?" the waiter said.

Everyone burst out laughing except for Douglas, our flummoxed waitperson, and yours truly. "No," Mama said, "but we'll take another basket of those rolls—um, make that two baskets. And more honey butter, please. I swear, I could fill up on just those rolls."

"I hear you, Mozella," Wynnell said. "Those rolls make my tongue want to come out and slap my head silly."

This time everyone, including Douglas, laughed— except for C.J. "Ooh, Wynnell, I know that's a good

149

Southernism, but I really wish you wouldn't say it. Cousin Cornelius Ledbetter really did have a tongue that long and it got him into all kinds of trouble. He went up North one winter—it was really cold up there—and his tongue got frozen to—"

"To a light pole." Mama sighed. "C.J., we all saw that movie."

"It wasn't a light pole, Mozella," C.J. said, somewhat piqued. "That just doesn't make a lick of sense."

"No pun intended," I said, and we all laughed—except C.J.

"Really, y'all," she said, turning red, "do you want to hear the story, or not?"

"Of course we do," Wynnell said quickly. I can't blame the poor woman for capitulating so quickly; after all, it was she who had to endure the ride up to Charlotte with my ex-sister-in-law. (A pouting C.J. is enough to drive a busload of optimists over a cliff on a sunny day.)

"Well, it's like this. It was actually both tongues that came out—"

"Now wait just one biscuit-baking minute," I said. "You really expect us to believe that your cousin has two tongues?"

The big galoot rolled her eyes. "Don't you ever wear tie-up shoes, Abby? Like sneakers?"

"Oh!"

"Cheese and crackers, Abby—I mean, you didn't really think I meant his *lingua*, did you?" Of the seventeen languages C.J. speaks, Latin gets the least use, so she is always happy when she gets to toss in a word that we'll understand by context.

"Of course not—" Thank goodness our conversation was interrupted by the delivery of two baskets of soft, warm yeast rolls, and freshly filled tubs of honey butter.

After Mama had inhaled two rolls she nudged C.J. "Let's go make a scene and embarrass the girls."

"This time you're keeping your clothes on, Mozella," C.J. said to my seventy-five-year-old mama.

"Whatever," Mama said.

I knew what they were up to. The Texas Roadhouse has a genuine saddle that you get to sit on if it's your birthday. Mostly children do this, and while they're in this photo opportunity the waitstaff sings the birthday song and onlookers clap. In short, everyone has a good time. However, my wee madre insists on climbing aboard the saddle every time we visit the restaurant (which is every time we're in Charlotte), and while I blush and look away, and no one officially sings, she hees and haws and has such a good time that when she finally climbs down, she somehow manages a standing ovation. Go figure.

"So tell me, Wynnell," I said, the second those two overgrown children were out of earshot, "how was your afternoon?"

"You should know, Abby," Wynnell said. "We seemed to hit every place you did—except that we arrived a few seconds *after* you stirred up the hornets' nests."

"I did no such thing!"

"Abigail Louise," Wynnell said, "don't you lie to me. That nice Melissa Ovumkoph said you pocketed all her Moon Pies but one, and she was so upset that she ate it herself, so she had nothing to offer me but a glass of rather strange-looking wine which, by the way, was really quite good."

"Oops," I said sheepishly. "I still have some of the Moon Pies. Would you like one?"

"Maybe later," Wynnell said.

"Were you able to learn anything?" I asked.

"She's not a natural blond," Wynnell said.

"You should work for the government," I said.

Wynnell smiled, and given that she now had two eyebrows and they were shaped, she was really quite attractive. Not jump-her-bones-attractive, of course, few women are—now where was I?

"The blond thing was a joke," Wynnell said. "But she really is an impostor; a fake."

"*What?*" I said.

"Maybe you didn't see it, Abby," Wynnell said. "That's only because you're always looking for the good in people."

"Yee-haw!" Mama whooped in the distance.

"Oh, I get it now," I said. "Melissa Ovumkoph is a Yankee pretending to be a native-born Southerner. What gave her away?"

"She kept addressing me as 'y'all.' When will they ever learn that 'y'all' is plural and stands for 'you all'?"

"When you put your guns down and surrender," I said. "Wynnell, the war has been over for almost one hundred and fifty years."

"Humph."

"Were you able to get any information that might pertain to the case?" I asked.

"She was fixing to fry up some chicken and take it over to her husband," Wynnell said.

"That's definitely the mark of a killer," I said.

"Abby," Wynnell said, "you're getting as smart-mouthed as your friend Magdalena. Frankly, honey, it isn't as becoming on someone as tiny as you."

"Why fiddle-dee-dee," I said. "Okay, dear, I'll zip my lips if you'll just cut to the chase."

Wynnell demonstrated that two brows can indeed be quite effective in denoting displeasure. "I *was* at the chase," she said. "Melissa was dredging chicken parts in flour as we talked, and that's when I happened to notice the empty package lying in the sink. Knowing that they are cash poor, I casually mentioned to her that it is cheaper to buy a whole chicken and cut it up oneself. Well, wouldn't you know she turned white as a sheet? She has an absolute phobia about knives. Turns out her twin sister committed suicide by—well, trust me, Abby, Melissa Ovumkoph did not stab her husband's aunt, and I very much doubt if her husband did either."

"Good job, Wynnell!" I said. Finally I had something to jot down in my notebook. "Was Mama any help?"

"Abby," Wynnell said, "your mama's a peach, and you know that I love her dearly, right?"

"Of course!" I said.

"She wouldn't come inside," Wynnell said, "all on account of she couldn't get her puffed up skirts through the door without getting them dirty. I whispered to her that she should slip off a few of her crino-lines so as not to appear rude, but you know that she can be as stubborn as a herd of concrete mules—especially to suggestions. So she stayed back in the car, listening to the radio. Now was that rude, or what?"

"What," Mama said breathlessly, having returned from her romp in the saddle. "What are you two talking about?"

"Your bad behavior at Melissa Ovumkoph's house: refusing to squeeze through the front door."

Mama has plucked her brows so much that what one sees now is mostly pencil. "Abby, that place was filthy," she said. "Besides, there is a lot that a good sleuth can deduce merely by quiet observation from afar."

"Such as?" I asked.

"Well," Mama said, "Aaron and Melissa might be dirt-poor, but they own a boat. I know because I peeked into their garage." Mama delivered her nugget of info with immense satisfaction. It wouldn't have surprised me if she'd commenced to purring just then.

"*Which* they are trying to sell," Wynnell said. "Neighborhood covenants don't allow them to keep the boat in their driveway. And it's a right shame that they have to sell it too, if you ask me. Melissa used to be a professional water-skier down in Cypress Gardens, Florida, before she got married. She's got a powerful grip; I told her she could rip a chicken into pieces. No need to cut it."

"Sounds like you two got along swimmingly," I said, "pun quite intended." I turned back to my mother. "Mama, is there anything else *extraordinaire* that you saw?"

"They haven't stopped their newspaper subscription," she said happily. "It seems to me that would be a luxury to someone in their situation."

"Unless they need it for the classifieds," C.J. said.

"Humph," Mama said, and reached for another yeast roll.

"Wynnell," I said, "did you pay Aaron a visit as well? If so, what did you think of his shop?"

"Abby, was that a dig?"

"Of course not," I said. Wynnell was never able to make a go of it with her shop, the Wooden Wonders, in Charleston. Yes, she displayed her merchandise in a jumbled, haphazard fashion, but at least she wasn't all over the board—pun also intended.

"I guess I'll have to take your word for that," she said. "Anyway, I didn't like that man at all. I thought he was trying to hide something from us."

That certainly piqued my interest. "Like what?" I asked.

"Like he pushed some stuff aside on the watch counter," she said, "and covered it with an apron, and then kept trying to move us away from there to where the cards were. Every time I took a step back toward the watch shop, so did he. And he got all nervous and his voice went up an octave. Oh, and he kept trying to sell me some face cream, or some gewgaw or another."

"I don't know what she's talking about," Mama managed to say, despite her left cheek being distended with a wad of yeast roll. "I think he was a charming man. Absolutely delightful, in fact."

"Argh," Wynnell said. "She's just being—"

"Ben Ovumkoph has a thing for you, C.J.," I said.

Mama managed to swallow the roll and speak first.

"Talk about a conversation stopper. How do you know this, dear?"

"He told me—well, not flat out; this isn't grade school. But he did say that he frequents my shop on account of he enjoys doing business with the tall gal with blond hair from Shelby. Who else could he mean?"

C.J. grinned happily. I don't blame her; it's always nice to be admired, even if nothing can come of it.

"Why I think that's disgusting!" Wynnell said. "C.J., how old *are* you now?"

"Twenty-nine—unless you're counting in goat years," she said. "In that case—"

"We're *not* counting in goat years," Wynnell snapped. "But Ben Ovumkoph is an old goat. How old is *he*, anyway? Sixty-something?"

"Probably close to seventy," Mama said. "I didn't smell a whole lot of testosterone when we shook hands."

C.J. slid out of the booth and appeared to inflate like the Michelin Man, so great was her anger. "Stop it, y'all! What matters is that I am a fully grown woman, and in charge of my senses. If a septuagenarian finds delight in my multitudinous charms, and I in his, it is none of y'all's beeswax."

"You tell 'em, girlfriend," I said evilly. Okay, so I wasn't really being evil; I was just tired of Mama and Wynnell judging C.J. so much. It was a generational thing, not a personality clash; Lord knows they were all three as nutty as a bridge mix.

But C.J. was momentarily vexed beyond mollification, and the big gal insisted that she'd be better off getting her supper elsewhere—perhaps at Carolina Place Mall—which was just an exit away down I–485. Unfortunately for her, no sooner did she pull out onto South Boulevard than two waitpersons arrived bearing plates of sizzling steaks and steaming baked sweet potatoes that were oozing butter and brown sugar. I know that it sounds impossible to believe, but time stood still for a moment and I was oblivious of the other diners as my tongue came out and slapped my cheeks silly.

16

When all was said and done, this was my battle to win; not Mama's, not Wynnell's, and not C.J.'s. Therefore, when a stuffed-to-the-gills Wynnell expressed a hankering to see a movie at the cineplex across the street, I insisted that she go. And Mama should go as well. It didn't take much to get them to agree. It was when they were arguing about which film to see while they were still in the parking lot of the Texas Roadhouse that I managed to slip away unnoticed.

My immediate destination was Carolina Place Mall. I have always been fond of this shopping mall for the following reasons: the concourse is open and two stories tall, and since there is only one concourse, it is impossible to get lost. I used to love it even more when flags resembling white puffy clouds were suspended from the glass domed ceiling, but alas, nothing seems to stay the same—especially the good things in life.

Carolina Place Mall has a rocking food court where

one can get falafel, as well as bourbon chicken, but I was so stuffed that I made my phone call from inside one of the stalls of the world's best public restrooms (there are fold-down infant seats inside each stall as well as paper liners!). Even just the smell of a Big Mac or the sight of a chocolate-dipped cone might set me off hurling.

C.J., bless her oversized heart, answered on the first ringtone. "You have reached the number of a deeply hurt individual," she said. "If you wish to leave an apology, you may do so now."

"I apologize, C.J. This is Abby, by the way. And I really have no problem with the septuagenarian thing, because it's not my business."

"Abby! How did you know where to find me?"

Now that perplexed me. "I'm on my phone, C.J. My phone finds your phone wherever you happen to be, just as long there are towers to transmit the right signals."

"No," she said. "I mean here—at the mall."

"You said you might come to the mall," I said.

"No I meant *here,* here," she said. I looked up to see C.J.'s oversized face peering down at me from above the right side of my stall.

"Aaaaaack!" I screamed. Yes, some folks actually do scream that way; I did. "Now look what you've done!"

"Hmm," C.J. said matter-of-factly, "you might want to work on your modesty issues. Using the lavatory is a universal need, and as such there is nothing to be embarrassed about. Why, some of the indigenous peoples of the Amazon—"

"C.J.," I said, "my cell phone landed in the toilet!"

"Ooh, Abby," she said, "you should really fish that out before—"

"You fish it out!"

"Okey-dokey," C.J. said. And she did fish it out. Just like that. She even rinsed off my cell phone and dried it as best as she could with paper towels before holding it next to a hot air dryer for a minute.

"Now what?" I said. "I can't get a signal." By then we had walked out of the restroom and into a lounge area equipped with sofas for the waiting loved ones of those who are inside micturating (did I not say that this was the world's best restroom, or what?).

"Take it back to the hotel, Abby—we're not that far—and use the hair dryer on it. I've done it before lots of times and it's always worked for me."

"You've dropped your phone in the pot repeatedly?"

"Ooh, don't be silly, you little goofball; of course not. I drop it in my Slurpee—not on purpose, of course. Except maybe that one time."

"Okay you big goofball; I'll try it." It's impossible to stay mad at Calamity Jane for more than a few minutes. The woman doesn't have a mean bone in her body. In fact I'm not sure that she has any bones; I wouldn't be surprised to learn that she is all heart.

"Abby?"

"Yes?"

"I think you should know that we're being watched," she said.

"Who? *Where?*"

"Shhh," she whispered. "It's Aaron Ovumkoph.

You'll see the top of his head sticking around the corner—there to your left any second."

And indeed I did. He was standing in the corridor that led to the food court, pressed up to the wall like a gecko, with only his bobbing head to give him away. His stance must have appeared totally bizarre to the folks who were constantly passing by him in the hall. Perhaps even a few of them were wondering how it was that he managed to keep his balance and not topple over backward.

"He's been following me ever since I left you guys at the restaurant. He was waiting out there in the parking lot. I feel like I'm a spy movie—you know, like one of those old spy flicks starring Sarah Palin: *The Guns of Wasilla, The Wasilla Candidate, North by Wasilla*—"

"C.J.," I said impatiently, "Sarah Palin has never acted in any spy movies."

"If you so say, Abby," she said, sounding not all convinced. Clearly this was not one of C.J.'s more lucid moments, so perhaps I'd given in to the power of suggestion and only imagined seeing the crown of a bulging head bobbing around the corner. Or not—because there it was again.

Well then the only way to test my own sanity was to lunge in the direction of the nodding noodle before it had the chance to get away. But what if there was indeed someone right around the corner (and either there was, or I was nuts)? What would I do? Grab him? Haul him into the lounge by his lapels and give him the third degree? Would I risk being embarrassed in front of the continuing parade of people?

And then there was an even worse scenario to consider: what if it *wasn't* the man with the bobbing head, but another man? What if I exposed some father playing hide-and-seek with his child? Or some pervert wishing to expose himself to women on their way to, or from, the facilities? Why on earth was I even contemplating charging a virtual stranger just because a dear, sweet friend—one who thought that she was part goat and swore that Sarah Palin and Cary Grant smooched atop a Mount Rushmore that was located in Wasilla, Alaska—claimed she was being followed?

But there it was again; the bobbing head! Somewhere—perhaps it was from watching sporting events or movies about Visigoths or Vikings—I'd picked up the notion that a head-on confrontation required loud sound effects. Like grunts or roars. That said, I decided to give the owner of this disappearing noggin a bit of surprise. While engaging in an animated conversation with my good buddy from Shelby (not a difficult task), I edged closer to the wall. Suddenly I stepped sprightly out into the hall. However, what emerged from my thrush-size throat was not a boot-shaking bellow, but a squeak that would have attracted any male mice (or teenage Japanese girls) within earshot.

"It *is* you!" I cried.

"Mrs. Timberlake," Aaron Ovumkoph said, "I have every right to be here; this is a public space."

"But you've been spying on us," I said.

"That's nonsense," he said.

"My friend here says that you've been following her."

Aaron glanced around. "This is a high-traffic area. Let's go to Penney's and talk in the luggage area. No one ever seems to purchase luggage."

"Yet somehow there are far too many people using the airport when I want to go someplace."

"Touché," he said. "Follow me."

17

I thought that women in my generation had moved beyond sexism. Certainly I had. Yet here I was, following a bobble-headed man through a crowded mall, simply because he'd issued an order. How crazy was that? Talk about a cop-out!

Well, at least it was *doing* something. It's sitting on my hands waiting for the guillotine blade to fall that turns me into a nervous Nellie. Poor Marie Antoinette; I hope she was allowed to have some needlework with her in those final hours.

But what do you know, Aaron Ovumkoph was absolutely right; we had the luggage nook all to ourselves—of course that might have been a fluke. At any rate, when we were approached by a friendly salesperson, Aaron introduced us as a happy family that was fixing to travel by supply ship to the island of Tristan da Cunha in the South Atlantic. This island, he said, which was halfway between Africa and South America, was the most remote inhabited place in the world. He also told the salesperson that C.J. was our daughter and that she was going to marry an islander and settle down on the island. After the wedding we would likely never see her again; so could we please have some privacy? And yes, when we were through talking, we just might purchase some luggage for our trip.

"Hey," I said, "your B.S. story worked like a charm."

"If only it were," Aaron said, bobbing more than ever. "We just got back six weeks ago. It took almost that long to get there."

"Why I'll be hog-tied," I said. "There really is such a place."

"I spent a year there," C.J. said, matter-of-factly. "Once you get on, it's hard to get off; no planes land there. I almost married one of those strapping hunks too, but aren't you glad that I didn't, Abby? Because then we wouldn't be ex-sister-in-laws."

In the words of Rob, I kvelled with happiness knowing that C.J. still loved me, despite any harsh words I may have thrown her way over the years. In fact, I was so moved that I hugged the lug from Shelby.

"Ooh, Abby," she said, "would you care for a breath mint?"

"Does my breath stink?"

"It smells like roadkill, Abby."

"In that case, thanks, but I'll pass on the mint, just to remind you of how you took honesty a mite too far."

Who knows, Aaron might have agreed with C.J. He took a few steps back and sat on a bright red suitcase, one easily large enough to contain my corpse, should I end up as one during the course of my investigation.

"Ladies," he said, "now that we have some privacy,

I'll get right to the point. As I'm sure y'all agree, my older sister Jerry was your consummate eccentric."

"I never met her," C.J. said.

"Trust us, dear," I said. "The woman could have been a character in a book."

"Abby here is a bit eccentric," C.J. said, with a straight face. "Was your sister more eccentric than Abby?"

"Oh much more," I said. "Wasn't she, Mr. Ovumkoph?"

His thin lips pursed as he struggled to say something, and then perhaps thought better of it. In the end he closed his eyes and bobbed his head to the tune of "Yesterday" by Paul McCartney.

"She was!" I said.

"Cheese and biscuits, Abby," C.J. said. "You don't have to bite our heads off."

"Anyway," Aaron said, as if nothing had happened, "she often did inexplicable things. And one of those things was to have a copy made of an emerald ring that she often wore—uh, you saw it, Mrs. Timberlake."

"Actually, I didn't; I saw the genuine article. That was when she gave it to me."

"I'm afraid you're incorrect; she gave you a copy."

"Look, Mr. Ovumkoph, I'm not a gemologist, and I only saw it for a few seconds, but I'd be willing to bet my friend's hooves here that it was the real McCoy."

"Pardon me?" he said.

"No, pardon me; I was being a smart mouth. But it *was* real, trust me. That's what took me by surprise so much. I mean, nobody wears big-ticket items out in public anymore—except maybe Queen Elizabeth II and a few lucky, but very nervous, stars at the Academy Awards. The insurance premiums would be through the roof. Most of the bling one sees is fake, although admittedly some of it is quite convincing to the untrained eye."

"And your eyes are trained, Mrs. Timberlake?" Aaron said.

"Last summer at the beach," C.J. said, "Abby told me she could spot a circumcised man from fifty yards away."

My face burned with embarrassment. I was guilty as charged, but it was girl talk, and it had to do with a visiting French swim team, and they were prancing around in their Speedos trying to impress a group of coeds from the College of Charleston. And just for the record, none of them was.

"I did not!" I said.

"Did too," C.J. said. "But just so you know, Mr. Ovumkoph, I am a certified gemologist."

That nugget of info nearly knocked me on my tiny tuchas. "No kidding, C.J.? Are you certified by the American Institute of Gemology, or something Granny Ledbetter cooked up?"

Uh-oh, I immediately regretted saying those words. Had they been words on paper—like in some whacky, totally unbelievable paperback novel—I would have ripped out the offending page, stuffed it in my mouth, and forced that sucker down my gullet. But these were spoken words, and there was nothing I could do. No doubt they would ring in C.J.'s ears for years to come.

The curious thing about spoken words is that they

have the power to morph, yet somehow remain the truth. Quite possibly, years from now, my dear, sweet friend from Shelby would play tapes in her head of things I'd never said, but which she could swear were true and still pass a lie detector test. Yes sirree Bob, I'd just screwed myself royally.

"Abby," C.J. said, interrupting my flow of self-chastisement.

"Oh, honey, I—"

"I want you to know," she said, "that I totally forgive you for that very insensitive and presumptuous remark."

I gasped. "You *do*?"

"Abby, with all your experience, I would have thought that you knew that since I belonged to LAGS—the Ledbetter American Gemological Society—there is no need for me to belong to anything else."

"Well, uh—yes, of course," I said. C.J., whose back was turned on Aaron, couldn't see that the man was making twirling motions next to his ear. Cuckoo, cuckoo, he was saying with his index finger; this woman is nertz to Mertz.

"Ooh, Abby, I love you," she said.

"I love you too, C.J.," I said.

Aaron walked so fast I had trouble keeping up; then again, I have trouble keeping up with most men without having to break into a trot.

But we caught up with him at his SUV—an old model that appeared to be filled with flea market junk.

"Merchandise," Aaron said with surprising curtness. "I don't have room for it in my shop. Mrs. Timberlake, you being smaller, would you mind sitting in back?"

"We could take my mother's car," I said politely.

"We're here, aren't we?"

"Yes, but her car is clean—I mean, empty."

"Mrs. Timberlake, are you insulting me?"

"No, of course not."

I crawled in the back and situated myself between a pagoda of stacked lampshades—some of them still in their original plastic wrap—and a tower consisting of old phone books. As we took the first turn onto Pineville-Matthews Road it became exceedingly clear why Aaron was so adamant about stuffing me into the backseat; essentially I was to act as a divider, a brace to keep the phone books from toppling over and denting the lampshades. This would have been a lot easier on me had the phone book tower not exceeded my height.

"You all right back there?" someone said a couple of times, but I was so busy trying not to get killed by *The Real Yellow Pages* that I didn't even have time to answer. At least my struggle to stay alive made the ride to Jerry Ovumkoph's house go by fast, even though I had no idea where we were, or how we got there.

"This is Amherst Green," Aaron said. "Very nice brick town homes, but hardly the place you'd think someone like Jerry would live."

"You're thinking more like Pastor Sam's house," I said. "Am I right?"

He stared at me. "You've been there?"

I returned his look. "I've been a friend of this family for years, just not of your particular branch."

169

"Good one, Abby," C.J. said, and then rightly gave her own mouth a light slap.

Aaron slammed the door and strode up the short walk. While C.J. trotted anxiously behind him, I took my time. Forsooth, I was awestruck.

Despite it being the dog days of summer, the massive terra-cotta bowl that baked in the sun just off the small front porch blazed with color. I identified orange, yellow, and white star zinnias, deep blue angolinas, and another variety of zinnia, this one hot pink. From a tall urn on the porch spilled dark purple petunias, and from another hung an equally impressive curtain of peach-colored million bells.

"Wow," I said.

"Yeah, yeah," Aaron said. "She had a green thumb. Wait until you get inside."

"How *are* we going to get inside?" I said.

"This is America," he said. "How else?" He flipped over the welcome mat, and finding nothing there but a roly-poly, ran his fingers along the lintel, and then after striking out again, tipped the urn containing the million bells.

"Bingo!"

When we stepped inside I knew exactly what he meant by Aunt Jerry's green thumb. One could see all the way through her town home and to the courtyard in back. The focal point of this vista was a lion's head fountain that spilled into a formal lily pool that was raised about two feet off the ground and surrounded by stone. It was flanked by raised planting beds that were also built with stone.

On either side of the fountain, and dominating the planting beds, were two spectacular palm trees. Their large fan leaves added such an exotic, tropical look that I forgot for a moment that we were still in Charlotte.

"Wow," I said again. I hurried forward to get a closer look through the bank of ceiling-to-floor windows. The lush courtyard appeared to stretch the entire length of the town home. It too was filled with a profusion of flowers, but what really impressed me was the number of palm trees. *Real* palm trees.

"I can't believe she was able to grow palm trees in Charlotte," I said.

"Ooh Abby," C.J. said, "those aren't just any palm trees; those are Windmill Palms. *Trachycarpus fortunei*. They're native to southern China, Japan, and the Himalaya Mountains. But they seem to do just as well in the clay soil of the Carolina Piedmont as they do back home. Westfield Road, right off Selwyn Avenue here in Charlotte, is practically lined with them."

"Well, I'll be darned," I said.

"Ladies," Aaron said impatiently, "can we stop talking about gardening and get to the task."

"Which is?" I said.

"We're here to look for Jerry's safe," he said. "Remember? To prove to you that ring she was wearing the day she was murdered was a fake. Honestly, Mrs. Timberlake, I had you pegged for brighter than that."

"You hold your brace of mules," C.J. said, matching his impatience. "Abby might not be the ripest grape on the bunch, but she's got an IQ of one twenty-five, which makes her totally adequate for just about any

171

job—even President, as far as the Electoral College is concerned."

"*What?*" I said. "How do *you* know my IQ score?"

"You told Wynnell and me once when you were drunk," C.J. said.

"That just goes to show you that you should never trust a drunk woman," I said.

"Amen to that," Aaron said. "And Aunt Jerry was often in her cups."

"I'm sorry to hear that," I said.

"Yes, well, she claims to have had a hard life, beginning with her childhood, but you don't hear Chanti or Ben complaining about that."

"I don't mean to be argumentative," I said, "but we all process things in different ways."

He responded with a soft grunt. "Yes, her husband died. That was all very sad, but she didn't stay a grieving widow for long. Oh no, not Jerry. She had a succession of failed love relationships. Sounds better than a parade of loser lovers, doesn't it?"

"Excuse me?" I said.

"Mrs. Timberlake, my sister may have been as old as the hills, but her heels were just as rounded—ha ha, what do you call that sort of wordplay?"

"Confusing."

"He means," C.J. said, "that he had a slutty sister."

"Ah, the big one is correct. And the men all seemed to be younger than her—some of them even extremely so. Now what does that make her in today's lingo?" He tapped his chin, which set his head to bobbing like a metronome. "Yes, a lioness!"

"A cougar," I said curtly. "It seems to run in the family."

"Oh, you must be referring to Ben's runaway wife in the Antipodes. Just so you know, she's not related by blood; we're Jewish, not Mennonites or Amish. We're not that into marrying cousins, even if they are just second or third cousins."

"Back to the boyfriends. Were any of them there at Ben's house the day she was killed?"

He shrugged, and the poor man's head practically became a blur. "Not that I could tell."

"What does that mean?" I demanded.

"It means," he said, "that I didn't go around peering behind each bush—hey, where's that goofy friend of yours?"

"Look here, buster, I'll not have you speaking like that about my friends—C.J., where *are* you?"

"She probably stepped out into in the garden," Aaron said. "Can you blame her? Sorry about that. The comment, I mean. I guess I'm kinda quick to pick on other folks' foibles, given that I'm—I'm, well, rather peculiar myself. Or so I've been told. Multiple times, in fact, by my near perfect wife, Melissa. She can't for the life of her remember why it is she married me, and not one of my handsome relatives."

"Hmm," I said. "Tell her that your brother Ben is too old for her, your nephew Rob is gay, and Sam is, well—she definitely came out ahead. You were the cream of the Ovumkoph crop—now there's a tongue twister for you."

He beamed. "You really think that I am?"

"Yes, I do. But for your Melissa. I still pick Rob, because he's my best friend."

"Oh."

I flashed him a charming smile. "Don't be hurt, silly. Just tell me what we do next. Look in Jerry's jewelry box?"

"That's actually not a bad idea. Sometimes the obvious place *is* the answer."

18

I guess I expected someone like Jerry Ovumkoph to have shockingly pink bedroom walls, so I was a bit surprised to see the warm yet soothing terra-cotta finish. But dominating the master bedroom was a massive king-size bed, and I had to work not to picture Jerry in it dominating her string of loser lovers. Other than the bed, the furnishings were simple: just two matching mahogany nightstands with drawers. The walls were decorated with a couple of paintings reminiscent of Tuscany landscapes, although there was one small stretched canvas that was covered only with orange and red poppies. On a small table opposite the monstrous bed perched a wooden Celtic harp.

"Did she play this?" I asked.

"Surprisingly well," Aaron said. "We all thought it was a phase at first, but I guess we should have known better. With Jerry, once something grabbed her imagination, it didn't let go. By the way, 'Greensleeves' was her specialty."

"I love that song," I said. "You sister and I had a lot

in common." Then a wicked thought grabbed my imagination, which I couldn't let go of.

"We even had the parade of loser lovers in common," I said.

That stopped his head from bobbing for a nanosecond. "Are you a cougar as well, Mrs. Timberlake?"

"Grrrrrah! Practically jailbait, all of them," I said. "But only practically, mind you—nothing illegal, I assure you."

"But immoral," he said.

"In whose eyes?" I asked. "The Bashilele tribe in the Democratic Republic of the Congo are polyandrous. At least they used to be in the 1950s. You should read *The Witch Doctor's Wife*—"

"Mrs. Timberlake, are we here to discuss literature, or find out where my sister keeps the real gem, and maybe—with a lot of luck—run across a clue that will point to her killer."

Unless it's one of us, I thought. And I'm pretty sure it isn't me. Really, what were we doing in Jerry Ovumkoph's bedroom anyway? Leaving fingerprints so that I could be arrested and spend the rest of my life behind bars playing maidservant to an amazing hulk named Big Selma? Odds are she would be anything but goofy, and not have one tenth the smarts of C.J. And another thing, I'm four feet, nine inches; whichever way you choose to run the stripes, it doesn't matter—they won't look good on me.

"It's a phenomenal book," I said. "The author's best."

He walked ahead into a divinely large bathroom. "Ah, the jewelry box. Would you care to open it, Mrs. Timberlake?"

"I'll pass, thank you," I said.

"What? Why not?"

"I'm too nervous, that's why." At least that much was the truth.

"Don't be silly," he said. "Whether or not the stone is genuine is not dependent upon whoever opens the box. Go ahead; give the top drawer a gentle tug."

"No. I'm feeling light-headed. I either need to sit on the edge of the tub, or go outside for a minute. You know what? I think I'll just step outside. I'll go join C.J.—wherever she is. Who knows what that goofy gal is up to."

"Dang it, Mrs. Timberlake, I thought we were past that." He grabbed a tissue from a faux marble box and used it to keep from leaving fingerprints. But although he opened every drawer—he even pulled them all the way out of the six-story box—we didn't find the emerald ring. We didn't even find any genuine jewels, other than a pair of commercial-grade ruby earrings, something undoubtedly meant as everyday wear by the deceased.

"I'll check the closet," I said, just as Aaron let loose with a string of invectives. Although I have reached a point in my life where mere words cannot offend me, I also feel that I have the right to protect my spirit from verbal garbage. Such vitriol does not just go in one ear and out the other—not with doing damage. A little bit of one's soul is worn away in the process, like sandstone in fast-flowing river.

I grew up in the house of a woman who I believed to be the South's most eccentric female. Yet, after only five minutes in Jerry Ovumkoph's spacious closet, I was ready to strip Mama of her title. It is my firm conviction that if I'd been shown Jerry's closet without any backstory, and been asked the following multiple-choice question, I might have given any of the three answers below.

Question: To what use is this space being put?

Answer A: *Storage room for a clown school.*

Answer B: *Closet for a seventy-five-year-old lady.*

Answer C: *Overflow storage for a fabric store run by very messy clerks.*

There were a few conventional pieces of clothing—Western-style, that is. Apparently Rob's Aunt Jerry was a great fan of Indian saris, which as a rule contain many yards of cloth. But these saris seemed to have staged a rebellion, and at least half of them had somehow managed to slip off their hangers to become jumbled with matching shoes. Now they were fighting it out in a death match over floor space.

It soon became apparent that the only way to effectively search the room (a closet this large could almost be a midsize room) was to pull everything out. For the time being, the nearby garden tub was as convenient a place as any to dump things, and that I did—willy-nilly.

"Mrs. Timberlake! Mrs. Timberlake, what are you doing?"

"Clearing out a few things," I said grumpily. I was no longer focused. Surely we were wasting our time sorting through this mess.

"Hey, that's my sister's stuff you're throwing around. Be more careful, will you?"

"Sorry," I said, "but I have this feeling."

He must have picked up on my mood. "Feeling?" he snapped. "What kind of feeling?"

"Call it a hunch," I said. "Woman's intuition. There's something back here under all this stuff—maybe a safe or something."

It was true, I did have a hunch, a very strong one in fact, but it had just come over me that second, even as I was telling Aaron about it.

"I don't mean to rain on your parade, Mrs. Timberlake," he said, "but I don't put too much truck in a hunch. At least not enough to mess with my sister's things like this."

"Mr. Ovumkoph, your sister's things *are* a mess, and as for my hunch, my friend Magdalena Yoder, up in Pennsylvania, says that a hunch from a woman is worth two facts from a man."

He reared back, no doubt surprised by the strength of my emotion. "Somehow I doubt that, Mrs. Timberlake."

I pulled aside a pile of assorted brightly colored silks. "Hunch verified," I said, taking care to keep any trace of smugness out of my voice. Attitude was not going to take me where I wanted to go.

"What?" he barked. "Let me see?"

I plopped my petite patootie right in front of the heavy metal box. "On the other hand," I said, "maybe we shouldn't be pawing through a dead woman's things."

"Move," he growled.

I scooted aside so that he could see the small safe that was bolted to the floor. "Well, I'll be damned."

179

"Any chance that you might know the combination?" I said.

"No need; the door isn't even closed all the way." He swung it open and I scooted back in to get a close-up view.

Jerry Ovumkoph had a collection of jewels guaranteed to make a duchess drool. There were two compartments in the safe: the top section was devoted to diamonds and gold set with diamonds; the bottom level contained pieces decorated with colored stones, such as sapphires, rubies, emeralds, and aquamarines. However, a cursory glance revealed that it did not contain a ring set with a monstrous emerald of the highest quality.

"Now what?" Aaron said. There was accusation in his voice.

"My hunch was that we'd find a safe somewhere in this jumble," I said. "I didn't claim that we'd find a smoking gun—so to speak."

He kicked at a pile of bras and underclothes at the other side of the closet. "Ow! Damn it!"

"What is it?"

He shoved aside the delicate underthings. Victoria had no secrets that evening.

"Another safe." He knelt.

"Let me see," I said breathlessly, "let me see."

He snorted. "Bit of a hypocrite, aren't you?"

"Well, the damage to our karma is already done. Now it's your turn to scoot."

"Cheese and crackers, but you're a bossy one. I bet Mr. Timberlake gets tired of you right quick."

"You've got that right; Buford generally can't stand me. Now scooch!"

But there wasn't much to see; just more of the same. Except that this safe had a couple of fabulous pieces of royal jade in it, plus a tsavorite garnet and diamond necklace that made me request a moment of silence so that I could seriously review my morals. Aaron Ovumkoph seemed like the kind of guy that could easily be talked into abandoning his morals. No one needed to know that we'd discovered the pair of safes, not even the mysteriously truant C.J.

"But we can't," he said out of the blue.

"*What?*"

"*You know*—what you're thinking."

"How do you know what I'm thinking? Maybe I'm thinking about what I had for breakfast."

"It wouldn't be right, and it's against my religion. I'm surprised it's not against yours."

My face burned. "Who says that it isn't—assuming you're even correct. Which, by the way, I most sincerely doubt."

"Now we add lying to the list."

"*List?* There is no list!"

"Of course *if* we did, I'd be the one to do the dividing, since you obviously can't be trusted."

I took a deep, cleansing breath. I swear that it was this extra second that allowed my eyes to settle on what looked to be a diamond pendant suspended from the green garnet necklace. However, at this angle light was passing through one of the planes, rather than being reflected back at me, which could mean only one thing: the magnificent diamond was actually a cubic zirconia. Braving the wrath of Aaron I picked up the entire necklace.

"Hey, what are you doing?" he demanded. "You put that back."

"Gladly," I said. "But first come have a look-see in the vanity light. This necklace isn't real."

"Yes, it is. I remember my sister wearing that with a green silk—whatchamacallit—"

"Sari?" I said.

"Yeah. Anyway," he said, "she wore it at the Purim Ball just last year, and you should have heard all the ladies complimenting her."

"As well they should have," I said, "because it *is* very beautiful; there is no denying that. However, I'm afraid that these stones are all cubic zirconia—even the large diamond."

"Bullhockey!" he shouted. "You'll say anything to get your hands on this stuff."

"Here, take this," I said. "I bet everything else in both safes comes under the category of replacement jewelry. Either Jerry had the real stuff stored somewhere else, and kept this just to remind her what she had, or else—well, she had this stuff made up because she was forced to sell the real jewelry."

When a bobble-headed man flies into a rage, it is wise to plan an escape route. Not being entirely foolish, I stepped slowly to my right, so that I was directly in line with the bedroom door.

"If she was that desperate, Mrs. Timberlake," he said through lips that were drained of blood, "how could she possibly leave millions of dollars to anyone in her will?"

I put one foot solidly behind me, ready to take off. "We don't know for sure that she *did*, do we?"

"What is that supposed to mean?" he demanded.

"Did you actually read the will?" I said.

The dome of his head was as white and shiny as a freshly peeled boiled egg. "Hold your horses there, little lady. Are you accusing my sister of making that all up? Of staging that will ceremony just for show?"

"I'm saying that it's possible," I said, as I made my escape into the master bedroom. "C.J.? Where are you, C.J.?"

19

But confound it, my gal pal could not be found. I even jogged all about the town home neighborhood, calling her name as loudly as I dared, but without the desired results. In fact, my only response at all came from one irate woman, fairly tall and with strawberry blond hair, who came running out of her house and demanded that I hush up at once or she was calling the police. This old crone claimed to be a successful writer, which I highly doubt, because if she were, she probably would have sent an assistant out instead.

At any rate, since life is not a science fiction movie, and there were enough Southern Baptists whizzing up and down Rea Road to let me know that the Rapture had not taken place, I concluded that C.J. had left the neighborhood and not simply disappeared. Perhaps she'd gotten bored and hoofed it—she is a country gal, after all—or maybe she'd called a cab—the woman claims to have dined at Buckingham Palace, so she's not a complete rube.

THE GLASS IS ALWAYS GREENER

Having satisfied myself that there was nothing amiss, I decided to call it a day. Sometimes it doesn't pay to play anymore, and I don't mean "play" in the fun sense. There are times when the wise thing to do is to pull up one's metaphorical drawbridges (in my case, the literal covers), TV remote in hand, and not answer the phone, or venture out of one's safe place, until one has been well rested. Of course lots of variables come into this mix: such as chocolate, purring cats, and sometimes warm-bodied snuggly-buggly husbands—unless they're the problem.

When I returned to the hotel I was loaded down with chocolate, and in lieu of my cat I had gossip magazines. I fully expected to find Greg in the room watching a detective show while practically tearing out his precious hair at all the gaffes in the writing. Greg is a vociferous critic of any TV show he watches, but crime shows in particular are the catalysts for these outbursts.

But when I opened the door it was the sound of the phone that assaulted my ears, not the swearing of my sweet hubby. And since the no-phone rule begins only after one has first checked in with principal loved ones regarding their safety (their happiness on drawbridge days is immaterial), I was compelled to answer it. Quite possible my minimadre had gotten her tiny self into trouble between the Texas Roadhouse and the hotel, as they were not attached. Even then, any long hallway poses problems for Mozella Wiggins, who has a nose for trouble and can sniff it out anywhere.

"Hello?" I said.

"Hon, it's Greg."

"Darling, you're on your way, right? Please say that you're calling from the lobby."

"I'm afraid not, Abby."

"Oh shoot, this sounds like a cell phone. And I think I hear a boat engine."

"Yeah, what's left of one. After I closed your shop, Booger and I decided we'd go out and meet a school of tuna that a small plane pilot had supposedly seen on his way down from Myrtle Beach. Unfortunately *The Charming Abby* decided that she had other plans. So, to make a long story short, we're being towed into Mc-Clellanville, where we'll be spending the night at Booger's in-laws. You remember Ted and Wilma Greer, don't you?"

"Oh Greg," I said, "I'm really disappointed. Things are going terrible up here in Charlotte."

"Terrible? How so?"

"I'm not making any headway; I'm just floundering in my investigation."

"That's because it's not *your* investigation, hon; it's the detectives' investigation. All you're supposed to do is cooperate."

I wasted precious minutes pouting. Meanwhile we could have lost our phone connection at any second. What an idiot I could be when it came to my ego.

"But I have discovered something interesting," I finally said.

"What's that?"

"Rob's Aunt Jerry was sort of an Auntie Mame on steroids. Throw in some Hugh Hefner as well."

"You mean she liked the ladies?"

"No! But she liked the men. And *loved* jewelry. She has—I should say *had*—two safes in her closet that were filled with fine pieces, but here's the catch: they were CZ copies."

"Holy shiitake mushrooms! Doesn't it cost a lot just to make a copy?"

"It depends on whether or not the piece is custom-made. If the finding happens to be mass-produced, then of course it is a lot cheaper."

"So what's a finding?" he said.

"The setting," I said tiredly.

"Then why didn't you just say so," he said irritably.

"Greg, I really have to go. My dogs are barking and all I want to do is take a nice long hot bath and then—"

"—and pull up your drawbridge. Do you have chocolate?"

"I have two bags of Peanut M&M's from the machine. They'll do. I'll find an old movie to zone out with and I'll be fine."

"Well, okay. If I was there, I'd give your dogs a nice rub—after you'd soaked them in the tub, of course."

"Of course. Good night, darling. I love you, and give my love to Booger."

"I love you too, hon. More than you love me."

"Greg, before you hang up; isn't Wilma the one who used to vacuum naked, and somehow managed to run over one of her own boobs with her machine, and sued the company for thirty million dollars and they settled for three million?"

"She's the one. Booger says to expect mighty nice accommodations tonight, so don't worry about me."

"I seldom do, dear."

It was C.J. who I was starting to worry about. And Mama too. The bridges hadn't been drawn up yet, so I tried calling one more time.

I didn't get the big galoot, but I did get Mama in her room. We ended up getting separate rooms as well on account of the fact that Mama snores like a chimpanzee on steroids. (Don't ask me how I know.)

"Abby, make it quick. The commercial just came on."

"What are you watching?"

"Big Brother. If only I could get on that show, I would clean their clocks."

"Mama! Where did you learn to talk like that?"

"Survivor. I could wipe their clocks clean as well; I've never seen such a bunch of whiners. There's only one area in which I couldn't compete and that's because my loins no longer quicken—"

"TMI! Too much information! I'm coming over," I said. Her room was next door.

"Oh Abigail, don't be such a prude," she said, as she let me in. "It's the bare-naked truth; isn't that something you young people are always accusing us old folks of avoiding? Ever since your father died—killed as he was by that dive-bombing seagull with the brain tumor the size of a walnut—I haven't felt a speck of, well, you know."

"No, I don't." Of course I did.

Mama glanced all around the room, and it wasn't until I obligingly checked under the bed that she spoke again. This time she whispered.

"The urge."

"*Oh.*" I nodded solemnly, wishing I'd never chosen to go there.

But before Mama could participate in reality TV, she needed to overcome issues besides that of learning to play a convincing temptress. For starters, she sets her hair in curlers each night and wears pounds of cold cream to bed. Her daytime costume consists of a dress that shows off a tightly cinched waist, and a full circle skirt buoyed up by yards of starched crinolines. Pearls and pumps that match the dress complete the outfit. Of course Mama never leaves the house without a hat. My point is that she couldn't last five minutes if her grooming opportunities were curtailed. Take the poufy skirts away from Mama, and poof, there goes her spirit.

"Mama, have you heard from C.J.?"

"I thought she was with you?"

"She was, but then she took off. You know how she is."

"You mean extremely inconsiderate at times? Remember how she held up her wedding to our dear, sweet Toy because she decided to run down to Poogan's Porch to have a bowl of bread pudding with brandy sauce?"

"Turns out the bread pudding was the smart choice."

"Abby, this is your brother we're talking about. Admittedly Toy was—and is—a ne'er-do-well—but at least he was *almost* ordained an Episcopal priest; it really isn't his fault that the Robinson twins moved in next door and put the make on him— Isn't that what you young people say these days?"

"I'm not so young anymore, Mama, and neither is Toy. He should have resisted the Robinson brothers."

Mama patted the bed. "Let's not argue, dear. The show is about to start, and I have a five-pound box of assorted gourmet chocolates that I have yet to open. I know that you like to do your drawbridge thing, so why not do it here?'"

"Well, I still have some Moon Pies that I guess I could contribute, but I'm calling first dibs on any chocolates with maple crème centers, *and* we watch *Design Star* at ten."

"It's a deal," Mama said, and scooted over on her king-size bed.

C.J. didn't answer her room phone in the morning, so of course I tried her cell, and when that didn't work I started to worry. Big time.

"Mama, close your eyes and tell me what you smell."

"Abby, I warned you about trying that generic deodorant. But if you don't shampoo again we can still meet the girls for breakfast at eight."

"That's just it, Mama. I mean, we might be meeting only one girl—one woman; C.J. seems to be missing."

"And you thought I could smell trouble!"

"That's what you claim—isn't it?"

"Abby, didn't I tell you? My special power has been diminishing ever since my last birthday. I guess it is just yet another thing that we gifted sexagenarians have to accept." Mama likes the word *sexagenarian*, but I'm afraid she hasn't been one for quite some time.

So I called Wynnell before she went down for breakfast, and Wynnell said that she had not seen or heard from C.J. since the Texas Roadhouse. That meant that I was the last one of the three of us, and in fact I'd had a feeling that something was amiss when I couldn't find her at Jerry Ovumkoph's townhouse in Amherst Green, but I hadn't given it enough credence. And to think that I was the one who kept preaching about the hunch from a woman carrying so much weight.

Well, I had the hunch now. But, what could I do? Absolutely nothing, that's what. C.J. was a grown woman, so a missing person's report was going to have to wait. And as nutty as she was—she could feed a tree full of squirrels through a New England winter—she was not in danger of hurting herself or anyone else.

Not wanting to come across as the perennial damsel in distress, I resisted calling Greg again. No matter, because no sooner did I make up my mind not to call him than he called me.

"Mozella's House of Earthly Pleasures," I purred into Mama's room phone. "How may I be of service?"

Mama was horrified. "Abigail Louise! How could you?"

"That depends," Greg said in his deep, manly, and quite unmistakable voice. "Do you have any openings today?"

"Sir, your innuendo is not appreciated at this hour of the morning. This is the room of an elderly scion of Charleston society. She doesn't care how young and handsome you might be, because her loins no longer quicken."

Greg chuckled. "You don't say."

191

Mama grabbed the phone from my hand. "Don't believe a word she says. My loins quicken like crazy—say, who is this?"

"Wrong number," my sweetie mumbled, and a few minutes later he called me back on my cell. By then I'd also returned to my room.

"Why did you even call Mama's room? How did you know I'd be there?"

"I didn't," my husband said. "I really wanted to speak to your mother."

"What on earth for?" I said.

"Hon, she's your mother, but she's also my mother-in-law. And my friend—I hope. Unless you told her it was me on the phone."

"No, I did not," I said.

"Good," Greg said. "And please don't tell her."

"So?" I persisted. "Why *did* you call?"

"What if I said it was personal?" Greg said. "Would you respect that?"

"Of course I would. Now tell me, *please* tell me. You're driving me crazy."

He laughed. "All right, but you just lost this argument; make a note of that."

"I wasn't aware that we were arguing," I said.

"Our clever banter, amusing though it is, does not serve the purpose of advancing this story."

"Too true. Proceed then with your explanation."

"I merely called to check in on you," he said.

"*What?*" I cried in indignation.

"Hon, you have to admit that you tend to go off half-cocked."

"I most certainly do not!" I said. "Okay, so maybe I do—*sometimes*," I said. "But no one likes to have her faults pointed out to her. No one I know, at least."

I gave him to the count of three to retract his assertion, or at the very least, cushion it somehow. When all I got was silence, I hung up.

20

Wynnell is a fiercely loyal friend, both to me and to C.J. There are times, however, when her clock starts keeping its own time. Once, when she was not feeling particularly appreciated, she ran off to Japan with some Japanese tourists and tried to become Japanese. It was then that she learned the same lesson that she used to try to drill into Yankees who have moved South: just because the cat has its kittens in the oven, that don't make them biscuits.

At any rate, Wynnell decided to spend her day in the nearby town of Waxhaw which is famous for its antiques shops, instead of blundering about with Mama and me—well, let's just say that I don't blame her. If I was in her size eight-and-a-half narrow shoes, I'd probably do the same.

"Now what?" Mama said, after she'd managed to drag breakfast out with a third cup of coffee.

"I go to the police station and turn myself in. Just promise me that you'll see that Dmitri gets fed. Sometimes Greg, bless his heart, forgets. I can't bear to think of my baby going hungry. And it's a shame to let someone as kind and handsome as Greg go to waste. So I think I'll ask for a divorce so that some other woman can be just as lucky as I have been."

"*What* other woman?" Mama had been in the act of applying fresh lipstick, but she snapped her compact mirror shut now and dropped it in her bag.

I shrugged. "Oh, I don't know. Someone who could keep him happy."

"Well, it couldn't be just any woman, Abby. You need to think about this more."

"Actually I have; I was thinking about you as my replacement, Mama. What with your loins that quicken like crazy—whatever that means."

Mama's face reddened. "Abby, that's sick and perverted. And it's probably illegal, unless you're a member of Congress. Then you can do anything."

"I'm just kidding, Mama, but don't you care about me going to jail? That didn't seem to bother you any?"

It was her turn to shrug. "You've done it before, dear. And in South Carolina, no less. I figured that Charlotte had to be a cakewalk. But I must say that I am disappointed that it was you who killed Rob's auntie. I thought surely I'd brought you up better than that. You know, dear, that if you'd have kept going to church with me, this probably wouldn't have happened."

"Mama, I didn't kill Rob's auntie! That was a joke; I was being sarcastic."

"Sarcasm killed the cat, dear," Mama sniffed.

"It didn't do much for Dick Cheney's career either. But it was curiosity that killed the cat, Mama, not sarcasm."

"You're so picky." Mama sniffed. "And I wish you'd lay off our former vice president. You know how I feel about him."

Indeed I did; it was time to back off. Mama is not a narrow-minded conservative; she's an open-minded Republican. There are indeed some around, but probably not many who find Richard Bruce Cheney to be their ideal sexual type. He's the one who really sets her loins to quivering.

"Let's get a move on, Mama. The traffic on I–485 must be cleared up by now."

"Where are we going, dear?"

"You'll see. But you might want to run back to the room first and grab a book for the ride."

"Should I bring you a book as well?"

"No thanks, Mama; I've given up reading while driving."

For the record, I have never, ever read a book while steering a moving car. But before we even got on the highway Mama spotted a woman driving while applying eyeliner. This aspect of grooming requires a very steady hand, a good deal of artistry, and one's full attention vis-à-vis a mirror. Mama watched in mounting horror as this woman—who was not even a young chickadee (her word, not mine)—continued to apply the black liquid as she maneuvered her car onto the ramp and merged into the highway traffic at sixty-five miles an hour. What was particularly mind-blowing was the fact that the beauty-obsessed driver managed to do this while steering with her knees.

Once the woman was done with her eyeliner, she brushed on several coats of jet black mascara. Suddenly, satisfied that she was the cat's pajamas, she pressed the pedal all the way to the metal and left us in her dust.

"Keep up with her, Abby," Mama said.

"What?" I said. "And get a ticket?"

"Don't be silly, dear," Mama said. "She's driving a red car with Michigan plates. As soon as you hear a siren, slow way down. Then we'll both start pointing like crazy up the highway. The police aren't stupid; they'll get the picture. In the meantime we get to drive—oh, just never you mind. Even if we had a rocket tied to our fannies, by now we could never catch up with her."

"That's too bad," I said, "because already the cops have caught up with us. And I was only doing six miles over the limit."

Mama undid her seat belt so that she could turn and kneel in her seat. It was my fault; I should have seen it coming. We'd been through similar situations dozens of times before. If I tried to force her to sit properly she'd simply refuse on the grounds that since she'd given birth to me (via a vacillating number of hours, all of them excruciatingly painful), she had a right to do as she pleased in my car.

"He's not a cop," Mama said.

"Mama," I said, "the car may be unmarked, but it's a Crown Vic, and the guy's right on my ass-cot. He wants me to pull over."

"No, he doesn't; he's on the phone. Trust me, dear.

This man is being yelled at by his boss. Or maybe a customer. He doesn't even know you exist. You need to change lanes because he's following *way* too close."

I changed lanes, all right. I got into the far right lane, and as soon as I got the chance I pulled over onto the shoulder, stopped, and in a movement just as smooth as a lizard's belly, I pulled on my hazard lights. Sure, I was speeding—a *little*—but I knew how to handle a vehicle.

"And there he goes," Mama said.

"What?"

"The man in the Cornish Vixen," Mama said. "He didn't even look our way."

"That's *Crown Vic*, Mama."

"That's what I said, dear."

"No," I said. "You referenced a female fox from extreme southwestern England."

"Picky, picky," Mama said, and made little hand motions in the air, as if she were gathering dust motes and putting them in an imaginary basket.

I kept my counsel—for a change. When we were growing up, and either Toy or I came to her with hurt feelings, Mama often consoled us by saying: "Consider the source." How strange, and sad, that now I thought it best to apply those words to her.

Yet she was totally cognizant of the fact that we were in Myers Park as I neared Chanti Ovumkoph Goldburg's home. When I pulled up in front of house and parked the car I swear that I could see her ears flatten just a little.

"You do know, Abby," she sniffed, "that I don't get along with that woman. Never have, never will."

"Why is that?"

"For starters," Mama said, "it's the way she treats her son-in-law."

"You mean Bob?"

"Does she have another?"

"Yes, Rob's sister is married to some guy named Antonio. He claims to be the son of a count—or something. It's just the kind of snootiness that Rob's mother eats up with a spoon."

Mama's eyes flashed. "Why didn't you tell me this before?"

"Because," I said, "Chanti comes to Charleston sometimes, and sometimes you're invited to the same functions, and I didn't want you to—"

"Why Abigail Louise!" she declared angrily. "How dare you treat me like I'm a child? Besides, this woman deserves to have the fecal matter forcefully ejected from her person, preferably with a fast-moving foot. The first time she came down I took her as my guest to my book club—the Blue Stockings—and she referred to Bob Steuben as 'my son's unfortunately effeminate roommate'—and this is *after* they had been legally married in Massachusetts."

I stared at Mama with a mixture of admiration and horror. It made me proud to see her stirred up over injustice, but the perpetrator of that injustice was just a few yards away, and since Mama already had her claws out, putting the two women in the same room was perhaps not such a good idea. A smart Abigail Louise would have driven away and rethought her next move. But I was tired, and no one has ever accused me of being a brainiac.

"Just remember that this is her home, Mama. Plus she's mourning the death of her sister."

"I'll just bet that she is," Mama muttered.

I shocked Mama by opening Chanti's front door and just walking in. I didn't ring the bell, nor did I knock.

"Hello?" I called.

"You!" Chanti said, swooping out of nowhere.

"You're sitting shivah, right? Rob said that one isn't supposed to knock; one just comes in and offers condolences. Chanti, my dear, I'm so sorry for your loss."

"I just bet you are. And for the record, I don't follow all the old customs; I don't sit shivah. If the door was unlocked, it's because I forgot to lock it. That's all."

"Now that we're here," Mama said, "we may as well sit down. I don't suppose you still have the coffeepot on. The coffee they serve at the hotel—"

"This isn't a restaurant and I'm not a waitress."

Mama settled into a high-backed armchair upholstered in red Chinese silk. "Of course not, dear. A waitress would be far more pleasant. Listen, when you get the coffee, please put in a lot of milk and at least two packets of sweetener. But not the pink stuff. Did you know that there is a certain percentage of the population that cannot taste the sweet factor in that stuff at all? In fact, it tastes bitter to some of us. Abby, how does that pink stuff taste to you?"

"It's okay."

"Oh, I find it bitter as well," Chanti said, thereby knocking the socks off me.

"What do you prefer then?" Mama asked.

"The yellow packets."

"You know, I haven't tried those yet. I still use the blue."

"You must try the yellow! Here, I'll get you some. How many did you say? Two?"

"Yes, thank you. And a lightly toasted bagel would be nice. Maybe with some cream cheese and raspberry preserves."

"Will some Entenmann's cheese Danish suffice instead?"

"That would be lovely."

And then just like that, the much despised, and despising, Chanti Goldburg waltzed off into the kitchen to wait on my minimadre. Or not. Most probably not. Why should she? This couldn't be good. I stewed on that for a few minutes, perhaps far too long.

"Mama," I said at last, "we have to get out of here before she gets back."

21

Don't be silly," Mama said. "It would be rude to just sneak out."

"Mama, that woman can't stand you. She's going to do something to your food."

"Now you're being ridiculous," Mama said. "How would she poison only me? What if you happened to eat it too?"

"Okay, so maybe she won't poison the food, but she might spit on it—*all* of it."

Mama made a face befitting just such a situation. "Nonsense. You watch too many of those college gross-out movies, Abby. Nobody does that in real life."

"Oh, you don't think so. You don't think that the White House kitchen isn't instructed to spit on the food of enemy heads of state before serving it at state dinners?"

"Who told you that? Some Democrat?"

Actually, I'd thought that one up myself—just that very second. And if they got a very sick kitchen worker to spit into the food, it might even influence the way negotiations went. Darn, but I was good. If the CIA wanted to hire me, they best hurry and get in line.

"Shhh, here she comes."

Chanti entered with a tray bearing the coffee items. Due to the fact that she was smiling, I didn't recognize her. I jumped to my feet.

"Abby Timberlake," I said.

Chanti's laugh may have been forced, but even then it was as beautiful as the song of a nightingale, or a babbling brook, or a babbling nightingale—take your pick. "My but you're a clever sprite, Abigail. Isn't she a treasure, Mozzarella?"

"That's *Mozella*," Mama snapped.

"Oh, I'm so sorry, dear; I'm absolutely dreadful with names. Please accept my apology."

I could see Mama take a deep heroic breath. "That's quite all right, Chanticleer. I have the same trouble with names."

"*Chanticleer?* Isn't that the name of a chicken in one of Chaucer's *Canterbury Tales*?"

"More specifically," this little sprite said, "it was a rooster. But isn't it nice that the two of you have at least a little education?"

Chanti fixed me with a glare that, if properly focused, could have warmed up the coffee nicely. "My name is Chanteuse."

"Well, you did start it," I said. "Anyway, we didn't come here to discuss literature or nomenclature, or sip coffee—no matter how delicious; we came to discuss your Aunt Jerry's two safes."

"Her *what*?" Chanti said.

"You heard her," Mama said. "You may be a sight older than you let on—"

"As are you, I understand," Chanti hissed.

"Biddies, please," I said, and dropped my Danish so that I could clap my hands. Then I clapped them over my mouth. "Oops, I meant to say *ladies*."

"The hell you did," the biddies said in unison.

I pretended to ignore them. "Yesterday afternoon your brother Aaron and I went over to your sister's house and looked around a bit."

"How did you get in?" Chanti demanded, her chin thrust forward. "You must have broken in. I'm the only one who has a key."

"This is America," I said. "How else?" Perhaps I was a bit too smug. Yes, surely I was. After all, she was a grieving sister.

"Huh? What is that supposed to mean?"

"They either found it under the mat, over the lintel, or somewhere around a flowerpot," Mama said somewhat more kindly.

"Humph," Chanti said, "that's still breaking in. But go on with your story. You didn't take anything, did you? Because that was Mama's good china, and I'm supposed to get that—what's left of it, at any rate. Same thing goes for the silver, even though it's not my pattern. But you can have all that crap in the safes, because that's just what it is: crap. The stones are glass and the metal is—well, I'm not sure what it is. They're the kind of rings you can buy for ten bucks in the gift shops at the beach."

"No way," I said. "These may have been copies of jewels, but they weren't those so-called fashion rings."

Chanteuse laughed again, and this time it was most definitely not a pleasing sound. "I was with her when she bought most of those. Heck, I even bought some of those and then gave them to her when I got tired of them—which was like when I took them off to wash my face, or changed my clothes, whichever came first. They're only meant to be viewed from a distance; so you can't wear them if you have a dinner date, for instance, or if you're playing mah-jongg."

"Why that's just silly," Mama said. "Why would anyone buy something so—"

"Fun?" I said. "Mama, would you like to share why it is you wear starched petticoats that make your skirt stick straight out like an open umbrella?"

"Why Abigail Louise, you're just like Aaron Burr!"

"So there you have it," Chanteuse said, as she passed a plate of pastry around, "it's all just costume; it's really *less* than costume jewelry. It's only pretend."

"Then why did she keep it in a pair of safes?" I asked.

"Yes, why?" Mama said, before taking a big bite out of a scrumptious-looking cheese Danish. Maybe it's because she keeps her waist cinched tightly with wide belts, or maybe she's been blessed with a fifteen-year-old boy's metabolism, but in any case, she eats like a lumberjack and never gains an ounce. I, on the other hand, can look at a photo of pancakes in a magazine and feel my hips commence to swell.

"Ah, the safes," Chanti said. "I was wondering when you'd get to that. Julio installed them. That was back in the seventies."

"Julio?" I said. "Are we supposed to know who that is?"

"Beats me," she said. She started to pour. "Tell me when to stop."

"Stop," I said. "Tell us who Julio was."

"One of a long string of lovers. A *very* long string of lovers."

Mama sighed. "Your sister must have been a happy woman."

"Mama!"

"Sorry, dear," she said. "You know that I loved your daddy very much, and Lord knows I was always faithful to him. Always. Even when—well, never you mind. But sometimes I wonder what it might have been like to lie in the arms of another man, to feel another man's kisses, to have another man—"

"Good grief, Mama, would you please stop it? Nobody wants to hear this."

"Au contraire," Chanteuse said smugly, "I find it quite amusing. I tell you, Mozella, the French say that sexual variety is our birthright. Or is it the Spanish who say that? Anyway, under no circumstances should you believe that the time for erotic discovery has passed you by. European men adore older women. That said, a woman with your classical good looks, and who has kept herself in top form, as you have obviously done, could own the day at any beach along the Riviera."

Mama dropped what remained of her Danish on her plate. "Are you pulling my size two petite leg, Chanti?"

"No, ma'am."

"Abby, did you hear that? We're going to France!"

"No, Mama, *we* are not going to France. I am quite happy with the man I've got, and my generation was smart enough to do our—call it what you will—before we had flab and back hair, so I'm not interested in squeezing the Charmin, no matter how charming the accent."

"Abby, that is so disgusting. Chanti, dear, please excuse my daughter's vulgarity; it certainly was not the way she was raised."

"I hear you," Chanti said. "It's the same way with my Rob."

"As long as I'm being rude," I said, "I'd like to interrupt long enough to ask about this Julio. Why did he install two safes?"

"Oh, we're back to that, are we? If you must know, then, Julio was Colombian. The safes were for drugs."

"Like aspirin," Mama said. "Now shush, Abby."

"Not aspirin," Chanti said. "Cocaine. Julio was a drug *runner*. You probably don't want to know how he brought in the drugs."

"I do," Mama said.

"Did it involve condoms?" I said.

"Yes."

"Then I have a good idea," I said. "I'll explain it to her later. Tell me, did your sister know about this?"

Chanti gave me one of her trademark withering

looks. "How do you think I know about this? Of course Jerry knew. I keep telling y'all: Jerry and I were very close. Why doesn't anybody believe me?"

"Do you want the truth?" I said.

"Of course," she said.

"Yes," I said, "but do you want the company truth, or the plain unvarnished truth—or, in other words— the *real* truth?"

"Just tell me, damn it!"

I swallowed; first a bite of cheese Danish, and then a lump of trepidation. "The reason that no one can believe that you two were close is because you have the personality of a frozen codfish. It's hard to imagine you being close to anyone." I swallowed again. "That was the company version. Hee hee—just kidding about that. But seriously, Chanti, you do strike me as being formidable, whereas your sister was very approachable."

"But you hardly knew her!"

"That's right, I didn't. Yet she was nice to me from the start. No preconceived notions of who I was, no judgments levied against my life partner."

"Well, I should say not! You're married to a very handsome heterosexual man. If my son was married to a beautiful heterosexual woman, we wouldn't be having this conversation."

"Honestly, Chanti," I said, "you're so shallow that if the sun came out for fifteen minutes you'd dry up and disappear."

"Huh? I don't get it," she said.

"Good one," Mama said.

"The other people in your life have their own wants

and needs," I said, "and they aren't always going to line up with yours. Learning that won't necessarily make you happy, but dwelling on the differences between your expectations and what they're likely to deliver is guaranteed to make you miserable."

The tears welled up in her eyes. Whereas I am definitely an "ugly cry," Chanti was a "heart-wrenching cry." What I mean is, here was a beautiful, well-dressed, older woman, who normally exuded extreme confidence, suddenly reduced to the most vulnerable and pathetic stance a person can assume. Before there were times when I'd been tempted to punch her in the knee pits in order to bring her down a notch or two, and now my instinct was to hug her.

"Life is s-so hard," she blubbered.

"There, you see what you've done," Mama said, and beat me to the hug. That was actually a very good thing, because Chanti was a rather tall woman, and being fashion-forward, was wearing heels that put her somewhere up in the stratosphere. Mama, of course, always wears pumps and thus is consistently three inches taller than yours truly. Had I hugged Chanti, I might have snatched my head away in acute embarrassment; enough said.

"What's going on?" a male voice boomed.

Three heads swiveled.

22

Bob!" I cried joyfully. "You're just the person we've been talking about!"

"I bet you have," he said.

Bob Steuben is Rob Goldburg's one true love, life partner, and business associate, but he is also the thorn in Chanti's flesh, the one that had just reduced her to tears. How fortunate she was that I had just gifted her with such powerful words of wisdom: pearls, rubies—she got the works! If only the universe had been this generous, and timely, with me when I was in need. Not that I'm complaining, mind you—okay, maybe a wee bit. I'm just saying that there was no Abigail Timberlake on hand when Buford announced that he was trading me in for a silicone-enhanced bimbo half my age named Tweetie.

"Oy vey," Chanti said, and started to turn away.

"Oh no, you don't," I hissed. Incidentally, hissing without an S is a skill that I've learned from Agatha Award–winning novelists, and it can be quite intimidating. It worked on Chanti.

210

"But he's ruined my life."

"I'll cloud up and rain all over you if you don't get over there and give him a hug. I mean it. I may be small, but I can tan your hide till it won't hold shucks."

Chanti, bless her heart, grinned. "I don't know what the hell you just said, but all right." She walked over to her son-in-law and gingerly put her arms around him. "Hey Bob."

"Hi Chanti."

She put her arms around him properly. "Just one little thing, Bob. In the South we say 'hey' or 'ha'; not 'hi-ee.'"

"So," Mama said, as we were pulling away from Chanti's house in her leafy Myers Park neighborhood, "all's well that ends well. Right, Abby? Franklin Roosevelt said that, I believe."

"He may have, Mama," I said, "but Shakespeare said it first. And *what* is it that ended so well?"

"Why just everything! We can cross Chanti off your list of suspects, and she's going to be pleasant to Bob from now on, thanks to you."

"Mama, what Toy says is true: you don't need rose-colored glasses, because your irises are already tinted that hue."

My peripheral vision has been waning in recent years, but it was still good enough for me to see Mama stiffen in her seat. "Why that little whippersnapper. I should tan *his* hide till it don't hold shucks—and Abby, you stole that line from your daddy!"

"Nah, I merely borrowed it," I said.

"Don't you get smart with me," Mama said. "Remember that it was me who birthed you."

"Yes, seventy-five years ago."

"Don't be silly; that's my age—wait just one cotton-pickin' minute! Hey, no fair tricking a senior citizen! There should be a law against that. When I get home I'm going to write to President Obama."

"Perhaps you should try writing Senator John McCain instead. He's closer to your age. He might relate to you better."

"Abigail!"

"Yes, Mama?"

"You're incorrigible."

"Yes, Mama, I am."

"Abby?"

"Yes, Mama?"

"The cop is behind you again."

"Very funny, Mama."

But since Mama can't duplicate the sound of a siren—believe me, she's tried—I soon looked in the mirror—and then immediately pulled over. Fortunately, by then we were out of sight of Chanti's house.

I asked Mama to get my license out of my purse while I arranged my lips into a pleasant formation and lowered the window on my side of the car. But when I snuck a peak in my side view mirror, I nearly had the big one.

"Oh crap," I squeaked.

"What's wrong," Mama said.

"Remember Tweedledee and Tweedledum down in Charleston? Well, Charlotte has its own version: Wimbler and Krupp."

"I'll start praying," Mama said. "They're only Episcopal prayers, so they may not be as effective as—"

"Exit your car, ma'am, with your hands above your head."

"Sir," I said, "may I use my hands to open the door first?"

"Very funny, ma'am. Now I said exit the car with your hands above your head."

"Abby," Mama whispered, "this one's a woman, and you just called her a 'sir.'"

"Oopsie daisy, ma'am. Would you please open the door for me?"

Much to my surprise, Detective Krupp actually did just that. Much to my continued surprise, I was not ready, and since I was shamefully in violation of a very important North Carolina state law—the seat belt law—I fell sideways, virtually into Detective Krupp's standing lap. That is to say, she had to catch me, and hold me to her, as she lowered me to the ground.

"Wow," she said, "you were really quick with that seat belt. I swear I didn't even see your hands move."

"That's because she—"

"I learned it from Tweetie—may she rest in peace. Oh the things that girl could do with her hands. And that's just for starters."

"Are you being crude, Miss Timberlake?" Detective Krupp said.

She made me stand on my own two little feet, which turned out to be a valuable source of inspiration. "Oh not at all. That's why I hate innuendo. It ruins things for us innocent folks. I was referring to the fact that

Tweetie was a superb soccer player. And ballerina. Why, you should have seen her stand *en pointe.*"

Mama snickered. "Are you referring to *our* Tweetie? Tweetie Timberlake?"

"Yes, Mama, our dear, sweet Tweetie, upon whom our very lives depended more than one occasion."

"Oh."

Detective Krupp, who was now standing an arm's length from me, beamed. "Cool beans. That sounds like the Tweetie I knew, all right; tell me more."

"Uh," Mama said, "Abby, this really is your baili-wick, not mine."

"Bailiwick," I said, "now there's an interesting word. I wonder how it came about."

"Quit stalling, Miss Timberlake," Detective Krupp growled.

"Okay, you only need to growl once. Well, you see, Mama and me were up at the top of Mount Mitchell in a blizzard—"

"I," Detective Krupp said, rudely interrupting me.

"Excuse me?" I said.

"It should be 'I,' not 'me.'"

"Does it really make that big of a difference?" I said. "After all, this is dialogue; this is how real people speak."

"That may be so," she said, "but if I read this in a book, I'd throw it across the room."

Thank heavens Detective Wimbler trotted over at that very moment, saving me from myself: my own worst enemy. "Mama," I said, gratefully, "Detective Wimbler's mother—she's passed on now—was a Wiggins."

"Well I'll be," Mama said. "My husband—may he rest in peace—was a Wiggins. Do you remember her daddy's Christian name?"

"Yes, ma'am, same as mine: Wallace."

"Abby! That's the same as your granddaddy's name!"

"Mama, I'm sure there was more than one Wallace Wiggins walking the earth in granddaddy's time."

"Son," Mama said, "what was your mama's name?"

"Formalda—short for formaldehyde. My grandpa was a funeral director who loved his work and he named his children after various aspects of it. He wanted them to take over his business when they grew up, but his son left home and cut off all contact with the family."

"Cry me a river," Detective Krupp said, "and then gag me with a spoon. This is not why we're here, Wallace."

"Shut up, dear," Mama said, "and let the boy talk. Wallace, was this runaway uncle's name Hyde by any chance?"

"Yes, ma'am! How did you know?"

"Oh Lord, Abby, this boy is your first cousin."

"I'm not a boy, ma'am," Detective Wimbler said.

"Mama, this is beyond ridiculous. Daddy's name was Clarence. In fact, he was Clarence Rufus Wiggins III. And he had only one sister, and that was Lula Mae Wiggins, who died as a maiden lady in Savannah."

"Abby," Mama said sternly, "now you need to shut up and listen. Your father, bless his now defunct heart, was a man who carried a lot of deep dark secrets with him; most of these secrets, I suspect, went to his grave

215

unrevealed to anyone. But every now and then, when he'd had one beer too many—this is after you children went to bed, of course—he'd let something from his past life slip. And yes, his real name was Hyde and he had a twin sister named Formalda."

"What a touching family reunion," Detective Krupp said. "Spare me any further details."

At that Mama got out of the car and stormed around to where the female detective was standing. With her puffed-up skirt she reminded me of a pink-and-white checked mother hen. Or perhaps a tom turkey with its feathers all fluffed out. I've been chased out of more than one farmyard by tom turkeys—but in my defense, they do stand nearly as tall as I do.

"Now what did I tell you?" Mama said. "Either you quit harassing my family, or I'll bring charges down on your head so quick that your eyes will spin out of their sockets faster than toy tops on a greased glass cutting board. *Capisce?*"

"Mama," I said proudly, "you're my hero."

"Auntie—I don't even know your name," Detective Wimbler said adoringly. "What *is* your name, if I may ask?"

"Mozella."

The new cousin giggled unbecomingly.

"What is it?" Mama said.

"No offense, Mozella," he said, "but that's kind of a funny name."

"Ooh," I said. "First offense, cousin, and you better start keeping track."

"Abby," Mama said, "I'm not *that* bad."

"Yes, you are." I clapped my hands, which produces the sound a five-year-old might make at her birthday party. "Everyone, I can't tell you how much fun this has been, but Detective Krupp is right. The family reunion, as lovely as it has been, must be put on hold until after Jerry Ovumkoph's killer has been put behind bars. And surely, dear cousin, you still don't think that I, your own flesh and blood, the owner of these minuscule mitts"—I held up my dainty hands—"am capable of murdering anyone. Do you?"

"Miss Timberlake, we're not here to arrest you."

"You're not?"

"If we were," Detective Krupp said, "do you think we would have let you babble on so long about all this nonsense?"

"Miss Timberlake," Detective Wimbler said, "we told you yesterday that it was our intention to help you, but clearly you didn't believe us. Do you know how hurtful that is? Especially now that I know we are kin?"

"Get to the point, nephew," my bantam mama said. "My daughter has been through enough already and the day is barely started."

"Humph," Detective Krupp said, as she dug a knuckle into my cousin's biceps, "I told you we should get right down to business." She did her best to focus her watery green eyes on me. "The coroner's report came in at six this morning. Miss Ovumkoph died of heart failure before she was put in the freezer. The heart attack was probably brought on by the ingestion— that means eating—of some sort of poison. The full report will probably not be out for another six weeks. At any rate, you are no longer a part of this investigation."

"Whoopee!" Mama cried, and tried to hug me, but I squirmed out of her embrace. She hugged Cousin Wallace instead.

"What about my prints being all over that knife?" I said, dumbfounded.

"Miss Timberlake," Detective Krupp said, "you're married to a former detective, you're supposed to know how this works: we wanted to keep our as—I mean *bases*—covered until the preliminary report was issued. So we said what we had to say. What was the harm?"

"That's *it*?" I said. "What was the *harm*? Are you idiots serious?"

"Abby," Mama said. "Please stop shrieking, dear."

I ran around the car and hopped back in. "Come on, Mama, let's go."

"Where, dear?"

"Anywhere these guys aren't is fine with me."

23

I hadn't been to Bubba's China Gourmet on Pine-ville-Matthews Road for the shelf span of a thousand-year-old egg. It may not serve up the best food in the Charlotte metropolitan area, but its dishes rank among the most interesting. Where else can one find stir-fried collard greens, sweet and sour okra, and moo goo gai grits? Adventurous diners may wish to sample General Tso's possum or the Hunan-style hog hocks. Finicky eaters need not dismay. There is always the dynamite salad bar with all the colorless iceberg lettuce you can eat, and if you're really lucky, Bubba will have gotten it into his hard Dixie skull to make lime gelatin squares that day.

It's almost impossible to find a parking space, thanks to Bubba's low prices, so I had to circle the lot for at least ten minutes before I found one that was more than half empty. Finally a Buckeye family of five waddled out and crammed themselves into a full-size van, which left me with plenty of room, along with the smug satisfaction that Bubba was beginning to get famous above the Mason-Dixon Line.

A faux Asian waitress with bottle-black hair and a Japanese kimono pounced on me the second I pushed open the greasy door. "I'm your waitress, Consuelo," she said in a heavy Spanish accent.

"You see, Mama! That's what I love about this place! Consuelo, is Bubba here today?"

"*Si*—no, *hai!* Is very hard this Japanese English, yes?"

"I thought this was a *Chinese* restaurant," Mama said.

"It is, but Bubba has this thing about kimonos, and fortunately his cultural confusion and fusion cuisine coincide nicely, hence the immense popularity.

We're actually here to meet a Mr. Ovumkoph," I said to Consuelo.

"We are?" Mama said.

"Yes, ma'am, and there he is waving at us."

"You didn't tell me that he was so cute," Mama said, as we made our way to the genuine faux leather booth Ben occupied.

"That gringo real hottie," Consuelo said. "Very rich, I think, but very old too. Not for me."

"Indeed," I said. "He played with Moses as a baby."

"What?" Consuelo said.

The concern in her voice belied her white-powdered persona. It also informed me that she hadn't understood my reference and was concerned that she might have been too hasty in her decision to dismiss the gringo because of his age.

"Never mind," I said.

"I want bring you complimentary *peech-er* of sangria," she said as she seated us.

"You bet," I said. "That's a yes."

"You want hear specials?" Consuelo said.

"Yes," Mama said. "But speak loudly. It's noisy in here."

Consuelo giggled. "Is no specials, is only buffet."

"Why that was meaner than one hen stealin' the eggs offen another," Mama said. She was born and raised on a farm between Rock Hill and York, South Carolina, and sometimes when she's under stress her country roots take over.

"So sorry," Consuelo said, and still giggling, trotted away with mincing steps.

"Welcome ladies," Ben said. He'd stood for us and now waited for us to sit. "Mrs. Timberlake, you failed to mention that your mother is such an attractive woman. Mrs. Wiggins, I hope that your husband appreciates the beauty that he is fortunate enough to gaze upon regularly. I myself am a divorced man, and no longer have such a pleasure."

Mama's giggle was annoyingly similar to Consuelo's. "My husband has been dead for almost fif— Many years, Mr. Ovumkoph. And though it's none of my business, your wife must have been out of her noodle."

"Mama!"

"Well, just look at him, Abby," Mama said. "He looks just like our Robbie, but older. Unless his man plumbing wasn't working back then, or he was beating her or something—I mean, sometimes women can be too fickle. That's all I'm saying, dear."

Poor Ben was blushing to the point that his skin appeared almost black. But then a moment later he roared with laughter, and soon his complexion returned to a healthy glow.

"My man plumbing was—and continues to work—just fine. And please call me Ben."

"Charmed, I'm sure," Mama said, and extended a well-manicured hand.

"Gag me with a pair of chopsticks," I said.

"Abby, don't be rude," Mama said.

"But Mama, you two are flirting like a pair of seventh-graders at a sock hop."

"Oh Abby, you silly thing, you couldn't possibly remember a sock hop; you weren't born until—"

"And neither can you, Mama," I said, "and not for the reason that I can't. Tell me, Ben, what is this meeting all about?"

"You may call me Mozella, by the way. I'm in the Charleston white pages."

Ben smiled broadly. "You two ladies are something else. Maybe if I'd have met you, Mozella, instead of that self-styled wildcat down in Australia—well, who knows."

This was getting ridiculous. Suspiciously so.

"I'm afraid Mama wouldn't make a very good Jew," I said. "She loves shrimp."

"But only kosher shrimp," Mama said.

Although Mama sounded clueless to me, Ben laughed. "You have a dry sense of humor as well. I like that."

"Too bad it's not rye," I said, "because she's been

222

known to ham it up."

"Abigail, are you making fun of me?"

"Should I be?" I asked.

"Ha ha," Ben said. "I just adore you two. My mother was so strict. The only time I ever saw my mother smile, it turned out to be a bowel obstruction."

That brought short-lived smiles to our lips. "I'm serious," Ben said. "We are taught to honor our parents, and one must never speak ill of the dead, but Mama is where Chanti got her scintillating personality."

"Shades of *Mommie Dearest*?" I said.

"Exactly," he said. "By now it must be clear to you that I had a favorite sister."

"In fact—"

Aiyee caramba! Just when the conversation was about to get interesting, along minced Consuelo on her platform shoes, toting the pitcher of alcohol-free Chinese sangria.

"Gringos, geet up," the waitress ordered. "Zee boofay, she not coming to you."

"Yes," Ben said, "but she is not going anywhere either."

"Don't make fun of her," I whispered.

But Consuelo didn't seem to have heard him. "Eez all you can eat," she said. I could hear the longing in her voice.

"Does Bubba let you eat here?" I asked.

"Only zee food that—how you say in English—smell bad."

"Why that's awful!" Mama said.

"That only sometime," Consuelo said. "Because the

rest of the time Bubba adds more spice and gives the food a new name. That's how he came up with Bubba's Pungent Pork Surprise. The surprise is a tummy ache."

"Whoa," Ben said. "What happened to your Hispanic accent?"

"Busted," Consuelo said, her voice dropping three octaves.

"And you're not even a real gal, are you?"

"Busted again, dang it."

At that point poor Consuelo looked so miserable that I had no choice but to intervene in his destiny. "Why don't you join us, dear? Lunch is on me."

"Bubba will fire my ass."

"Consuelo—uh, that isn't your real name, is it?"

"It's Conrad, ma'am."

I smiled. "Conrad. What's going on? What was with the accent?"

Mama raised her hand and like a Goody Two-shoes schoolgirl waved it impatiently. "I bet I know!"

"Mama, *please*," I said.

"He's an illegal alien," Mama said, whereupon Conrad blanched.

Ben chuckled politely. "Mozella, you are indeed droll; there is no doubt about that."

"Oh, can the droll," Mama said. "Abby, my sniffer is working again. This young man is from Manitoba and he slipped across the U.S. border up in North Dakota without documentation. Somehow he made it down to Charlotte. He likes it in this country and wants to stay, but of course he can't, not without a green card. Then he read an article in the *Charlotte Observer* that Bubba hires Hispanic waitresses to play the part of geisha waitresses in his Chinese restaurant. Conrad—who is no stranger to drag, but had never met a Spanish-speaking person before arriving in the Carolinas—thought he could make this work. Am I right so far, dear?"

Conrad clumped over to the next table, swiped an empty chair, and threw his narrow butt gratefully down in it. "I can't believe this woman. Everything she said is absolutely true—well, except I come from Saskatchewan, not Manitoba."

"Don't you miss your family and friends?" I said.

Conrad had large, expressive brown eyes. "Have any of you read a book titled *A Complicated Kindness* by Miriam Toews?"

Amazingly, all three of us had. "I do have a sensitive side," Ben said when he saw my reaction to his affirmative response.

"Well, anyway," Conrad said, "that was exactly the way I was raised. From the moment we were born the whole object was for us to gain admittance to the afterlife. In other words, to get saved. And we started early getting used to the idea of dying. I'm sure you know the prayer that goes: 'Now I lay me down to sleep, oh Lord I pray my soul to keep.'"

"Yes, and I refused to teach it to my children," I said. "'If I should die before I wake, I pray the Lord my soul to take!' What a gruesome thought to put into a small child's head just before they nod off."

"Exactly," Conrad said.

"This is very interesting," Ben said. "This is a Christian prayer, I presume."

"Yes," Mama said, as she patted her pearls indignantly. "Call me old school, if you wish, but I see nothing wrong with it. I found it very comforting as a child."

"What I find so interesting about it," said Ben, "is that my sister had her own version of it that she used to say all the time. I just didn't know it was part of a real prayer."

"What was it?" I said. "Do you mind sharing?"

Ben cleared his throat. " 'If I should die before I wake, tell everyone my jewelry's fake.' "

Mama and Conrad stared at Ben, as if waiting for a punch line to be delivered. I, however, felt like I had just been punched in the tummy. Of course! That was it! That was the key. Jerry couldn't afford the genuine article, but she had found someone skilled enough to make copies that could pass for the real thing. And now, just six days before her predicted demise, she was dead.

"Excuse me," I said, as I pushed my chair back and stood. "And please, y'all, don't try to stop me."

"I wouldn't dream of it, dear," Mama said, although she was reaching out to block me with her left hand at the same time.

Ben, being a good Southern gentleman, was on his feet by then. Conrad, who was somewhat restricted by the bulk of his obi, made only a token attempt to rise.

"Please don't go," Ben said. "Mrs. Timberlake, I apologize if I have offended you in any way. I realize that religion is one of the three taboo topics for the dinner table—"

"Give me a break," Mama said. "There aren't any

taboo topics at my table, or Abby's either. Now sit down, the both of you, and as soon as the line clears a little at the buffet, then we'll all get up and fill our plates."

I'm afraid that Ben had very persuasive eyes. "Your mama has spoken, Abby. You would be breaking a commandment in both of our faiths if you were to disrespect her."

I at least gave myself the satisfaction of rolling my eyes before retaking my seat. "Since *you* insist, Ben."

"Hey guys," Conrad said, "I want to know what the other two forbidden topics are."

"Politics and sex," I said. "Which, here in the States, often go hand in hand."

"Jerry and I never agreed politically," Ben said. "Then again, she never quite agreed with anyone on that score. I swear, the woman was trying to get a rise out of her siblings—especially Chanti. They had a thing, you know."

"A *thing*?" Mama said. "What does that mean?"

Ben suddenly looked miserable. "I shouldn't be talking ill of the dead; it isn't right."

"Of course not," Mama said. "But you weren't; you were talking about Chanti. Am I right? The woman is a pain in the tuchas."

"Mama!" I said.

Ben laughed. "You can bet your bottom dollar on that. Jerry and Chanti were always at each other's throats. As far back as high school it had to do with guys."

"Figures," Mama and I said in unison.

"Jinx," I said. "You owe me a Coke."

"Then Chanti fell in love with this one guy—they were engaged to be married—but then Jerry steals him away. And then dumps him!"

"Men are jerks," Mama and I said, speaking in tandem again.

"Hey," Conrad said, "I feel that I must protest. Not all guys are like that."

"Would you be speaking from experience?" Ben said. "You might sound more convincing if you take off that dress."

"It's not a dress; it's a kimono."

"Anyway," Ben said, "and then Jerry had a minor heart attack; but still, you would think that it would be a good time to let go of grudges and come together as a family, right?"

"My family never wants to speak to me again," Conrad said.

"Hush up," Mama said, not unkindly, "and let the man speak."

"But it didn't mean squat for this family. Not squat. Chanti never showed up at the hospital. Neither did our brother Aaron. Of course no one ever expected our famous cousin, Pastor Sam, to show up."

"And did he?" I asked.

24

Ben shook his head and chuckled. "No. But if he had, he would have been under a lot of pressure to perform. There were two rabbis and a cantor there until she was out of the woods."

"Well, good," I said. "So then their prayers were answered."

Ben shrugged. "Maybe. In my faith we don't pray for miracles. We pray for strength and peace. We pray for hope and guidance. Most of all we give thanks for what we already have."

"Just don't make them prayers too obvious," someone said. "Unless them's Christian prayers."

I looked up over my shoulder into the immense jowly face of Bubba himself. It was like looking into the maw of a bloated hippopotamus sans the enormous teeth. (Bubba has only store-bought teeth and usually he forgets to wear them.) Whether from smoking at home, or crying over country lyrics, Bubba's red eyes resemble maraschino cherries about ready to pop out of the slits in which they are housed. His numerous chins, every one of them as soft and smooth as a bag of freshly kneaded dough, sway with each syllable of the spoken word. In short, it is almost impossible not to stare at this legend of Pineville, North Carolina.

"We're done with the praying," Mama said. "Now we're about to sample your delicious cuisine."

"That's what I like to hear, ma'am, a fine Southern accent like yours. Where are you from, if you don't mind me asking?"

"I'm from Rock Hill, Bubba. Born and bred."

Then the squished red cherries settled on the soon-to-be unemployed geisha. "What are you doing, girl, sitting with the customers?"

"I quit," Conrad said.

"You can't quit," Bubba said. "I have to fire you."

"Don't be mean," Mama said.

"He's not being mean," I said. "He wants to make sure Conrad can file for unemployment." I tried my best to maintain eye contact with Bubba. "But you're forgetting that this boy is an illegal alien."

"*What?* He don't look like no kind of Mexican to me."

"I'm not," Conrad said. "I'm from a rotten little town called Moose Jaw, Saskatchewan."

"You take that back!" Bubba roared. "Don't nobody call Moose Jaw a rotten little town."

Conrad was on his feet so fast that the beautiful, genuine faux polyester kimono split up the rear. He threw off the heavy black wig. Unfortunately, the lad tossed it a mite too far and it landed in another diner's moo goo gai grits.

The diner whose grits had been violated by polyester locks was none too pleased. "Hell's bells!" he shouted.

I swear I didn't see Ben move, but like the true Southern gentleman that he is, he had both his hands over Mama's ears, protecting the dainty things from being polluted by such crude language. And Mama, being the fragile Southern belle that she is, was so overcome at hearing Satan's homeland referenced that she was on the verge of a swoon.

It just so happens that Mama has turned swooning into an art form. She puts one delicate hand up to her forehead, palm out, the other to her bosom, palm inward, closes her eyes halfway, and commences to sway. Because she's vertically challenged, she can't achieve a whole lot of lateral motion, so she makes up for it vocally. Her sighs and moans are reminiscent of the film *When Harry Met Sally*, and have no place in an eating establishment. When she started with the unseemly sounds, Ben let go of her ears and cradled her shamefully in his arms.

"Mama, stop that," I begged, "or I'm leaving."

Bubba was oblivious both to the profanity and to Mama's theatrics. He'd blown himself up like a giant puffer fish and was looming over the boy from north of the border.

"What do you know about Moose Jaw, boy?" Bubba demanded.

Conrad had begun to back up. It was a tricky task, given the platform shoes and ripped kimono.

"I'm from Moose Jaw," he said, his voice quavering. "But that's in Saskatchewan, *not* North Carolina."

"You know a woman by the name of Emma Rae Corntassel?" Bubba blubbered.

"Yes, sir, she plays the organ at my church. She's like a hundred years old or something."

"She's eighty-nine, and she's my mama."

"Give me a break," I moaned. "Is everyone on this trip going to turn out to be related to someone else up here? First it was Tweetie and the detective, although they weren't relatives but bath mates, and then it was—"

But Mama had stopped mid-swoon. "Do you know what all this means, Abby?"

"No, what? You're going to tell me that we're related to Ben? Because if that's the case, he's going to have to drop his mitts. I'm sure that I read somewhere in the Good Book that we're not supposed to lie with our relatives, and I'm not talking about misrepresenting the truth."

"Don't be such a smart aleck, Abby. That too is a commandment—and one of the Big Ten."

"Touché," Ben said.

"Shhh," Mama said. "I prefer to handle my daughter alone. No, Abby, the significance of Bubba's hidden Canadian origins means that he's not a *true* Southerner—nor even a real Bubba. In other words, this restaurant is a sham."

Mama is no fool. And she'd spoken quietly so that only our immediate party was privy to her words. As they registered in Bubba's well-padded brain his face went from rage red to a shade of gray not included on most color wheels for obvious reasons.

"I'm going to be sick," he said.

"No, you're not," Mama said. "We're all entitled to our own deceptions. You didn't kill anyone, did you?"

"No, ma'am. I stopped here overnight on my way to Disney World. It was Christmas Eve, thirty years ago this past December. I wanted to try some Southern food, but the only restaurant open was this Chinese place, so I bought it, brought in a local chef, and voilà, that's how Bubba's was born. It was in the paper, but folks have kind of forgotten about it over the years, which is just fine with me. I think it helps that they think I'm Southern."

"Moose Jaw *is* in the southern part of the province," Conrad said kindly. After all, the boy didn't need to be helpful.

"Well, in that case," Mama said, "your secret is safe with us, but we expect free meals in perpetuity. And Conrad gets his job back."

"With a twenty-five percent raise," Conrad said, proving that he was adapting to American ways really well.

"*What?*" Bubba said.

"That means," Mama said, "that we'll be dining—"

"I know what it means," Bubba said, resorting to his old self. "It's called extortion."

"Mama, what do you know about false advertising?" I said in a voice loud enough to rouse Daddy from his permanent resting place over the South Carolina border in Rock Hill.

"Okay," Bubba said, "but no alcohol."

"I know plenty," Mama shouted, attracting the attention of the Clintons, who were vacationing on Hilton Head.

"Dang, y'all drive a hard bargain—eh?" Bubba was clearly a beaten man.

Wynnell was on her way back from Waxhaw so we agreed to meet at the South County Library to further strategize. Charlotte, by the way, has the best library system of any city I have set foot in. South County Library, for instance, is open seven days a week and has ample parking. For a book lover like myself a library card is the next best thing to getting a gift certificate with unlimited credit at your favorite bookstore. This library even has a muffin and coffee stand.

While I waited for Wynnell I sat outside in the courtyard, by the fountain, and chowed down a blueberry cheese Danish, which I washed down with a café latte grande with brown sugar sweetener and cinnamon sprinkles. I'd asked for full-fat milk. My friend Magdalena Yoder, a Mennonite farm woman up in Pennsylvania, lives by the motto that "fat is where it's at." Of course she's lucky and has genetics on her side. But sometimes it is nice to give the tongue the full treatment: to reacquaint it with the joy of living—so to speak. At any rate, this was my lunch, so it needed to have a "stick to the ribs" element.

Having satiated myself on just half the Danish, I shamefully shared the other half with a flock of boldly advancing sparrows. I'm not sure that the library personnel would have approved, and I may have shortened the life of some of the more cholesterol-challenged birds, but how could I say no to those cute little faces? A pushover, that's what I am. So what the heck was I doing trying to investigate a murder if I couldn't even

shoo away a bunch of "mice with wings"? Acting foolishly, that's what. Well, that seemed to be the story of
my life.

I brushed the last of the crumbs off my lap and because the fountains and street traffic rendered it too
noisy to make a phone call in the courtyard, I made
my way through the library and out to the parking lot
again. This time the "victim" of my paranoia was the
member of the Ovumkoph-Goldburg clan who was
least affected by Aunt Jerry's death.

"Hey Abby," Bob whispered, "I can't talk now, we're
with the rabbi."

"Oops. Sorry. Rob's that broken up, is he?"

"Not really. Hang on a second while I step outside."

I hummed the theme from *Exodus* to myself as I
waited. The movie, starring Paul Newman and Eva
Marie Saint, is one of my favorites, and one that I think
the younger generations of today would do well to
watch.

"Abby? I'm back."

"Bob, really—"

"It's all right. We were going over the final plans for
the funeral service. It's tomorrow afternoon, by the
way, at two P.M."

"You're kidding! I mean, obviously you're not, but
how can this be? A memorial service, maybe, but the
morgue won't release a murder victim until—"

"That's just it, Abby. Aunt Jerry wasn't murdered."

25

"S he died of natural causes."

"*What?*"

"I bet that word's been said a lot this week-end."

"*What?* You're not making a lick of sense, Bob, which is unfortunate. I called you because you are—were—the sensible one in the gang."

"The dull Yankee from Cleveland?"

"You're not dull; you're just not as eccentric as the rest of us."

"And I'm not from Cleveland either. I'm from *Toledo*."

"Oops again."

"What I'm trying to say is that you're the most normal."

"Thanks, I guess."

I took a deep breath as I chose my words carefully. "Please tell me, Normal Bob, what were Aunt Jerry's natural causes? Did she have a heart attack?"

"Bingo. It turns out that she had a very bad heart

this time. According to her hospital records she'd been coded four times in the previous year."

I gave my gray matter a second or two to process this information. "Are you saying that she almost died four times in the previous year?"

"Technically she did die, but, of course, thanks to modern science, was brought back each time. Aunt Jerry knew that she was literally a heartbeat away from meeting her Maker at any given moment. That's why she gave herself the going-away party."

"Okay. Now it all makes sense. So at some point during the party, maybe when folks are eating and therefore distracted, the Angel of Death decides to code her for a fifth time."

"Abby, you're so dramatic!"

"There, you see? I'm definitely not normal. Anyway, she must have been somewhere off by herself—like maybe the restroom. Then someone comes along, but instead of helping her, takes the ring off her finger and stashes her body in the freezer."

"Exactly. In fact, the coroner ruled that she was already dead when she was put in the freezer. The odds are that she went peacefully, and was robbed afterward. At least that's what we prefer to believe."

"Of course. But what happened to her is still a crime, right?"

"Of a major sort. If you ask me, whoever it is should be bound hand and foot with duct tape and laid across a fire ants' nest."

"Bob! How terribly Southern of you: fire ants indeed!"

"Abby, you know me. You know that I'm such a

pacifist—well, I am not a vegetarian, I will admit that, as I do love my emu and musk ox meat—but I would never wish physical harm to another human being. But Aunt Jerry was the beloved flesh of my beloved, and besides, the thought of robbing the dead is just so revolting that it makes me spitting mad."

"Well then let's spit together, Bob, and leave the fire ants alone. They can turn on one another, you know. Tell me, were the police as forthcoming about any leads? The two dingleberries I spoke with this morning were on my tail. As if I could lift a hundred pounds of deadweight—oh goodness, excuse the pun. It was inadvertent, I assure you."

"I believe you, Abby. You're not that droll; trust me on that. The police wouldn't tell us a thing, Abby. Not a dang thing. Abby, do you think that I'm being too sensitive?"

The right answer was "probably." "I'm sure you're not, sweetie. What is it?"

"Rob's mother is, of course, the prime organizer, and she's putting all the family in the front row. That includes Rob, but it doesn't include me. I'm supposed to sit in the second row, in what she calls the close friends section."

"Screw that," I said.

"Why Abigail, I knew I loved you for a reason," Bob said.

"What does Rob say about that?" I said.

"We haven't had time to talk about it," Bob said. "She's in there flapping her jaws right now. Say Abby, you wouldn't happen to know the whereabouts of this Uncle Ben character, would you?"

"Actually I do. He's at Bubba's."

"As in China Gourmet?" Bob said in amazement.

"Righto," I said. "But without the Bubba, eh?"

"What?"

"Never mind," I said. "But what about him?"

"Well, apparently the entire family is here at the temple meeting with the rabbi and cantor, everyone that is except for Uncle Ben. He's the one who supposedly looks like Rob, right?"

"Not supposedly," I said. "He's a dead ring— Oops, hush my mouth!"

"And a bit of a scoundrel from what I've been led to believe," Bob said.

"By whom?" I asked. I was honestly surprised.

"Everyone—I guess," Bob said. "Well, not the clergy. They're not into badmouthing anyone. But the rest of the family—whew! Talk about dysfunctional!"

"Is the pastor there as well?" I asked.

"You bet your bippy. And with that weird wife of his. Then there is that bobble-headed uncle with the trophy wife—"

"Except that they're as poor as temple mice and she really does love him, so despite her store-bought parts—the sum of which is marginally attractive—I'm not sure she can legitimately be called a trophy wife. Is Ben's daughter Amy there?"

"The chubby girl? Yeah, along with three friends and they're all weeping copiously, although according to Chanteuse those girls wouldn't have recognized Aunt Jerry if they saw her walking at the mall."

"We're supposed to call her Chanti now."

"Oh, are we? Well, I think that will be—"

Tamar Myers

"Careful what you say, dear. A mother is a hard person to distance oneself from, no matter how badly she behaves."

"What are you saying," he asked. "That you think she's guilty?"

"No. Simply that you don't want to put out too much negative energy to the universe because it has a way of coming back to bite you. Rob doesn't see the same woman that we do; he never will."

"Abby, how did you get to be so wise?"

"You've got to be kidding," I said. "If I was wise, my husband wouldn't be stuck on a broken-down fishing boat with a man named Booger. Anyway, it's your counsel I'm seeking now."

"Ah yes, words of wisdom from the Toledo dullard," he said.

"Stop that!" I laughed nonetheless. "Do you have wheels?"

"Yes, but they're back at the hotel."

"The *hotel*? You mean you're not staying with Rob's mom?" I asked.

"No, and neither is Rob. You should have seen the steam come out of her ears when he told her."

"Well, good for him. Okay then, I'm coming up to get you, if that's okay, and we'll talk on the way over."

"Over to where."

"Over to where C.J. was last seen alive."

Temple Beth El is located in Shalom Park off Providence Road. Shalom Park is home to two synagogues, the Jewish Community Center, the Jewish Family Service, Charlotte Hebrew Day School, and the Jewish

240

Federation of Charlotte. This is a fine example of inter-organizational cooperation, and in fact many of the events held on the campus are open to the community at large. When I got to the light I saw Bob leaning against the sign; he was gasping for air.

"I would have driven all the way to the temple to pick you up," I said.

"Girl," he rasped, "haven't you noticed that I'm getting a bit flabby?"

"Uh—no."

"Too long of a pause," he said, clearly disappointed.

"Then eat less," I said, "or else exercise more. It's just physics."

"Exactly," he said. "And that's what I just did. Now where are we going?"

I filled Bob in on everything I'd done since coming back to Charlotte—well, just about everything. There are a few things I don't even share with my husband.

"Finally I get a chance to scope out the pastor's palace—and I do mean palace. Bob, you're not going to believe this place. If you want to get rich, heal people on TV. Charlotte, by the way, is *the* place to do that kind of thing. There seems to be something in the air that's very spiritual."

"Why Abby, you didn't even sound sarcastic when you said that."

"I didn't intend to; I meant what I said. Every year thousands of people move here from all over the country. And you wouldn't believe how many of them start referring to this as 'God's country,' and they aren't being sarcastic either. Tell me, do you feel that way about Toledo?"

"Shut up and drive, Abby."

"At least I'm not on the phone, and I'm not texting," I said. "I think that people who text while driving should serve mandatory jail sentences."

"Let me guess; you don't even know how to text, do you?"

"I prefer conversation, thank you."

"Spoken like an old fart—I mean, friend. So, Abby, what are you going to do when you find your guilty party? Lasso them and dump them in the lake?"

"Hey, that's not fair. That's exactly what Tweetie had planned for me. I was just defending myself."

"I know; I'm sorry. That was uncalled for. I'm just worried that you're going to get in way over your pretty little head and then I'm not going to have anyone to pal around with."

"I'm only collecting pieces of a puzzle, Bob. So far I haven't even attempted to assemble them."

"What are some of the pieces if you don't mind me asking?" he said.

I waited to answer until the poor woman in front of me, who stopped suddenly, turned right. I could have gotten into the other lane had she been allowed to use her signal. However, anyone caught using his or her turn signals in Charlotte is immediately driven out to the city dump and executed via a firing squad. It is a very effective law, and one of the few that is consistently obeyed.

"Well," I finally said, "except for the pastor and his wife, who seem to be raking in the moola by the offering plateful, the Ovumkoph clan appears to have a cash-flow problem. Perhaps even the pastor does;

that's sort of what I'm anxious to see. It's hard to tell from just the outside of their McMansion."

"Even Aunt Jerry?"

"Her too. From what I gather, she liked to taunt her sister with her over-the-top jewelry—but it was all fake. At least most of it. Jerry was a show woman—no different really than her nephew, except that she didn't steal from anyone. But I don't have any reason to think that she was living beyond her means. That's something her bank records can prove."

"Aaron and Melissa, on the other hand—well, the Joneses left them in the dirt two facelifts ago."

Bob laughed so hard that he was rude to my upholstery. "Abby, what if I was to tell you that Chanteuse—"

"Chanti," I interrupted. "Remember?"

"What about Charade?" he said. "I like that even better."

I laughed. "Go on."

"Well, it's no secret that she's what we on the coast call shabby chic. Rob has to send her a check every month to keep the wolf from her door."

"Forgive me," I said, "but you sound a mite resentful."

"Abby, how can you be so wrong sometimes? I am *not* a mite resentful; I'm might*ily* resentful. Yes, we're doing very well with The Finer Things, but the downturn in the economy has really hurt high-end stores like ours. No offense."

"Only a minimal amount taken," I assured him.

"You see, Rob and I were hoping to hear the pitter-patter of little feet—"

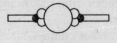

26

"You plan to get a Chihuahua?"

"Remind me why I like you so much?"

"Oh Lordy, you weren't planning to adopt me, were you? Mama wouldn't like that."

"Shut up and listen. I intend to stay home when we get our baby—well, I did. But Chanti keeps taking cruises and having these so-called *necessary* procedures to that unrecognizable minefield of a face, and my dear husband keeps forking over the dough whenever she asks. Do you think she could have a gambling problem?"

"Gambling? Chanti? I don't know; I never thought about it before."

"The reason I ask," he said, "is that the way she burns through our money is one thing. But when I was in her bedroom I saw two lottery tickets tucked into the mirror on the vanity, and—"

We happened to be passing the Fairview Avenue entrance to South Park Mall, so I pulled into the nearest parking spot. "You were in her *bedroom*?" I shrieked.

I'm sure that to some people Bob might appear as ugly as homemade sin, but he has many very attractive attributes. For instance: he is totally without guile. He removed his thick, horn-rimmed glasses and looked me straight in the eye.

"Last Mother's Day, in addition to a sizable check, Rob and I gave her a studio portrait of us in a silver frame. She said she was going to put it beside her bed so that it would be the first thing she saw in the morning, and the last thing she saw at night.

"Abby, it was my marital duty to see if indeed it was on display. What if Rob thought to check, and it wasn't there, and he got his feelings hurt— Why, I just couldn't bear that."

"Yeah, I bet you couldn't. And if he took it up with his mother and it led to a big brouhaha, it would just break your heart, wouldn't it?"

"I'm tearing up now, Abby, just thinking about it."

"Ah, there, there." I gave him a couple of pats on the back that bordered on friend abuse. "So, was the picture on display?"

"Of course not."

"Figures. Still, shame on you, Bob. You shouldn't be invading someone's privacy that way. Even a woman like Cruella De Vil deserves a modicum of respect."

"There were shackles hanging above the bed. And leather restraints tied to the bedposts."

"Get out of town and back!"

"And that's just for starters. But you're not interested in that kind of talk; you made that clear."

"Keep talking. A gal has a right to change her mind."

"Well, I lied. I made that all up, just to see how you'd react."

"And you caught me red-handed; I'm as guilty of being a hypocrite as John Edwards is of making a baby with Rielle Hunter while his poor wife was suffering from cancer."

"Shhh, Abby, someone might hear you and you'll get sued."

"Don't be silly. He admitted it. It's been in all the papers and on 20/20. Plus we're in my car, for crying out loud. You sound almost paranoid."

"You think? Gee Abby, you're a lot kinder than my shrink."

"Sorry, Bob. I didn't mean to go off on you like that. I didn't get much sleep last night and my nerves are frayed."

"You want to talk about it?" he said.

"No," I said. "We should be talking about your plans to add poopy diapers to your daily routine."

"Whoa! I take it back. Dr. Freidman may be kinder than you after all."

"Oh Bob, don't get me wrong; I said it in jest. You know that I think that there could be no better dads than you and Rob. But face it, neither of you is much at home with icky things. And your baby is going to give you ick—every single day; you can count on that."

"*Every* day?"

"Every day—just as long as he or she is healthy."

"Hmm," Bob said. "Maybe we should think about adopting an older child."

"Or perhaps a change of attitude. Being a parent

guarantees that you're not going to live an ick-free life."

Bob rolled his eyes dramatically. "Yes, Mom. Can you stop with the lecture?"

"Sorry. They too come with the territory, as you'll find out soon enough. But back to Cruella De Vil and the lottery tickets she has tucked into her mirror— Do you really believe they might mean something?"

"I checked the dates, Abby. They were purchased several years ago. They also look creased and a bit shopworn, like they've been carried around in someone's purse or wallet since then. What happens to unclaimed prizes in North Carolina anyway? Is there a statute of limitations on collecting them?"

"Are you suggesting that Chanti might have taken the tickets out of Jerry's wallet and is waiting for a more appropriate time to cash them in?"

"Well, that is possible, isn't it? Maybe Jerry confided to her sister that she'd won a big prize, but for whatever reason, was afraid to cash in the ticket. In the case of a lottery ticket, I should think that possession would be more than nine tenths of the law."

I nodded. "More like everything."

Bob loosened his seat belt so that he could get to his wallet. "I wrote the numbers down, in case anyone would be interested."

I studied the numbers. "Holy Toledo," I almost shouted. "Those, my dear, look like they could just as well be the combination to a safe."

"Or some secret spell she uses to make her broom fly."

"Stop being catty, Bob, and listen."

* * *

"Hmm," Bob said when I was through telling him about the safes at Aunt Jerry's Amherst Green house, "you might just have something there. Do you think that Chanti knew about the safes?"

"I don't know. Maybe this dog won't hunt and the lottery tickets are meaningless. But until I try those numbers, I won't be satisfied. But first, we're heading directly over to the Wicked Witch of the West's house. Those tickets are just crying out to be liberated from that cramped spot behind the mirror, and you, as a newly minted Southern gentleman, have been given the honor."

"Abby, you know that I love the South—well, parts of it, at least. I'm not particularly fond of no-see-ums and sweat getting in my eyes in April. But I absolutely adore y'all's way of life."

"Bob, do you really think that Chanti is capable of murder?"

"Aren't we all? If circumstances were exactly right?"

"No."

"Oh, come on, Abby. What if you had to choose between saving the life of a loved one—like your mama, or one of your children—and a stranger. Let's say that by pushing a lever, somewhere someone on the opposite side of the world dies, but the life of one of your loved ones is saved. What would you do?"

"Bob, stop that! That's an awful thing to contemplate, and it doesn't have anything to do with the subject at hand."

"Yes, it does. Babies on the other side of the world

die every day because we don't send them our pocket change for formula. We tell ourselves that it's not our responsibility, it's their government's, whatever, and we can put them out of our minds because they're so far away.

"But you see, it's just a matter of degree. Maybe Chanti didn't do anything to cause Jerry's heart attack, but she could have intervened. Instead she watched and waited while her sister died. It may have been a passive act, but it's still a crime, and in my book it's murder. And why did she do this? Not to save the life of someone she did love, but simply because she hated her sister so much."

"Bob, you know that if we can prove this, your partner might never speak to you again."

"I know, Abby. That's why *you're* going to prove this. I'm just along as your bodyguard."

Then, without further provocation, my tempestuous friend from Toledo burst into a deafening rendition of the theme song from the Whitney Houston movie *The Bodyguard*. Unlike Miss Houston, Bob sings bass. *Poorly.* I'm sure that he reached decibels so low that they were inaudible to the human ear, but which may have caused serious psychological damage to the elephants at Riverbanks Zoo down in Columbia. I shouted at him to stop, but to no avail, so I turned on a CD of Moroccan love songs as loud as my car player could go without blowing out on me.

I had a little practice sneaking out of Mama's house as a teenager, and as far as I know, my comings and goings were never detected. But breaking and entering was taking it to a new level.

"I have to pee," I said.

"You should have thought of that before," Bob said.

"I would have," I said, "if I'd had the urge. I didn't then; I do now."

"Well, hold it in for a few minutes. It was your idea to come here; I'm just along to protect you, remember?"

It turns out that we didn't have to really break into the house per se, because Rob had a key, which he'd left behind in the motel room. That said, we decided that entering through the front door was the least suspicious thing to do in the eyes of the neighbors. We—or I should say, Bob—even scooped up the morning paper on the way in.

"Bob, be a dear and hand me the paper."

"Abby, you said *pee*. I want to get out of here as fast as I possibly can." Nevertheless he handed me the *Charlotte Observer* still neatly folded in its protective bag.

I whopped him up the side of the head with all the news that was fit to print. "Coming here was *your* idea. You convinced me that Chanti was capable of murder—remember?"

Having spoken my piece I headed off to the downstairs water closet, which I knew to be located just off the kitchen. In my humble opinion this more recent addition is in a terrible location, being so close to food preparation. The one advantage it has is that one need not miss out on kitchen gossip just because nature compels one to use the facilities.

Of course there was no one in the kitchen at the time. There was, in fact, no one home at all, except for Bob. Chanti has a large house, and it's on a quiet street, so it can get rather spooky in there—or so I imagine. It was on that account that I didn't latch the bathroom door, but instead left it open just a crack; just enough to make me feel connected to Bob and the world beyond.

So there I was, blithely minding my own business, when I began hearing the voices. First a buzz, then loud and clearer, until they were in the kitchen, and finally just outside the bathroom door.

"This is the last time I'm asking you," Chanti said. "What are you doing in my house?"

"Rob gave me the key," Bob said.

"I don't care if Moses gave you the key. Who said you could come in?"

"Your son," Bob said.

Chanti snarled; I think she intended to laugh. "Whose house is it: his, or mine?"

"Yours," Bob said.

"Then why do you think—" Chanti said. "Never mind, you're not going to tell me, are you?"

"I love your son, Mom," Bob said. "May I call you Mom?"

"You most certainly may not!"

Way to go, Bob. Chanti was livid. What a brilliant way to deflect her. I couldn't have thought of a better way myself.

"Do you play the lottery, Chanti?"

What? That wasn't part of the plan. Not yet, for Pete's sake.

"What are you talking about?" Chanti said.

"Don't deny it. I found those tickets on your vanity mirror."

Chanti's mouth flew open and her hands formed talons; from what I could see through the crack in the door, she brought to mind an eagle swooping down to face its prey. "You were in my *room*?"

"Or," Bob said, bravely feigning indifference, if not boredom, "the numbers on the tickets may be a code for something else."

The eagle suddenly recoiled, afraid of the mouse. "Of course they're just lottery numbers. Who would be stupid enough to put a safe combination on a lottery ticket?"

"You."

"Oh crap," Chanti said. She still had her pocketbook with her—a lovely beaded number that had to cost an arm and a leg—which she set on the kitchen table. "You might as well take the ring too. It's here in my purse."

I watched, spellbound, as Bob found himself staring into the barrel of a revolver for the first time in his life.

27

Then I got angry: how dare she threaten my friend! I foolishly flung open the bathroom door to confront her, which startled Chanti so badly that she almost jumped out of her Jimmy Choos. Fortunately, I found my tongue first. "Chanti, sweetheart, you don't want to hurt us. If you do, Rob will never forgive you. Never, *ever*."

"Yeah? Well, maybe if I kill you, he won't, but him—he can be easily replaced."

"Don't be ridiculous—I mean, so sure. Your son loves this man. They've been partners for over ten years."

"Twelve years, three months, and six days," Bob sniffed.

"Shut up, dear," I said softly.

"My Robbie wasn't even gay until he met this man," Chanti said. Her eyes narrowed. "I should have shot you at the beginning; I would have grandchildren by now."

"*No*," I said, "you would have an unhappy, lonely

son who probably *wouldn't* visit you at whichever prison you were in."

"Even you would have been better than nothing," Chanti said, nodding in my direction. "A dozen years ago you might still have been young enough to be fertile. And although you're about the tiniest thing I've ever seen, you do have nice wide hips—proportionally, I mean. Birthing hips, I think they're called."

"Why, thank you," I said. "That's the nicest thing you've ever said to me."

"Abby," Bob said plaintively, "are you making nicey-nice with this woman?"

"Shut up, Robert," I said.

"Thank you," Chanti said. "I've been wanting to say that to him since the day I met him."

"Well, now is certainly your chance," I said. "There's nothing that annoying little man can do but listen—and lump it."

"Ha! And lump it!" Chanti laughed and the gun wavered.

Bob's eyes bulged and his Adam's apple bobbed several times before he managed to speak. "Abby, I can't believe you're turning on me like this! We're friends! And she—this woman—Rob's mother is—well, I can't even say it to her face. I wasn't brought up like that."

"Are you trying to say 'bitch'?" Chanti asked.

"There!" Bob said. "She said it herself. You heard her!"

"And I should kill you just for wanting to say it," Chanti hissed. "I despise you, Bonnie."

"It's Bob," Bob said through clenched teeth.

THE GLASS IS ALWAYS GREENER

I shook my head sadly, as if having arrived at some disappointing conclusion. "Chanti, I totally understand where you're coming from. But like I said, it is so not worth it to kill a schmuck like this. Disposing of the body is going to be a major hassle. I suppose we could stick him in the attic and just let him dry out for several years before discarding him in a cornfield. But let me tell you something: Bob Steuben eats a lot of weird animals, and when he decomposes he's going to smell something awful. You're not going to be able to cover his stench up with room deodorizers. No sirree Bob, Spring Bouquet and Tropical Mist are not going to cut the mustard for this bad boy."

As I wound up my little speech I gave Bob a whack across the back that sent him sprawling headlong into Chanti. The little revolver she'd been holding slipped from her hand and went skittering across the marble tiles of the kitchen floor and ricocheted off the baseboard of the dishwasher. Like a boomerang it arced back in our general direction, but this time it was my tiny hand that closed around the mother-of-pearl inlaid grip.

In the meantime Bob remained sprawled on top of his pseudo-mother-in-law, in what can best be described as an indelicate position. A stranger finding the two of them on the floor, with their limbs arranged thusly, might be forgiven for jumping to a conclusion far different from what was really going on.

"Don't let her up, Bob," I said between gasps for breath.

"What? Suddenly you're on my side?"

255

"I always was," I said, "and I still am—but now with the gun."

"Let me up, or I'll sue," Chanti rasped.

"Well, it's time to call in the posse," I said. "Chanti, any last words?"

"Huh?"

"Bob and I have both known you for a long time. Therefore I'm giving you a chance to tell us something about how you felt about Jerry and her death, before the police get here. We may not be a sympathetic audience, but we are familiar, and who knows, maybe we will understand after all."

She wasted no time. "Do you have a sister, Abby?"

"No, but I have a brother who is aptly named Toy."

She didn't seem to really care about my sibling issues.

"Jerry was an extrovert so she got everything," she said. "Dance lessons, piano lessons, riding lessons—hell, she even got a pony for her eighth birthday. Of course we had to keep it out at a stable somewhere in Union County, but it still counts. Did I mention that she got all the new clothes? Everything she wanted, that girl got.

"Then Ben was born, and he got everything. But a girl like me, nobody notices."

"I bet your mother did," I said, "even if she had 'birthing hips.'"

"Go ahead, make fun of me, if you want. But you haven't lived my life. You haven't had the only man you'll ever love stolen out from underneath you—then crushed by a man-eating carnivore—and spit out to die."

"Your mixed metaphor intrigues me," I said. "How did she crush him?"

"Alfred was a sensitive man—but an ambitious man. He would have gone very far in life. He was going to be a nuclear physicist. In high school he was voted most likely to win the Nobel Prize."

"You were high school sweethearts?" I said.

"When Alfred was just finishing up his doctoral degree, and we were finally talking wedding dates, in Jerry sweeps like a bird of prey and carries him off in her talons."

"What had she been doing in the meantime?"

"Working as a shopgirl as she ate up men and shit out the parts she couldn't digest—just like an owl."

"Pardon your French," said Bob.

Chanti glared up at him. "It isn't French. It's an old, respected Anglo-Saxon word."

"Not among the cozy set," I said. "Now get on with your pathetic tale."

"*Pathetic*? We'd been soul mates for a dozen years, and then along came Jerry, and her only motive was to *steal* him away from me. That's all she wanted. The moment she knew she had him in her clutches—her talons—she dumped him."

"But wasn't it your fault that you didn't take him back?" I said.

"I never saw Alfred alive again. That very same night he hung himself in the physics lab after hours. The janitor found him at four in the morning." Chanti began to sob. "When I confronted Jerry, all she did was shrug," she eventually managed to say.

In fact, Chanti was producing such a copious

amount of tears and phlegm that Bob was forced to let her off her back, otherwise the scorned yet scornful woman was in danger of expiring there in her own kitchen.

Was it the right call? Who knows? Would I do it again the same the way, knowing what I do now? Probably not. Greg often says that although I'm a little thing, I'm a big softy, and Bob—well, he may as well be made out of whipped cream. Together we're hopeless.

We extracted a sacred oath out of Chanti, on beloved Alfred's grave, that she would turn herself in to the police immediately following Jerry's interment at Charlotte Hebrew Cemetery. In the meantime she would conduct herself as properly befits a grieving sister, *and* allow Robert Steuben to sit with his partner in the section reserved for family.

Rob was thrilled at his mother's improved attitude and patted her arm throughout the service. Frankly, it made me sick to see him fawning all over her when she was the cause for us being there in the first place. Had there been an unscripted spot in the service, one where just anyone could get up and eulogize, mother and son would have been in for a rude surprise.

As soon as the last *"ah-mein"* was sounded, the family was ushered out to a caravan of cars for the trip to the cemetery. Mine was the second row to be released by the ushers, and even though I did my best to maneuver my way up a side aisle through a sea of elbows and pocketbooks, by the time I got outside, the hearse and accompanying caravan were no longer to be seen.

Figuring that there was no point in trying to fight my way out of the parking lot, I ducked in to use the restroom before driving out to the cemetery on my own. When I got there, the first person I saw was Bob. He was standing just inside the tall wrought-iron gates, and when he recognized my car he waved his suit jacket as if it was a matador's cape. I pulled over into the nearest available spot, which happened to be in the shade of an ancient willow oak. Bob ran to catch up.

"Abby," he panted. "We've got big trouble."

28

"You lost her, didn't you?"

"No! Of course not! Why would you say that?"

"Then where is she?"

"With the rest of the family—over by the gravesite."

"Then I don't get it. What's the problem?"

"The problem is— Abby, I need to sit down. May I get in?"

"By all means." I threw my handbag in the backseat. "Ow!"

"Mama?" I shrieked. Trust me, being surprised from behind by another person is even worse when it happens in a cemetery.

"That's my name, dear; just don't wear it out. Abby, that thing hurt like the dickens!"

"I'm sorry, Mama—no, I'm not." I'd unbuckled my seat belt and was on my knees confronting the maxime. She wasn't bleeding that I could see. "Did I hit you in the eye?"

"No, you hit my shoulder, thank goodness. But you could have hit my eye."

"Well, I'm glad I hit your shoulder. How long have you been sitting there?"

"Too long; I thought that service would never be over."

"How did you get here—to the temple, I mean?"

"Well, if you must know, after you so rudely ducked out on our lunch, I decided to date Ben; he drove me. But my goodness, look around, will you? Apparently Rob's aunt was a popular woman."

"At least she knew a lot of people," I said. I felt my lungs compress as the air was sucked out of them. "What do you *mean* that you've decided to date him? You can't, Mama. He's your own age and entirely normal; it would be unseemly. What kind of Charleston eccentric dates a normal man?"

"Oh, Abby, I've never been happier."

"Does Ben know that you're dating him?"

"He will soon enough, dear," she trilled.

"Oy vey," Bob said. "Abby, I can see it now; you and I will be in-laws."

"So anyway," Mama said, "since this is my car, I thought we'd carpool."

"Thanks for the heads-up, Mama," I said, still grousing. "But what gives? Why aren't you sticking with the new love of your life? Every funeral has its widow snatchers—you know, folks who prey on the bereaved. And handsome brothers fall into that category. Some lithe young thing with fake blond hair is liable to put the moves on Ben right there at the gravesite; some women aren't above that, and you know it."

"Don't answer, Mozella," Bob said. "It's my turn to talk first."

"That's right, Mama. We have a non-escaped killer on our hands."

"Don't be so jocular, Abby," Bob snapped.

"I'm not," I said, quite taken aback by his outburst. "I'm merely cynical. I get like this every time a gun gets pulled on me."

Mama, bless her heart, didn't say a word. She's been through the wringer with me enough times to know that as long as I'm still standing (or even sitting upright, and flapping my gums), she has all she needs to know for the time being.

"In that case," Bob said, "be prepared to get even more cynical. Do you hear a police siren right now?"

"Yes. But I must say it's awfully early in the schedule of events for that. Chanti was going to wait until it was all over, but half the entourage has yet to arrive."

"That's because it's Ben who the police are taking away."

"Say what?"

"The four siblings rode over in the same limo—no spouses—and on the way over Chanti fed them some version of the story, and then—Abby, you're going to love this—Ben, being the loving brother that he is, offered to take the rap for her."

"What the heck?"

"Yeah, isn't that a bummer? But it gets better; he did so because he has prostate cancer and is afraid of chemo, and figures that sooner rather than later, the state isn't going to want to keep a dying old man incarcerated just because he didn't take measures to prolong his sister's life."

"And she told you this?"

"As soon as we got there, she dragged me away from Rob and told me the real deal. She also said that if I ever as much as hint to Rob that she had anything to do with her sister's untimely death, she will string me up by my cojones, after which she will tell Rob how I assaulted her in her kitchen. Abby, did you know that she has a security camera in every room, and that she can edit the tapes?"

"No, and I don't believe her."

I felt Mama's soft hand on my shoulder. "Whatever this is about," she said, "I think you should both sleep on it before deciding your next course of action."

One of the things that has really disappointed me in life is the discovery that what little wisdom I've managed to accumulate for the years has been of interest to no one. Not once has anyone positioned himself or herself at my feet and begged for a pearl of wisdom. What's more, the pearls that I've thrown at my children in passing (they were running to avoid them) rolled off them like water off the back of an Alaskan duck.

Maybe things will change, given more time. I say this because I am just now realizing that Mama may possess a smidgen of wisdom. A pinch of perspective. At the very least, she is so much smarter now than she was when I was a teenager. If Mama advised waiting, then that's what I would do.

"Mama's right," I heard myself say. "We'll sleep on it for now."

"But Abby," Bob protested, "the woman's demonic. You saw how she behaved when she had the gun. We have to find some way to tell Rob!"

"For now is not forever," Mama said quietly.

"Has anyone seen C.J.?" I asked.

Mama, Bob, and Wynnell all shook their heads in the negative. It had been a strange supper at the Olive Garden in Pineville to say the least. Bob was furious at Rob for agreeing to stay at his mom's overnight, and he was outraged that Chanti should have asked. His anger, of course, spilled over onto Mama and me, but being the polite sort, he expressed it by remaining mum.

"You know C.J.," Wynnell said, with the wave of a breadstick. "She's young and impetuous. By now she could be halfway to China."

C.J. has always been like a second daughter to Mama. In fact, she is her ex-daughter-in-*law*.

"Sort of like you dashing off to Japan," Mama said. "Right, dear?"

Wynnell, who is guilty of having done just that, had the decency to blush. "Touché, Mozella. Have you tried calling Toy?"

"You bet I did," Mama said, as she snapped a breadstick in two. "Some little tart named Tiffany had the temerity to answer his cell phone."

"Alliteration is frowned on these days, Mama," I said.

Mama frowned. "Echo schmeko," she said, in response to a raised red pen somewhere, for she was practically on the verge of swearing. "I'm not done talking. The ink is barely dry on Toy's divorce papers, and he's already shacking up with a bimbette who had the nerve to then ask me who I was. Can y'all believe that?"

"We can't," we chorused.

Before anyone could gain the floor again, Wynnell snapped her breadstick, then *another*, and then waved a third one pointedly at each of us. "So, as I was about to say," she said, enunciating each word as if she was teaching a class of immigrants (perhaps from countries where non-Indo-European languages were spoken), "being in Waxhaw yesterday has reminded me where my priorities lie."

"They lie with your husband, Ed," Mama said. I'd never heard her speak that sharply—at least not in a public place.

"And that's where you should lie too," Bob said.

It was clear just by the various contortions of her forehead muscles that Wynnell sorely regretted giving up her unibrow. "What are you two driving at?"

"The same thing that you are, dear," I said. "You're homesick for the Charlotte region. And when you were wandering around all those lovely antiques shops in Waxhaw, you began to envision a life there for yourself."

"So what if I have?"

"But everyone knows that your husband Ed loves fishing and that he's becoming a little—uh—set in his ways. To leave him now would be cruel."

Wynnell aggressively poked the air in front of Mama with the last remaining whole stick. "It's not definitive that he has Alzheimer's," she said. "All his doctor will commit to is that he is slowing down some. But I ask you, aren't we all getting slower?"

"Still, you would divorce him *this* late in the game? Honestly, Wynnell, I thought you were better than this."

"Why look who's talking, Mozella! First of all, I'm not divorcing him; he's free to come along if he wishes. And secondly, I wouldn't be throwing stones if I were you, given that you live in a palace of the finest, most fragile crystal ever created."

"You wouldn't dare," Mama squawked, and actually threw both halves of her breadstick in my friend's triumphant, and until recently hirsute, face.

Of course, as far as I was concerned it was all over now except for plucking the chicken. "By the way," I said to Wynnell, "first you might try Sun City just over the border in Lancaster County, South Carolina. I've been told that they have every kind of activity imaginable, so I bet that they have fishing—or at least fishing trips. With all that stimulation, you might find that Ed won't decline that fast.

"Now on to you, Mama."

"What?"

"If you added the word *ever* you'd have the most annoying word in the English language. I heard it on NPR—but I forget *their* source. Anyway, Mama, what's your glass castle yet again this time?"

She took a deep breath. "Well, I might as well get this out now. And just so you know, even Toy isn't privy to this information."

29

S pit it out, Mama. The longer you try to drag it out, the harder it will get."

"I'm not a widder woman," she said, cringing.

"Please, Mama," I begged, "we're being serious here."

"She is serious," Wynnell said. "Go on, Mozella, tell her the rest."

"When your father died—well, he didn't die as quickly as you thought he did. After that gull hit him and he crashed the speedboat, how long do you reckon it was until I buried your daddy?"

"A couple of days, Mama. I was eleven years old. I remember; you can't tell me different."

"You remember a private prayer service that we had at the church—just family—but that's all, because by then your daddy had been airlifted up to Duke. They were working on a new procedure—something that might reverse brain damage in people thought to be brain dead, who were being kept alive only by ma-

267

chines. You see, I was desperate, and I couldn't pull the plug."

I began to cry. Silently. All these years later I didn't even want to know how long Daddy may have lived after the accident. Because that wasn't really *my* daddy hooked up to the machine, even if it wasn't my right, or Mama's right, to pull the plug.

"What is your point, Mama?"

"My point is that I couldn't afford any of this. I was going to lose the house, and then most probably you kids, so when a lawyer suggested that maybe I divorce your daddy and let the state take over payments, I— Abby, I want you to know that I really struggled with that decision. So anyway, I guess then that my point really is that by the time your daddy passed on his own, I was a divorced woman. Technically, I guess, I have no right to call myself a widow woman."

I jumped out of my chair and hugged Mama so tight that she started to choke. Then I patted her back and made her take a couple of sips of her sweet tea.

"Wynnell Crawford," I said, measuring each word as carefully as I would the ingredients of a sponge cake, "that was so unfair. I didn't need to hear that, and Mama certainly didn't need to tell me that."

My intent was to stare across the table at Wynnell and make her feel so guilty that she would cry as well. But Wynnell is essentially a good woman, with a heart as big as the Piedmont, and she was already crying. The problem with my oldest friend is that both her conscience and her common sense buttons are located slightly to the right, and behind, her impulse button. If she were a car she would be recalled.

"Mo-z-ella, Ab-b-by," she blubbered, "I don't know what I was thinking. I am so sorry. So, so sorry! Can you ever forgive me?"

"We'll try," I said. "Won't we, Mama?" I answered first, partly because I didn't want Mama to jump in with an immediate pardon. Wynnell might be feeling the deepest remorse possible, but she still needed to swing in the breeze for a few minutes. *Needed*, not deserved.

"Sun City does sound like a good fit for Ed," Bob said.

I smiled at him gratefully. "Yes, I think we should all take a look at it on our way home."

There still remained the not-so-small problem of Calamity Jane. As a means of penance I took Wynnell with me on my after-dinner hunch. Unlike on the coast, there are evenings in the Piedmont, even in August, where the temperatures become almost bearable after dark. This was one of those occasions.

So as not to be too obtrusive, we parked in the public spaces adjacent to Amherst Green's mail kiosk and around the block from the late Aunt Jerry's townhouse. The shrill sound of cicadas screaming in the woods behind the development seemed to add a layer of protection to our adventure. If we could barely hear each other talk, then surely nobody else could.

"How are we going to get in?" Wynnell all but shouted. "Don't tell me you have a key."

"No, no key. We're going around to the back. The garden gate is unlocked. And so is the bedroom window. I made sure of that."

She grinned. "You deserve your gumshoes. Abby, you've gotten to be as good as your husband at this."

"What?"

"Never mind, I'll tell you later."

"Okay." The truth is I'd heard just fine. It was also true that I was developing quite a reputation for solving mysteries, which was a good thing, given that an uncanny amount had come my way over the past few years. At any rate, everyone likes a compliment, right?

Wynnell was likewise impressed to see the beautiful palm garden, but she wasn't surprised. She had a cousin over in Five Knolls who was also into palms, and had spotted several on her trip to Waxhaw.

"Abby," she said, after we'd let ourselves through the window, "I'm surprised that this is as tasteful as it is. I thought that maybe she slept in a giant pink clamshell supported by a quartet of blackamoors."

"Yeah, well, I guess you had to have met her. Jerry Ovumkoph was—uh—"

"Tasteful?"

"Yes. I'm telling you, Wynnell, I only knew her for five minutes, but it's like she's been burned in my brain."

"Abby, you're sort of like that—to me, at least. When I walk into a crowded room and you're there, somehow I immediately seem to find you."

"Aw shucks, Wynnell. That's the nicest thing you've ever said to me."

"Does the same thing happen to you?"

"Absolutely," I said. It was the truth too, albeit for different reasons.

"Abby, what is that sound?" Wynnell said.

"I hope and pray it's my hunch," I said.

"Abby, you know I have a hard time with Apparition Americans. I'm not like you or C.J. in that regard."

"They won't hurt you," I said. "Not usually. Besides, if we find my hunch in time she'll remain a very large, pleasantly annoying American—the apparition part will just have to wait."

"You think that C.J.'s in here someplace?"

"That's what I'm betting on: that she never left the house. Now all we need to do is be quiet and listen."

"There!" Wynnell whispered loudly. "I hear it again. Do you think that's Morse code?"

"Whatever it is," I said, "it's coming from upstairs. Let's go!"

"Shouldn't we call 911 first?" Wynnell said.

"No. If it's squirrels—"

"Yeah," she said, agreeing from experience. "Then they'll think that we're squirrelly."

We weren't totally stupid, however. Wynnell carried a small fire extinguisher that she found sitting on the counter next to the oven in the kitchen, and I carried a croquette mallet from the hall closet. If need be, together we would club and smother whatever type of American awaited us upstairs, and if on the odd chance it turned out to be of the apparition variety, then we were psyched to run out the front door screaming.

Trust me; screaming really is just about all that one can do with a ghost. The carrying on, by the way, is merely for his or her ego. Apparition Americans can be quite flattered by excessive attention, and thereby rendered malleable. It is the ignored spirits that tend to be destructive and end up throwing things. But no ghost, *ever*, is capable of doing physical harm to a human being.

At the top of stairs was a loft area that had been outfitted with a pair of antique couches. Both were upholstered in orange cut velvet with about a million puffs and buttons—really rather splendid if you got over the gauche factor. On the largest wall hung a large framed copy of the oil painting by Lord Frederic Leighton titled *Flaming Jane*, which depicts a reclining woman dressed in a flowing orange gown. The only other piece of furniture in the loft was a child's rocking chair which appeared to date from Edwardian times.

From the loft one needed to cross a bridge to reach the bedrooms, all of which were on the left front side of the house. But on the right, just past the bridge, was a door that presumably led to storage—perhaps even an attic. It was from there that the strange noises seemed to be coming.

"Wynnell," I whispered, "you're older than me, right?"

"What does that have to do with anything," she snapped.

"Just that you've lived a longer, fuller life. Therefore, you wouldn't mind opening that door, would you?"

"In your dreams," she said, and gave me a push.

One can either spend a night quivering under the covers, or waste no time in leaning over the bed to face the monster beneath. Sometimes it's not a matter of choice. When Wynnell pushed me, I landed against the door with a thud. A second later whatever lay beyond responded with a multitude of thumps and groans. To be honest, I was a mite miffed that Wynnell had actually laid hands on me, and since I would never touch her in return, I decided to channel that anger to help me slay the dragon.

"Come on out!" I roared, as I flung open what was indeed an attic door. (And yes, this mouse *can* roar—well, sort of.)

"It's C.J.!" Wynnell actually did roar. "Look at her. She's all bound up!"

I looked. If it wasn't for the top of the big galoot's shaggy head of dishwater blond hair, and her enormous hands and feet, I wouldn't have recognized her, so thoroughly was she wrapped in duct tape.

"Call 911," I said, and leaped forward to begin the rescue process. I may not be a Boy Scout or a Saint Bernard, but I am a well-prepared antiques dealer, which means that I carry a Leatherman around in my purse wherever I go. This handy-dandy tool can do just about anything, except write good reviews in *Kirkus*.

"Hold it right there!" a deep voice said.

I didn't have to turn my head as much as a millimeter to identify the speaker. "Go ahead and do your worst, Bob."

30

ob! Bob! Bob!" Wynnell seemed to be barking her alarm.

"You can kill us, dear," I said, feeling remarkably calm, "and then go your merry way. It might be days before we're found. But it might be hours. Who knows, depending on which buttons Wynnell pressed on her phone, it might be minutes."

"Abby, shut up, will you?" The order came from Wynnell, who'd found her voice; not from the criminal Bob.

"I'm not done speaking. If this was a book—"

"Which it's not; so you're going to piss him off. Then we're going to end up like C.J.—big balls of duct tape. Except that you'll be a little ball."

"Both of you just shut up," Bob boomed. "You're giving me a headache."

"Remind me to feel sorry for you," I said. "How do you think C.J. feels right now? You can do what you like to me, Robert Steuben, but I'm going to cut her loose."

Without as much as throwing a single glance to the lout from Toledo, I pulled out my trusty Leatherman tool and began to liberate my ex-sister-in-law with the questionable DNA.

"Stop that! I'm warning you!"

That's when I did turn to him. My eyes must have been flashing with anger, because I remember him recoiling.

"Shame on you, Robert. Shame, shame, shame! I am one of your very best friends—no, I will go so far as to say that next to Rob I *am* your very best friend. You can't hurt me. You are a man of integrity. Whatever you did here, you did because you temporarily lost your way; it wasn't because you're an evil man."

"Yes, he is," Wynnell said. "He's a bad, bad, man."

"Chanteuse is the bad, bad woman," Bob said, his voicing cracking like an adolescent's. "I saw her take the ring off Aunt Jerry's finger. God forgive me," he sobbed. "I don't know how I managed to get caught up in this."

"Help me get C.J. unbound," I said. "Then we'll talk."

"Abby, don't listen to a word he says," Wynnell yelled. "Run for your life!"

I bent my head so that the microphone taped to my chest picked up every word clearly. "Did you get everything you needed?" I asked.

I nestled back against my husband's strong, tanned arms, and took pleasure in the gentle rocking of the boat. Across our laps sprawled fifteen pounds of happily purring pussycat. Dmitri loves being aboard *The*

Charming Abby because it means that there will eventually be fresh fish on the menu—even for him. These two very important men in my life and I were on our way to the Florida Keys. The trip would last however long it took; there were no rules *except* that at no time were either Mama or Booger allowed across the gangplank.

"Hon," my beloved said. "Have you gotten over the shock yet?"

"Not really. I can be doing the most mundane thing—like sifting Dmitri's litter box—and then poof! Suddenly it hits me."

"I never would have pegged that boy for a criminal," Greg said.

"That's because he's not!"

Greg sat up in our bunk, an act which made Dmitri jump off and trot away. "Darling, you can't be defending him. Not after he stuck the old lady's body in the deep freeze."

"But she was already dead by then. And he wasn't thinking, Greg. Bob has always had a problem with jealousy. That's why he followed Rob up to Charlotte, after saying that he didn't want to go along. And even though he was invited to the party. Anyway, he showed up just as Chanti was robbing the dead, so he thought—and yes, it was wrongheaded thinking—but he thought that he could blackmail her into accepting him fully into the family."

"And she was caught with her pants down, so what could she say—"

"But you can never blackmail someone into feeling a certain way," I said.

It had been Chanti who followed Aaron, C.J., and me to Jerry's house, and when C.J. got too close to discovering the safes—which Chanti thought contained real jewels—Chanti forced her into the attic at gunpoint, and then tied her up. Bob really hadn't known about that until much later. But the scene in Chanti's kitchen—that was all a put-on. Bob and Chanti were in it together as thick as thieves. Small wonder, that; they *were* thieves. There really was no excusing Bob that, but how much pain did Rob need in his life? And if Chanti's dying brother, Ben, thought he was doing something noble for his sister, then who was I to intervene? Besides, if Ben went to jail, it might stop Mama from marrying him, and Mama *was* my business.

"Oh Greg," I said. "I'm so confused."

"You need a beer, hon," Greg said.

"No, I don't," I said. "I think I need to talk to Mama's priest."

"Well, I need a beer," Greg said. "Be a doll, babe, and make a run to the galley and bring me back a cold one."

"Cold what, dear?"

His sapphire blue eyes widened in surprise. "A beer, of course."

"But darling, you are just as capable of carrying a can of beer as I am."

"Touché," he said, and hopped out of bed to fetch his own refreshment. But when he returned he was carrying a second beer, one intended for me.

I drank the proffered libation before calling Mama's clergyman. But rest assured, the appointment I made

Tamar Myers

to talk with him was for *after* Greg, Dmitri, and I returned from the Florida Keys.

I received two postcards today from loved ones that have put me in a reflective mood. It's funny that the postcards should arrive at the same time, because they came from such faraway, unrelated places.

One postcard was from Mama. She's finally found her calling, albeit somewhat late in life. It's a long story, but the gist of it is that she was discovered by the talent director of one of the many cruise ships that dock in Charleston harbor. He was looking for a "mature" torch singer. He must have been having a particularly good day when he hired Mama because she fit exactly one third of his requirements.

Anyway, she styles herself the Lounge Lizardess and somehow manages to sing Doris Day songs with the achy-breaky undertones of Hank Williams. It's a very small ship that now pretty much restricts its run to the rough seas between Punta Gorda, the southernmost city in the world, and the northern ice shield of Antarctica. Mama claims to never have been happier; in fact, she's so happy that she's thrown out all her crinolines and full circle skirts. When Greg asked me how I felt about this, I said, "To each his own and *que sera sera*."

The other postcard was from the Rob-Bobs, who are taking their second honeymoon in Europe. The card was mailed from Andorra, a tiny country tucked up in the Pyrenees Mountains between France and Spain. Rob had pleaded guilty to stashing Aunt Jerry in the freezer—his motive was greed—but since it was his first offense, and the court had yet to see anyone quite

278

so contrite—or white—as the immigrant from Toledo, he was given a five-year sentence, which was then instantly commuted.

At any rate, the Rob-Bobs had swung by Andorra specifically to see C.J. and her Andorran husband, Guillermo Chevron. C.J. was on the Internet searching for angora sweaters (frankly this seems a little macabre to me, given her supposed DNA). Instead she came across a site advertising a "sweaty Andorran," and not being one who reads postings carefully, C.J. contacted the listing, and the next thing you know we were all welcoming this handsome brute of a man—six feet four with Mario Lopez dimples and abs—into the family.

Oh, and did we know, the Rob-Bobs asked, that C.J. and Guillermo were going to have a kid come March?

What?

I dashed up the walk and burst into the house. "Greg," I shouted. "Pack your packs! We're going to Andorra!"

Welcome to the
Den of Antiquity

*Home to rare antiques, priceless artwork—
and murder!*

Celebrated author Tamar Myers invites you to enjoy
her hilarious mystery series featuring Charleston's
favorite shopkeeper-turned-detective,
Abigail Timberlake.

"A very funny mystery series ... a hilarious
heroine."

Charleston Post & Courier

"Professionally plotted and developed, and fun
to read."

San Francisco Valley Times

"Rollicking!"

The Washington Post

"Who do you read after Sue Grafton or Margaret
Maron or Patricia Cornwell? ... Tamar Myers!"
Greensboro News & Record

Step into the world of Tamar Myers, and see what
mysteries the Den of Antiquity has in
store for you ...

Larceny and Old Lace
For whom the bell pull tolls . . .

As owner of the Den of Antiquity, recently divorced (but *never* bitter!) Abigail Timberlake is accustomed to delving into the past, searching for lost treasures, and navigating the cutthroat world of rival dealers at flea markets and auctions. Still, she never thought she'd be putting her expertise in mayhem and detection to other use—until a crotchety "junque" dealer, Abby's aunt Eulonia Wiggins, was found murdered!

Although Abigail is puzzled by the instrument of death—an exquisite antique bell pull that Aunt Eulonia *never* would have had the taste to acquire—she's willing to let the authorities find the culprit. But now, Auntie's prized lace collection is missing, and somebody's threatened Abby's most priceless possession: her son, Charlie. It's up to Abby to put the murderer "on the block."

Gilt by Association
A closetful of corpse . . .

Abigail Timberlake parlayed her savvy about exquisite old things into a thriving antiques enterprise: the Den of Antiquity. Now she's a force to be reckoned with in Charlotte's close-knit world of mavens and eccentrics. But a superb, gilt-edged eighteenth-century French armoire she purchased for a song at an estate auction has just arrived along with something she didn't pay for: a dead body.

Suddenly her shop is a crime scene—and closed to the public during the busiest shopping season of the year—so Abigail is determined to speed the lumbering police investigation along. But amateur sleuthing is leading the feisty antiques expert into a murderous mess of dysfunctional family secrets. And the next cadaver found stuffed into fine old furniture could wind up being Abigail's own.

The Ming and I

Rattling old family skeletons . . .

North Carolina native Abigail Timberlake is quick to dismiss the seller of a hideous old vase—until the poor lady
comes hurtling back through the shop window minutes
later, the victim of a fatal hit-and-run. Tall, dark, and
handsome homicide investigator Greg Washburn—
who just happens to be Abby's boyfriend—is frustrated
by conflicting accounts from eyewitnesses. And he's just
short of furious when he learns that the vase was a valuable Ming, and Abby let it vanish from the crime scene.
Abby decides she had better find out for herself what
happened to the treasure—and to the lady who was dying to get rid of it.

As it turns out, the victim had a lineage that would make
a Daughter of the Confederacy green with envy, and her
connection with the historic old Roselawn Plantation
makes that a good place to start sleuthing. Thanks to her
own mama's impeccable Southern credentials, Abby is
granted an appointment with the board members—but
no one gives her the right to snoop. And digging into the
long-festering secrets of a proud family of the Old South
turns out to be a breach of good manners that could
land Abby six feet under in the family plot.

So Faux, So Good
Every shroud has a silver lining . . .

Abigail Timberlake has never been happier. She is about to marry the man of her dreams AND has just outbid all other Charlotte antiques dealers for an exquisite English tea service. But an early wedding present rains on Abby's parade. The one-of-a-kind tea service Abby paid big bucks for has a twin. A frazzled Abby finds more trouble on her doorstep—literally—when a local auctioneer mysteriously collapses outside her shop and a press clipping of her engagement announcement turns up in the wallet of a dead man. (Obviously she won't be getting a wedding present from him.)

Tracing the deceased to a small town in the Pennsylvania Dutch country, Abby heads above the Mason-Dixon Line to search for clues. Accompanied by a trio of eccentric dealers and her beloved but stressed-out cat, she longs for her Southern homeland as she confronts a menagerie of dubious characters. Digging for answers, Abby realizes that she might just be digging her own grave in—horrors!—Yankeeland.

Baroque and Desperate
Good help is hard to keep—alive . . .

Unflappable and resourceful, Abigail Timberlake relies on her knowledge and savvy to authenticate the facts from the fakes when it comes to either curios *or* people. Her expertise makes Abby invaluable to exceptionally handsome Tradd Maxwell Burton, wealthy scion of the renowned Latham family. He needs her to determine the most priceless item in the Latham mansion. A treasure hunt in an antique-filled manor? All Abby can say is "Let the games begin!"

But when Abby, accompanied by her best friend C.J., arrives at the estate she receives a less than warm welcome from the Latham clan. Trying to fulfill Tradd's request, Abby finds she could cut the household tension with a knife. Only someone has beaten her to it by stabbing a maid to death with an ancient kris. Suddenly all eyes are on C.J., whose fingerprints just happen to be all over the murder weapon. Now Abby must use her knack for detecting forgeries to expose the fake alibi of the genuine killer.

Estate of Mind

A faux van Gogh that's to die for . . .

When Abigail Timberlake makes a bid of $150.99 on a truly awful copy of van Gogh's *Starry Night*, she's just trying to support the church auction. Hopefully she'll make her money back on the beautiful gold antique frame. Little does she expect she's bought herself a fortune . . . and a ton of trouble.

Hidden behind the faux van Gogh canvas is a multimillion-dollar lost art treasure. Suddenly she's a popular lady in her old hometown, and her first visit is from Gilbert Sweeny, her schoolyard sweetie who claims the family's painting was donated by mistake. But social calls quickly turn from nice to nasty as it's revealed that the mysterious masterpiece conceals a dark and deadly past and some modern-day misconduct that threatens to rock the Rock Hill social structure to its core. Someone apparently thinks the art is worth killing for, and Abby knows she better get to the bottom of the secret scandal and multiple murders before she ends up buried six feet under a starry night.

A Penny Urned

Pickled, then potted . . .

All that remains of Lula Mae Wiggins—who drowned in a bathtub of cheap champagne on New Year's Eve—now sits in an alleged Etruscan urn in Savannah, Georgia. Farther north, in Charleston, South Carolina, Abigail Timberlake is astonished to learn that she is the sole inheritor of the Wiggins estate. Late Aunt Lula was, after all, as distant a relative as kin can get.

Arriving in Savannah, Abby makes a couple of startling discoveries. First, that Lula Mae's final resting place is more American cheap than Italian antique. And second, that there was a very valuable 1793 one-cent piece taped to the inside lid. Perhaps a coin collection worth millions is hidden among the deceased's worldly possessions—making Lula's passing more suspicious than originally surmised. With the strange appearance of a voodoo priestess coupled with the disturbing disappearance of a loved one—and with nasty family skeletons tumbling from the trees like acorns—Abby needs to find her penny auntie's killer or she'll be up to her ashes in serious trouble.

Nightmare in Shining Armor
The corpse is in the mail . . .

Abigail Timberlake's Halloween costume party is a roaring success—until an unexpected fire sends the panicked guests fleeing from Abby's emporium. One exiting reveler she is only too happy to see the back of is Tweetie "Little Bo Peep" Timberlake—unfaithful wife of Abby's faithless ex, Buford. But not long after the fire is brought under control, the former Mrs. T discovers an unfamiliar suit of armor in her house. And stuffed inside is the heavily siliconed, no-longer-living body of the current Mrs. T.

Certainly some enraged collector of medieval chain mail has sent Abby this deadly delivery. But diving into their eccentric ranks could prove a lethal proposition for the plucky antiques dealer turned amateur sleuth. And even a metal suit may not be enough to protect Abby from the vicious and vindictive attention of a crazed killer.

Splendor in the Glass
Murder is a glass act . . .

Antiques dealer Abby Timberlake is thrilled when *the* Ms. Amelia Shadbark—doyenne of Charleston society—invites her to broker a pricey collection of Lalique glass sculpture. These treasures will certainly boost business at the Den of Antiquity, and maybe hoist Abby into the upper crust—which would please her class-conscious mom, Mozella, to no end. Alas, Abby's fragile dream is soon shattered when Mrs. Shadbark meets a foul, untimely end. And as the last known visitor to the victim's palatial abode, Abby's being pegged by the local law as suspect Numero Uno.

Of course, there are other possible killers—including several dysfunctional offspring and a handyman who may have been doing more for the late Mrs. S than fixing her leaky faucets. But Abby's the one who'll have to piece the shards of this deadly puzzle together—or else face a fate far worse than a mere seven years of bad luck!

Tiles and Tribulations
Supernatural born killer . . .

Abigail Timberlake would rather be anywhere else on a muggy Charleston summer evening—even putting in extra hours at her antiques shop—than at a séance. But her best friend, "Calamity Jane," thinks a spirit—or "Apparition American," as ectoplasmically correct Abby puts it—lurks in the eighteenth-century Georgian mansion, complete with priceless, seventeenth-century Portuguese kitchen tiles, that C.J. just bought as a fixer-upper. Luckily, Abby's mama located a psychic in the yellow pages—a certain Madame Woo-Woo—and, together with a motley group of feisty retirees known as the "Heavenly Hustlers," they all get down to give an unwanted spook the heave-ho.

But, for all her extrasensory abilities, the Madame didn't foresee that she, herself, would be forced over to the other side prematurely. Suddenly Abby fears there's more than a specter haunting C.J. And they'd better exorcise a flesh-and-blood killer fast before the recently departed Woo-Woo gets company.

Statue of Limitations
Death by David . . .

Abigail Timberlake, petite but feisty proprietor of Charleston's Den of Antiquity antiques shop, stopped speaking to best friend and temporary decorating partner Wynnell Crawford a month ago—after questioning her choice of a cheap, three-foot-high replica of Michelangelo's *David* to adorn the garden of a local bed-and-breakfast. But now Wynnell has broken the silence with one phone call . . . *from prison!*

It seems the B and B owner has been fatally beaten—allegedly by the same tacky statue—and Wynnell's been fingered by the cops for the bashing. But Abby suspects there's more to this well-sculpted slaying than initially meets the eye, and she wants to take a closer look at the not-so-bereaved widower and the two very odd couples presently guesting at the hostelry. Because if bad taste was a capital crime, Wynnell would be guilty as sin—but she's certainly no killer!

Monet Talks

Birds of a feather die together . . .

Abigail Timberlake is thrilled to purchase an elaborate Victorian birdcage that is a miniature replica of the Taj Mahal. However she's less excited by the cage's surprise occupant—a loud, talkative myna bird named Monet. But Monet soon becomes a favorite with Abby's customers—until one day he goes mysteriously missing. In his place is a stuffed bird and a ransom note demanding the real Monet painting in exchange for Abby's pet. "What Monet painting?" is Abby's only response.

Abby tries to put the bird-snatching out of her mind, dismissing it as a cruel joke—until Abby's mama, Mozella, is taken too. This time the kidnapper threatens to kill Mozella unless Abby produces the painting.

What do a talking bird, Mozella, and a painting hidden for hundreds of years have in common? Abby must figure it all out soon before the could-be killer flies the coop for good.

The Cane Mutiny

Abigail Timberlake Washburn understands the antiques game is a gamble—so she doesn't know what to expect when she wins the bidding for the contents of an old locker that has been sealed for years. It's a delightful surprise when she discovers inside a collection of exquisite old walking sticks—and a not-so-delightful one when she pulls out a decrepit gym bag containing . . . *a human skull!*

The last thing the diminutive South Carolina antiques dealer needs is to be suspected of foul play. So she grabs her chatty assistant (and future sister-in-law), C.J., and heads out to search for a killer they can stick it to. But this cane case will be no walk in the park—with its arcane clues hinting at poaching, counterfeiting, smuggling . . . and homicide, of course. And when a fresh corpse turns up, things are about to get *really* sticky for Abby and her staff of one.

TAMAR MYERS'

THE GLASS IS ALWAYS GREENER
978-0-06-084661-9

Abby Timberlake is the prime suspect when her friend
Rob's aunt turns up dead with a priceless emerald ring
missing from her lifeless finger.

POISON IVORY
978-0-06-084660-2

Abby never expected her online purchase of an exquisite
seventeenth-century rosewood linen chest to place her in
federal custody for ivory trafficking.

DEATH OF A RUG LORD
978-0-06-084659-6

While investigating the brutal murder of a local rug
store, antiques dealer Abby Timberlake Washburn discovers
that the prized Orientals of Charleston's society dames are
cheap fakes.

THE CANE MUTINY
978-0-06-053519-3

When Abby discovers a human skull in a sealed locker she
bought she heads out in search of a killer.

TAMAR MYERS'

DEN OF ANTIQUITY MYSTERIES

LARCENY AND OLD LACE
978-0-380-78239-0

GILT BY ASSOCIATION
978-0-380-78237-6

THE MING AND I
978-0-380-79255-9

SO FAUX, SO GOOD
978-0-380-79254-2

BAROQUE AND DESPERATE
978-0-380-80225-8

ESTATE OF MIND
978-0-380-80227-2

A PENNY URNED
978-0-380-81189-2

NIGHTMARE IN SHINING ARMOR
978-0-380-81191-5

SPLENDOR IN THE GLASS
978-0-380-81964-5

TILES AND TRIBULATIONS